D1265713

A
RELUCTANT
BRIDE

Center Point
Large Print

Also by Kathleen Fuller and available from Center Point Large Print:

Letters to Katie
Faith of Her Own

This Large Print Book carries the Seal of Approval of N.A.V.H.

A
RELUCTANT
BRIDE

Kathleen
Fuller

CENTER POINT LARGE PRINT
THORNDIKE, MAINE

This Center Point Large Print edition is published
in the year 2016 by arrangement with Thomas Nelson.

The Voice™. © 2008 by Ecclesia Bible Society.
Used by permission. All rights reserved.

The text of this Large Print edition is unabridged.
In other aspects, this book may vary
from the original edition.
Printed in the United States of America
on permanent paper.
Set in 16-point Times New Roman type.

ISBN: 978-1-62899-830-6

Library of Congress Cataloging-in-Publication Data

Names: Fuller, Kathleen.
Title: A reluctant bride / Kathleen Fuller.
Description: Center Point Large Print edition. | Thorndike, Maine :
Center Point Large Print, 2016. | ©2015
Identifiers: LCCN 2015037821 | ISBN 9781628998306
  (hardcover : alk. paper)
Subjects: LCSH: Amish—Fiction. | Married people—Fiction. | Large
type books. | GSAFD: Love stories. | Christian fiction.
Classification: LCC PS3606.U553 R43 2016 | DDC 813/.6—dc23
LC record available at http://lccn.loc.gov/2015037821

To my husband, James.
I love you.

The deepest pains may linger
through the night, but joy greets
the soul with the smile of morning.

PSALM 30:5, THE VOICE

GLOSSARY

ab im kopp: crazy, crazy in the head
ach: oh
aenti: aunt
Amisch: Amish
appeditlich: delicious
auld: old
bann: shun, shunned
boppli/bopplis: baby/babies
bruder: brother
bu/buwe: boy/boys
daed: dad
danki: thank you
Deitsch: language spoken by the Amish
dochder: daughter
dumm: dumb
dummkopf: dummy
Englisch: non-Amish
familye: family
frau: woman/wife
geh: go
Gott: God
grienhaus: greenhouse
grossmammi/grossmutter: grandmother
grossvatter: grandfather
gut: good
gute nacht: good night

haus: house
herr: man/mister
kaffee: coffee
kapp: head covering worn by Amish women
kinn/kinner: child/children
kumme: come
lieb: love
maed/maedel: girls/girl
mamm: mom
mann: Amish man
mei: my
mudder: mother
nee: no
nix: nothing
onkel: uncle
Ordnung, the: rules the Amish follow
schee: pretty/handsome
schwester: sister
sohn: son
vatter: father
ya: yes
Yankee: non-Amish (Middlefield only)
yer: your

PROLOGUE

Sadie Schrock gripped the four heavy ice bags, struggling to keep them from slipping out of her hands and crashing to the ground on the side of the road. She wished it hadn't been her turn to fetch them from the ice cooler nearly a half mile from her family's grocery store. She also wished she'd taken her mother's suggestion and brought their small pull wagon. That would have been the smart thing to do. Instead she was stuck hauling the bags with her hands, the ice seeming to grow heavier with each step she took.

As she plodded along the road, the summer sun pressed down on her sweat-soaked body. Her dress clung to her back, and heat radiated from the asphalt beneath her tennis shoes. She couldn't get home fast enough and into the cool building that housed Schrock Grocery and Tools. Her dry mouth longed for a huge glass of iced tea, heavy on the ice.

As Sadie walked along a cornfield, the tall, lush stalks standing still and proud under the blazing August sun, she hummed a simple tune of her own invention.

The stalks beside her suddenly rustled.

She paused. Her scalp tingled beneath her white *kapp*, signaling some kind of warning she couldn't discern. The road stretched out in front of her, surprisingly deserted for midmorning. Sadie turned and looked at the cornfield. The stalks were moving, gently pushed by a weak, hot breeze. She blew out a breath, feeling ridiculous. Last night would be the last time she and her sisters, Abigail and Joanna, stayed up late telling foolish ghost stories. None of the stories were real. They all knew that. They weren't even that scary, just made-up tales about some old legends in the Birch Creek area. Still, it had been fun to be a *little* frightened in the safety of Abigail's room, the three of them sitting on the floor in low candlelight as they tried to see who would scare first.

Sadie glanced at the cornfield again. From now on she was done with scary stories. She quickened her pace, dangling the plastic bags of ice that had grown slick with condensation.

"Whatcha doing, Sadie?"

She nearly dropped the bags as Solomon Troyer jumped out of the cornfield and blocked her path. She took a step back and breathed in. "Good grief, Sol. You practically scared the life out of me."

But instead of offering an apology, he moved toward her, a wolfish expression creeping over his long face. He'd turned nineteen last month, and from almost the day she'd turned sixteen earlier that year, he had looked at her in a weird, unnerving way whenever she saw him. Today wasn't any different. He wasn't wearing his straw hat, and another shift of the sultry breeze lifted the damp ends of his reddish-brown hair. He took a step toward her, his lips curving into a leer. "A *maedel* shouldn't be walking down the road by herself."

"I walk down this road by myself all the time." She scowled, then wrinkled her nose. He smelled. Not just of sweat and sawdust, but of some kind of alcohol. He'd been drinking. Again. She didn't have time for his nonsense. "I have to get back to the store, Sol. *Mamm* and *Daed* need this ice and it's melting everywhere." She couldn't keep the bite out of her tone. "In case you haven't noticed, it's really hot today."

"That's not the only thing that's hot."

Ugh. Not only was he creepy, he was corny too. "Sol, I'm serious. Get out of *mei* way."

His bloodshot leer wandered from her eyes to her lips. "Don't you have a little time to talk?"

He was making her skin crawl. "*Nee*. Now let me by." She moved to walk past him, but he blocked her again.

"You could be a little nicer to me." He blew stale breath in her face as he leaned over her. "Let's *geh* in the cornfield. I have something to show you."

Her blood stilled in her veins. Sol was at least six inches taller than she was, and although he

11

was lean, she knew he was strong. Still, she wasn't afraid of him . . . at least not too much. Although the sun was bright, his pupils grew wide. Dark. She definitely didn't want to see whatever it was he wanted to show her. He was taking a risk, being bold like this. A car could come by at any minute. She suddenly prayed that one would. "I don't think so," she said, tightening her grip on the slippery plastic bags.

He licked his dry lips. "Oh, I think—"

"Sol!"

Sadie turned to see Sol's younger brother, Aden, appear from the cornfield. She let out a relieved breath. She'd never been so glad to see Aden. The Yoder family owned this field, and Sadie was sure they wouldn't appreciate the Troyer brothers taking a shortcut through it. But they were the bishop's sons, so no one would say anything.

"*Daed*'s waiting on us, Sol." Aden's apprehensive look met Sadie's for barely a second. "Hi, Sadie." Then he glanced away, his eyes fixed on the ground.

"Hi, Aden." She managed to keep her voice even despite the panic stirring inside her. They were the same age and had grown up together, attending the same school and seeing each other at church services. But Aden was shy, painfully so. She'd never paid much attention to him. Most of the time she didn't realize he was even there. Aden Troyer had always blended into the

12

background, always kept his distance. Right now she was happy he'd chosen this moment to make his presence known. Sol wouldn't try anything with his brother as a witness.

Feeling more confident now that Aden had arrived, she started to push past Sol. "See you all later," she said, striving for a light tone she didn't feel.

Sol took a step to the left, blocking Sadie again. "Not until you and I have had our . . . talk."

"Sol," Aden said, his voice cracking on the last letter. His voice wasn't as deep or as confident as his older brother's. It wasn't cruel or lecherous either.

Sol turned to him, smirking. "You *geh* on home. Tell *Daed* I'll be there in a little while."

Aden paused. "But—"

Sol looked at Sadie again, a spark of anger replacing the leer in his eyes. "*Leave,* Aden." His mocking stare never left Sadie as he spat out the words.

Despite sweating from a mix of heat and anxiety, her body shivered. She shot Aden a pleading look, begging him silently to do something. Sol's determination to get her alone was starting to frighten her. Surely Aden could convince his brother to let her be. But when Aden looked at her again, she saw her fear reflected in his fern-colored eyes.

His mouth opened, as if to say something. Then

he clamped it shut, turned around, and ran back into the cornfield.

"Aden!" she called out. But the only response she heard was the whispering swish of the cornstalks as he left her and Sol together. Alone. Just like Sol wanted.

Coward. There was nothing she could do but try to escape on her own. She started to run, but Sol grabbed her around the waist, making her drop the ice bags. She pushed against him as he dragged her deep into the cornfield and set her down hard on the ground. Sadie looked around wildly, unable to see the road through the veil of endless corn.

Sol's fingers dug into her arms. "You're not going anywhere."

"You're hurting me!" she said, struggling against him.

"Settle down." His voice was low, menacing. His face moved closer to hers. "All I want is a little kiss."

She shook her head, trying to pull back from him. "Let me *geh*!"

"Just one kiss." His grip lessened slightly. "Then I'll do whatever you ask."

She stilled, searching his reddened, sweaty face, looking for deception, unsure what the upward curling of his top lip meant. *Lord, I hope he's telling the truth.*

"Okay." Her mouth trembled. If he kept his

word she would be free of him. "One . . . one kiss—"

He slammed his sour mouth down on hers, mashing so hard it hurt. His lips moved as she winced against him. When she tried to stop him, he kept pressing closer until there wasn't any space between them. She managed to insert her hands between their bodies and shoved against his chest. When he didn't move, she bit his bottom lip. Only then did he stop.

"You kissed me." She gasped for fresh air. "Now let me *geh*."

But Sol only grinned in response, a drop of blood forming where her teeth had clamped down. He licked it away, clutched her arms, and squeezed until she cried out. He ran the back of his rough hand down her cheek, as if he owned her face. As if he owned *her*. She could see flakes of sawdust in his hair, evidence of his carpentry work. Why wasn't he at his job? Why had he been drinking? *Why* was he doing this to her? The questions darted around in her mind as she tried to wiggle out of his grip.

"We're alone, Sadie." He whispered the words. "I can do whatever I want . . . and no one is going to stop me."

He was right. No one would. Aden had disappeared. And if she screamed, Sol might lose his temper and do more than kiss her. A white-hot rage she'd never felt before consumed her. She couldn't let him touch her again. Desperate, Sadie brought up her knee and rammed it into his crotch.

Sol cursed at her as he folded over in pain and dropped to the ground. She raced away, not caring if he was hurt. *He deserved it.* As she fought her way through the cornstalks, she prayed she was going in the right direction. When she cleared the field, she saw the road. Somehow she managed to be near the ice bags. She snatched them up and ran as fast as she could toward the store, throwing one last glance over her shoulder to make sure Sol wasn't following her.

When she got inside the store, she slammed the door behind her, gasping for breath. *Mamm* looked up from behind the cash register.

"Sadie. What on earth?"

"I'm . . . fine." Sadie forced a smile. *I'm fine . . . I'm fine.*

"I'm glad you're fine, but why did you slam the door?"

"Didn't . . . mean to."

Mamm moved from behind the counter and took the ice. "What did you do, run all the way from the cooler?"

"*Ya.* Didn't want the ice to melt."

Mamm looked at the dripping bags. "Sadie, you didn't have to run. Whatever melts will freeze right back up." She gave her a concerned look. "Why is *yer* dress dirty?"

16

Sadie glanced down and saw the dust and hay from the cornfield scattered across the pale blue fabric of her dress. "I tripped," she said flatly.

"Are you hurt?"

Yes. "*Nee.* Just clumsy."

"*Ach, yer* cheeks are red and you're sweating." She lifted her lips in a kind smile. "*Geh* to the house and cool down. Change *yer* dress too. Next time, don't be in such a hurry."

Sadie nodded and left. She rushed to the house, locking the bathroom door behind her even though she knew Sol wouldn't—he *couldn't*—follow her home. She'd left him curled up on the ground in the cornfield.

She went to the sink, turned on the tap, and splashed water on her hot face. She touched her lips with wet fingertips, shame and disgust filling her. *My first kiss . . .*

She switched off the tap and gripped the sides of the counter, fighting back tears. Her arms ached from Sol's hard grip, and she knew her skin would show the bruises soon. She'd have to hide them with long sleeves, then come up with a plausible explanation when people asked why she was wearing a cold-weather dress in the harsh heat of summer.

But she refused to cry. Sol wasn't worth her tears. She let the anger pulse through her, not just anger toward Sol but also toward his brother. Aden knew what was going to happen. She'd seen the fear in his eyes. But he'd turned tail and deserted her. In her mind, he was just as guilty as Sol.

Clenching her fists, she knew she could never say anything about what happened. Not to her parents or to Sol's. If she did, Sol would lie about what happened, and his father, who had been the bishop in Birch Creek all her life, would believe him. The bishop was held in high regard in the community. No one would go against him.

She had no choice but to forget it ever happened and make sure she would never be taken advantage of again. She spat into the sink, trying to purge the memory. She lifted her head, glared at the mirror . . . and vowed never to let Sol or Aden Troyer near her for the rest of her life.

CHAPTER 1

Six years later

"Sadie, hurry up! We're going to be late!"

Sadie lifted an eyebrow as the door to her room opened. Her sister Abigail huffed in frustration.

"You're not even ready." Abigail walked into the room, Joanna close on her heels.

Sadie returned her attention to the book spread out on her lap. "I'm not going." She crossed her ankles as she stretched out on her bed.

"But you promised you'd *geh* this time." Abigail looked down on Sadie, her forehead furrowing above her thick light brown eyebrows.

"I don't recall promising." Sadie turned a page, pretending to be absorbed in the book she was reading. "I recall saying maybe."

"Maybe is close enough."

"Maybe means *maybe*." Sadie glanced up at her youngest sister. Joanna stood a few steps behind Abigail, quiet as usual, her chestnut eyes wide and filled with innocent sweetness. Sadie peered at her around Abigail's shoulder. "You're not going to say anything in *mei* defense?"

"I'm a neutral observer."

Sadie chuckled. "Chicken." She looked at Abigail again. "Just so we're clear, I have no plans to *geh* to the singing tonight. I do have plans to spend the evening reading this fascinating book."

Abigail smirked as she peered down at the title at the top of one page. *"The Basics of Accounting?"*

"We all have to start somewhere." Sadie lifted the book in front of her, blocking her view of Abigail. She heard her sister blow out an exasperated breath.

"Sadie, please. You never *geh* to the Sunday singings anymore. Or too much of anything else, other than church. How are you going to get a *mann* if you don't make an effort?"

For the past two years her sister had been singularly focused on her own dating life. But that didn't mean she needed to extend that interest to Sadie's. "Who says I want a *mann?"*

"You *need* a *mann."*

Sadie set down the book, her mirth evaporating. *"Mamm* sent you up here, didn't she?"

Abigail shook her head, while Joanna nodded. Abigail turned around, glanced at Joanna, and rolled her eyes. "Fine. *Mamm* sent us. She said if you didn't *geh* tonight, we couldn't *geh* either."

Sadie sat up and dropped her book on top of the quilt. "That's not fair."

"That's what I said." Abigail put her hands on her slender waist. "But she was serious."

Sadie paused, stifling a groan of frustration. For

the last couple of years, the same two years Abigail had been so focused on her own prospects, their mother had been after Sadie to be more serious about finding a husband. Sadie wasn't interested in finding a husband, or even dating. Just the thought of being alone with a man, even a nice man, made her want to run in the opposite direction. But her mother had other ideas. Sadie swung her legs over the side of the bed and stood. "I'll *geh* talk to her."

"It would be easier if you'd just *geh* to the singing." Abigail dropped her arms. "C'mon, Sadie. It will be fun. You'll see *yer* friends."

"The ones who haven't gotten married yet. I think that adds up to two."

"So? There are still a couple of guys who aren't dating anyone."

"For the last time, I'm *not* interested."

Joanna moved to stand beside Abigail. A few inches shorter and three years younger than Sadie, she'd always tried not to get involved in her sisters' arguments. "You don't have to be interested in the *buwe* that way." She smiled sweetly. "Just be nice."

"In other words, don't be yourself," Abigail added.

Joanna elbowed Abigail in the side. "You're not helping."

"I don't care." Abigail crossed her thin arms over her chest, acting more like a twelve-year-old than a twenty-year-old. "If we don't leave soon we're going to be late." She glared at Sadie.

Sadie ran her palms over the skirt of her old sage dress. She and Abigail were evenly matched in the stubbornness department. But so were Sadie and their mother, and Sadie knew even if she went downstairs and tried to convince *Mamm* to let her sisters go to the singing without her, *Mamm* wouldn't change her mind. Appealing to her father wouldn't work either. He would say, "That's between you *maed*," and then find a way to escape the room.

"Fine," Sadie said, a knot forming in her stomach. "I'll *geh*. For a little while."

Abigail and Joanna both grinned. "*Danki*," Abigail said.

"Now, you two *geh* downstairs while I get ready." She started for her dresser. "Where's the singing again?"

"Sadie, don't you ever pay attention?" Abigail said. "It's at the Troyers'."

Sadie froze, and by the time she turned around to make an excuse—any excuse—for changing her mind, they had both left.

Her hand curled over the edge of her dresser, and the knot that had started to form in her stomach transformed into a full-blown ache. Why was her mother choosing *this* singing to take a stand?

She willed her pulse to slow. When that didn't

work, she silently asked God to do it. Sadie looked at her reflection in the small oval mirror above her dresser. Her normally fair complexion was now paper white, and her stomach lurched at the thought of walking into Bishop Troyer's house.

When Abigail and Joanna were old enough to go to singings, she'd forced herself to go to the ones held at the Troyers' to ensure Sol stayed away from them, and she'd been relieved for the last year or two when he hadn't even made an appearance. To his credit—which he deserved very little, in her opinion—Sol had stayed away from her, and her sisters too, even at church services. Maybe he'd get married soon, since he was nearly twenty-five years old. Not that she'd wish Sol Troyer on anyone.

She knew why Abigail was so insistent on going tonight. It was no secret that she and Joel Zook were interested in each other. Joanna, as usual, just went along with whatever everyone else wanted. She was the most easygoing person Sadie knew.

She loved her sisters, and she didn't want to disappoint them. She didn't want to argue with her mother, either.

But the Troyers . . .

If she protested too much, her family would be suspicious and would start asking questions she didn't want to answer. And she couldn't risk

23

the chance that Sol would be there. He couldn't be trusted. Abigail had Joel, but what if Sol tried to talk to Joanna?

She had to do this. Sadie closed her eyes, then opened them again as she straightened her shoulders and lifted her chin.

She would get through it . . . somehow.

Lord . . . help me.

Sadie quickly slipped into a nicer dress, black stockings, and her black shoes. She checked the pins on her dress to make sure they were straight, ignored the trembling in her hands, then headed downstairs.

"I'm ready," she said, tamping down her anxiety as she entered the living room.

Her mother looked up from the cooking magazine she was reading and smiled. "I'm glad you changed *yer* mind, Sadie."

"I didn't have much choice," she muttered. Even if she was going now with a purpose of her own, she didn't like her mother's slightly underhanded methods, although she understood *Mamm* had the best of intentions.

Although Sadie was certain her mother had heard her, *Mamm*'s smile remained in place. "I'm sure you'll have a nice time, *dochder*. It will do you *gut* to get out of the *haus* and be among friends."

Sadie forced a smile and nodded. "We won't be gone long."

"Speak for yourself," Abigail huffed.

"I am," Sadie said, giving her a look.

"You *maed* take *yer* time." *Mamm* glanced at *Daed*, who was lying back in the hickory rocking chair, his eyes closed and his mouth partway open as he quietly snored. *Mamm* shrugged. "I'll say good-bye for him and let him sleep."

"Bye, *Mamm*!" Abigail tugged on Sadie's sleeve as they walked out of the house. Joanna was standing by Sadie's buggy, the horse already hitched and ready to go. Sadie had bought both the buggy and the horse a year ago, after saving her money from working at the family store. Of course, her mother complained she worked too many hours, but Sadie loved to work. She enjoyed all aspects of the job—stocking shelves, ordering product, serving the customers. She'd started reading the accounting book and hoped she could convince her father to let her start managing the books, or at least help him with the store's accounts.

But most of all, and something she'd never admitted to anyone, was that the store was *safe*. When she was there, she didn't have to worry about Sol or Aden. By some miracle neither had stepped foot inside the store in years. Even if they had, between her family and the customers, she and her sisters were almost never alone. And when Bishop Troyer and his wife stopped by, she could always put on a smile and pretend she didn't resent their sons. She was happy with her life the way it was. She didn't want a man . . . and she certainly didn't need one.

"Sadie, hurry up," Abigail said as she climbed into the buggy. Joanna scooted in next to her.

Sadie patted her horse's nose as she trudged by. Apple gave her a nudge and Sadie sighed. Even her horse was rushing her along. She got in the buggy and grabbed the reins, which nearly slipped from her slick hands. All she'd wanted was to spend the evening learning a little about accounting. Instead she'd be forced to dodge people she didn't want to see.

Abigail leaned forward, resting her chin on Sadie's shoulder as Sadie guided Apple out of the driveway. "Tonight will be fun," she said. "I promise."

Sadie clutched the reins and managed a nod. As her sisters started to talk about Joel and the other young men they'd see at the Troyers', Sadie tuned them out. Maybe she would be lucky tonight and Sol wouldn't be there. Maybe she'd be double lucky tonight and Aden wouldn't be around either. To her, one brother was as bad as the other.

Aden Troyer pushed the porch swing back and forth with the toe of his boot as he watched the buggies file one by one into the driveway. He didn't want to be here, but his father insisted— and he didn't dare refuse his father. He was past the age of attending these things, but his father persisted in having them, more for the youth of the community than for his own son. Yet every year Aden had to endure this mandatory attendance. He was getting sick of it.

The back-and-forth motion of the swing calmed his nerves a bit. If he had to be here, he didn't have to be inside. Not yet. At least Sol wouldn't be here. His father had stopped making his brother attend the past year or two. He thanked God for small favors.

He thought about Sol, about how the drinking was getting worse, along with his temper. He suspected his father knew about Sol's vices, although he never said anything about them in Aden's presence. Probably because he was too busy pointing out Aden's flaws. His many, *many* flaws.

He pushed the swing in motion again, lifting his head to see the latest person arrive to the singing. He watched as the buggy parked in front of the barn, neatly lining up with the rest of the buggies. The driver exited the vehicle.

Aden stopped the swing. What was Sadie Schrock doing here?

He leaned forward as Sadie's sisters, Abigail and Joanna, got out on the other side of the buggy. But Aden barely paid attention to them. Why would Sadie come here? This was the last place he'd expected her to show up.

But his surprise at seeing her wasn't the only

reason he couldn't tear his gaze away. To him, not only was she the prettiest *maedel* in Birch Creek, she was also the most interesting. Sadie wasn't like other girls. He could always tell she was fiercely devoted to her family and to their business. She was serious minded, but there were also times he'd seen her lovely smile, heard her sweet laugh when he saw her talking with her sisters or her friends. He appreciated her. He *admired* her. He could easily see himself falling for her . . . if things were different. If he hadn't run off and left her with Sol that time by the cornfield.

Maybe then she wouldn't hate him so much.

The front screen door opened with a squeak. "Aden."

Aden pulled his gaze away from Sadie at the sound of his father's voice. *Daed* was standing in the doorway, his face placid, nearly inscrutable. But Aden could see the glimmer of disappointment in his father's eyes, so small that Aden was sure only he could have detected it.

I've had enough practice.

"You need to be inside, *sohn*, to greet our guests."

He didn't look at his father. At twenty-two he shouldn't have to be talked to like he was a kid. "I'll be inside in a minute."

Daed paused. "I haven't received the money from this week's honey sales."

"I'll get it to you tomorrow."

"See that you do. And see that you come inside. Now."

Aden flinched as the screen door slammed shut. He kept watching Sadie as she lagged a few steps behind her sisters. From the pinched look on her face, he could see she didn't want to be here either. *At least we have that in common.*

He stood and went inside the house. He wasn't ready to face anyone, not yet. He snuck upstairs to his room and opened the bottom drawer of his small dresser. Beneath a layer of socks was the envelope that held the money. *His* money, despite his father's insistence that Aden give every penny to him as recompense for putting a roof over his head and meals in his stomach. But it wasn't his father who had built the beehives, or tended to them, or collected and packaged the honey, or read dozens of books from the library on pollination and gardening. His father was too busy. Too important.

Aden would never say such a thing to the man's face. He was the bishop, and he had been since his family and five others had moved to Birch Creek a little over twenty-five years ago. Aden was born here, but his parents were from Holmes County. Over the years their small community had grown to twenty families, all under Emmanuel Troyer's watchful, and out-wardly caring, eye. Aden had a difficult time understanding how a man who was so revered and respected by the rest of the community could be so hard and unyielding to his own son.

He was old enough to leave. He could strike out on his own and make a decent living raising bees and selling honey and other hive by-products. But he wouldn't leave his mother here with his father and Sol. As long as Aden stayed, he would be the one to bear the burden of Sol's temper and his father's derision. Neither his father nor his brother had ever turned on *Mamm*, but Aden didn't want to risk the chance of that happening if he weren't here.

He sighed and opened the envelope that held almost three hundred dollars. He took out fifty, put the envelope back, and pulled out a small metal box from under his bed. He put the fifty dollars inside and shoved the box back until he heard it hit the wall. His father trusted Aden to be honest, and in almost every aspect of his life Aden was. But he had to have something for himself. He needed the security the money he set aside without his father's knowledge gave him. He couldn't convince himself that withholding some of the money he'd earned was a sin, not when his father demanded everything from Aden—even when Aden's everything wasn't close to good enough.

He stood, brushed off his black pants, took a deep breath, and went downstairs.

•••

Sadie *really* didn't want to be here.

She stood in the corner of the Troyers' basement, which seemed so similar to her parents'— gray cement floor, cinder block walls, and a small horizontal window at the top of the back wall to let in a bit of light. There were several gas lamps in the room, which gave adequate lighting. Sadie held a red plastic cup filled with apple cider and tried to be as inconspicuous as possible. She kept her eye out for Sol, who fortunately hadn't shown up. Still, she had to stay on guard.

"Sadie," Abigail muttered, "stop looking like you've got tacks in *yer* shoes."

"What?" She turned to her sister, who was standing close beside her.

"You could at least try to be friendly." Abigail glanced around. "Everyone's pairing up already, and Joel's waiting for me." She looked at Sadie again. "You're going to end up alone tonight."

Sadie ignored her and Abigail sighed. "Look, Aden's standing all by himself over there. Why don't you *geh* talk to him? He always looks so lonely."

Sadie spied Aden in the opposite corner of the room, partially shrouded by the shadows. He leaned against the cinder block wall, but his posture was rigid. Unwelcoming. She had the sense he was as lost as she felt.

She turned her gaze from him. She didn't care

31

about Aden. But she did catch out of the corner of her eye his sudden departure from the room. *Good. Hopefully he won't come back.*

As Aden walked away she said to Abigail, "I'm fine right here."

"But—"

"Don't worry about me," she added, softening her tone and managing a smile. "*Geh* see Joel. He's waiting."

Abigail looked over her shoulder at Joel Zook, who was standing a few feet away holding two cups of cider. When he smiled, she said, "He's very *schee*, don't you think?"

With a shrug Sadie glanced at him. He was tall—very tall, at least a head taller than everyone else in the room. But that was the most remarkable thing about him, in Sadie's opinion. "What's important is that you think so."

Abigail flashed an excited grin before walking toward Joel, who held out a cup of cider to her.

With Abigail content, at least for the moment, Sadie scanned the room again, on the lookout for Sol. Fortunately he was keeping his distance, like he did at church services. Maybe being under his father's roof was keeping him at bay. Whatever it was, she was glad for it.

She spied Joanna, off to the side and talking to Andrew Beiler. In contrast to Joel Zook's towering height and slight frame, Andrew was on the short, stocky side. He leaned closer to Joanna and spoke. Joanna pulled back, a delighted smile on her face, a rosy blush on her cheeks.

Good. Sol wouldn't be able to get to her with Andrew in the way.

Sadie turned away, an odd emptiness coming over her. As Abigail had predicted, everyone had paired off, with the exception of her and Aden, who'd had the good sense to leave. It shouldn't have bothered her to be standing apart from everyone else. That was what she wanted.

Wasn't it?

She was about to take a sip of her drink, but froze as she saw Sol enter the basement. He'd grown broader over the past six years, his muscular biceps straining against the short sleeves of his yellow shirt. If he'd been that size when he'd restrained her in the cornfield, she might not have gotten away. A shiver coursed through her.

She watched as he threaded through the small crowd of young people, pausing to talk to Irene Beiler, Andrew's older sister. Then he looked up, and his gaze met Sadie's—and held.

The cup slipped from her hand. She barely caught it before it hit the floor. Her throat constricted, her heart hammering in her chest. Despite Sol keeping his distance, she felt invaded as he continued to look at her. The memory of his forceful, sweaty kiss came slamming back, and it took everything she had not to grab her sisters and go home. But they were having a good time, and she didn't want to spoil it for them.

That didn't mean she had to stay in the same room as Sol.

Sadie hurried out the back door of the basement, then up the four steps that led to the backyard. She paused at the edge of the simple concrete slab that served as the Troyers' patio and drew a sharp breath into her panicked lungs. Dusk had descended, cloaking everything in dim light. Wanting to put as much distance between her and Sol as she possibly could, she blindly hurried from the house, not caring where she ended up. She'd spend the rest of the evening in her buggy if she had to. Anything to get away from Sol and the desperate fear his presence ignited.

By the time her pulse slowed, she found herself behind the Troyers' barn and realized she had made a foolish choice by coming outside alone. What if Sol had followed her out here? If he did, she'd scream herself hoarse this time. She wasn't a naïve sixteen-year-old girl anymore.

A buzzing noise appeared near her ear, briefly distracting her. She turned and saw four stacks of beehives a few yards away. In the fading light of dusk she could barely make out a few bees hovering above the hives. Great. On top of everything she would probably get stung. She took a few steps back, ready to bolt again if the bees came near her.

"They won't sting you."

She whirled around to see Aden standing inches away. Closer than he'd been in years.

"They're coming home for the night," he said, his voice soft, low, and deeper than she remembered. "As long as we don't bother them, they won't bother us."

She didn't care about his stupid bees. She glared at him. His russet hair almost brushed the collar of his shirt, and she thought for a bizarre moment that he needed a haircut.

"Sadie, I . . ." He clamped his mouth shut.

She stepped back, desperate to put space between them. Another step. When she took the third, her ankle twisted.

"Careful!" He grabbed her upper arm and moved to her side, preventing her from falling. "The ground is uneven here."

She regained her balance as their eyes met. His other hand skimmed the back of her waist before he released her. "Are you okay?"

His concerned tone and gentle touch stole her words. She balked, expecting to recoil from the gesture.

She didn't. And that scared her more than anything.

"Sadie?"

When he stepped toward her, she rushed past him, confused. The surge that went through her when he touched her, when he showed her unexpected kindness, didn't make sense. She wasn't going to stick around and contemplate what had happened.

She hurried back inside the basement and went straight to Abigail. "We have to leave," she said, breathless and still reeling from her reaction to Aden.

Abigail cast a bewildered look at Joel before addressing Sadie. "We just got here—"

"Now."

"All right." She looked at Joel again. "I'm sorry."

"Is everything okay?" he asked, his words directed at Sadie.

"Everything is fine," Sadie said through clenched teeth. "We just need to *geh*."

Abigail nodded. "I'll get Joanna." As she walked by Sadie she leaned over and whispered, "What's going on? You look white as a sheet."

"I'll be in the buggy." She brushed past Abigail and walked out the basement door. As she raced to the buggy, she looked to see if Aden, Sol, or their father was outside. But the yard seemed deserted. *Thank you, Lord.*

She climbed inside the buggy and sat on the bench seat, placing a steadying hand over her chest. She gripped the leather reins and fought for calm, praying her sisters would hurry up so she could get away as fast as possible.

I shouldn't have come tonight.

36

I shouldn't have touched her.

Aden stood by his beehives and watched Sadie as she ran from the basement and straight for her buggy. He had to fight the urge to follow her, to ask her if she was okay. He could kick himself for touching her, but it had been instinctive on his part. And for that brief moment when his hand rested on her waist, he hadn't wanted to let her go.

For years he'd wanted to apologize to her for what had happened, for running away and leaving her with Sol. He wasn't sure what actually had happened between Sadie and his brother in the cornfield that day, but Sol had returned home a couple of hours later, fuming and more sober than he'd been earlier in the day. Aden had known better than to question him.

And if he were honest with himself, he'd have to admit he didn't want to know what had transpired between Sol and Sadie. Which made him just as cowardly now as he was back then, when he was sixteen and afraid of Sol's fists and his father's retribution.

If he was a man instead of the weak-willed boy his father always called him, he'd go after Sadie right now. He'd ask her forgiveness. He'd tell her she'd never have to worry about Sol again.

But something more powerful than guilt and fear held him back. He'd observed Sadie during the singing, watching her as she stood in the corner, looking alternately pained and anxious. The only thing more surprising than her coming tonight was that she stayed as long as she did. And he knew part of the reason she was leaving was because of him.

He couldn't approach Sadie again. He didn't have the right to.

He heard the back porch door hinges creak and saw his father step out onto the patio. The flicker of a match glowed in the near darkness as he lit his pipe, smoke coming out in puffs from his mouth. Aden ducked out of sight farther behind the barn. Eventually he would sneak back into the house before his father noticed he was missing.

Aden heard the sound of a buggy leaving, and he knew it was Sadie's. Someday he would find a way to apologize to her . . . and he could only pray that she would find it in her heart to forgive him.

"That will be four dollars." Sadie smiled as she handed Naomi Beiler a paper bag filled with Fuji apples.

"That's a bargain price," Naomi said, handing Sadie the money. "Cheapest I've found anywhere."

"We aim to have the lowest prices," Sadie said. *Sometimes too low.* But she trusted that her parents knew what they were doing when it came to their grocery and tool business. Even now they were out with Joanna picking more apples from a local orchard to sell in the store. She gave Naomi her change. "Come back soon."

"I definitely will." Andrew and Irene's mother smiled and left.

Sadie picked up a broom and started sweeping the front of the store, which had seen quite a bit of traffic today. The customers had kept her and Abigail busy, and that had kept last night off Sadie's mind. Abigail had been irritated about what happened, but Sadie couldn't help that. She didn't say anything to either sister when they continued to ask her why they had to leave the singing early. Eventually they both gave up and went to their rooms, leaving Sadie alone.

She'd spent part of the night trying to forget Sol's stare and Aden's light touch. Finally she was able to get the Troyers out of her mind and get some much needed sleep.

"The cereal is all stocked," Abigail said, coming from the back of the store. "*Mamm* and *Daed* should be back soon." She grinned. "Joel said he might stop by today."

"That's nice." Sadie continued to sweep, pushing away the small carpet remnant from the store entrance and sweeping the dust from underneath.

"If he does, would you mind if I went with him for a little bit?"

Sadie stopped mid-sweep. "Where?"

She shrugged. "Wherever he wants to *geh*."

"Abigail—"

"To lunch, Sadie." Abigail chuckled. "You're always so serious."

"Someone around here needs to be." She leaned the broom against the wall behind the counter, then went to one of the shelves nearby and straightened several packages of cookies.

Abigail stood beside her. "I don't suppose you feel like talking about last night?"

"Like I said last night, *nee*. I don't feel like talking about it."

Her sister sighed and went back to the counter. "There's a picture of you next to the word *stubborn* in the dictionary. I'm sure of it."

"I'm flattered." Sadie focused on the packages of chocolate-cream sandwich cookies in front of her. Hopefully Joel Zook would walk through that door any minute and relieve her of dodging any more of Abigail's questions. When she heard the bell over the door ring as a customer came in, she smiled. *Perfect timing.* She turned to say hello, only to choke on the word as both Sol and Aden walked into the store.

CHAPTER 2

Sadie's hand remained on the package of cookies as she saw Abigail approach the Troyer brothers. As soon as she saw Sol move closer to her sister, Sadie regained her senses and went to stand between them. "What are you doing here?" she asked, her narrowed gaze bouncing from Sol to Aden.

"Sadie," Abigail said, stepping to the side. "That was rude."

But Sadie moved her glare back to Sol.

"We're just here to pick up an order," Aden said quietly.

She glanced at him for a second. Whatever she thought she'd felt last evening when he'd kept her from tripping in his yard had disappeared. She focused her sights on Sol again. Although he hadn't so much as glanced at her sister, she wasn't taking any chances. He wasn't getting near her or anyone else in her family.

"*Mamm* talked to *yer mudder* about it," Sol added, taking a step toward Sadie. "Food. Tools. Some other stuff. Too much for *Mamm* to take home on her own."

Aden did move to stand beside his brother, but his eyes never met Sadie's. Instead they remained focused on the tops of his boots, much in the same way they had when he had arrived in the cornfield six years ago.

Her nails dug into her palms, but Sadie didn't move, standing her ground. If he thought he was going to intimidate her again—

"I'll check the order sheet," Abigail said, moving toward the counter, which put her in closer proximity to the Troyer brothers.

"I'll do it." Sadie nearly pushed Abigail out of the way to get behind the counter, keeping her attention on Sol.

Sol leaned his hip against the counter. He was only a foot away from Sadie. At least he hadn't been drinking, from what she could tell. Sadie forced her hands to stay steady as she thumbed through the order sheets, praying she'd find the Troyers' order quickly. When she found it she held up the yellow page. "The boxes are in the back."

"I can get them," Abigail said.

Sol turned to Abigail and smiled. He suddenly looked genuine. Even slightly charming.

If a snake could be called charming.

"Actually," Abigail continued, looking from Sol to Sadie, then back to Sol, "I could use some help. Aden, would you mind?"

Sadie shook her head while Abigail grinned and gave her a knowing look. Her sister might have good intentions, but they were pointed in the wrong direction. Sadie started to move from behind the counter. "*Nee* need to bother Aden," she said quickly. "I'll help you."

Abigail held up her hand. "That's all right, Sadie. Aden and I can handle it." She glanced at Aden before winking at Sadie.

Sadie looked at Aden, a horrible sense of déjà vu washing over her. Would he leave her alone with Sol again? Indecision was written on Aden's lightly freckled face, and she realized she still couldn't trust him any more than she could Sol.

Lord, please, do something. Send a customer through that door . . . anything to distract Abigail.

The bell over the front door rang, and Sadie nearly fainted with relief. *Thank you, God.* She turned to see a stocky man with a black mustache walk into the store. He wore a brown uniform Sadie didn't recognize. Her gaze went to his belt . . . and she saw the gun.

Sol immediately stepped away from the counter.

The man walked toward Sadie, his expression somber.

Strange. He was obviously a law officer of some sort. But why would he be in their store? Their community had little to do with the outside world, something Bishop Troyer always stressed in his sermons. While they had *Englisch* customers and were always friendly toward them, Sadie and her family didn't interact with the *Englisch* beyond that.

As the officer removed his hat, Sadie's chest tightened. Something was wrong. Very, very wrong.

"I'm looking for Sadie Schrock."

Her throat went dry, as if someone had stuffed it with cotton. She swallowed, somehow finding her voice. "I'm Sadie."

"I'm with the sheriff's office." He took in a deep breath and laid his hat on the counter.

And that's when Sadie's world came crashing down.

Aden stood in shock as the officer spoke to Sadie.

"An accident?" Sadie's beautiful brown eyes grew round. "What do you mean, an accident?"

"A car hit your parents' buggy. Your sister was thrown from the vehicle." He paused, glanced away, and ran his finger across his mustache in a nervous gesture.

"What about *mei* parents?"

The officer hesitated. With each passing second Aden's chest seemed to grow heavier. "I'm sorry," the man said, barely able to look at Sadie. He picked up his hat from the counter and started fumbling with the brim. "They . . . they didn't survive."

Sadie's lips turned stark white.

"*Nee!*" Abigail rushed at the officer, halting right in front of him. She looked up, her complexion as ashen as Sadie's. "That can't be true."

He turned, looked at Abigail with sympathetic eyes, and slowly nodded.

Abigail put her hands over her face and burst into tears.

"We'll do our best to find the driver," he said. But he didn't sound confident.

"You don't know who hit them?" Sadie asked, her voice surprisingly steady, her expression disturbingly calm.

"They fled the scene."

Sadie didn't move. She didn't shed a tear. Aden gazed at her, taking in her stoic face, her beauty marred by pain that she was trying so hard to hide.

"C'mon, Aden."

He felt Sol tug at his arm. In slow motion he turned toward his brother. "What?"

"We need to get out of here."

"But—"

"Now."

Aden's feet wouldn't move. How could they leave Sadie and Abigail alone at a time like this? But what could he say that Sadie would want to hear? *I'm sorry* wouldn't be enough. It wouldn't scratch the surface. If anything, he would make everything worse. But what choice did he have except to leave?

Reluctantly, Aden followed his brother out of

the store and hurried to catch up with him. "We have to tell *Daed*," he said, matching his brother's long-legged stride.

"*Daed* will find out soon enough."

Aden halted. "So what are we gonna do? Just *geh* home and say nothing?"

Sol spun around and glared at him. "*Nee, dummkopf.* We'll kill some time, wait until the news gets to *Daed*, and then we *geh* home. We'll tell *Mamm* the store was closed by the time we got there."

"That doesn't make any sense." The Schrocks never closed their store except on Sundays and the holidays their faith acknowledged. His gut suddenly lurched as he thought about his mother. She and *Frau* Schrock were close friends. *Mamm* would be devastated when she heard the news. "We can't leave," he said to Sol.

"It's none of our business, Aden."

"Sol . . . they just lost their parents." He looked at the sheriff's car parked in the small gravel lot that separated the grocery from the Schrocks' home. "*Herr* and *Frau* Schrock—"

"I know what happened to them." Sol rubbed his hand over the back of his neck. "I heard the sheriff, plain as you did. That doesn't change anything. Let *Daed* handle it." He started for the buggy again.

Aden paused and looked at the store, his stomach churning with shock and grief. Leaving them alone was wrong. Sadie might not want him here—he was solidly sure she didn't—but he couldn't walk away after hearing the worst possible news. He planted his feet on the ground and called after his brother. "I'm not leaving."

Sol stopped and looked over his shoulder. "What?"

"I'm going back inside the store." He started to turn. "Sadie . . ." He cleared his throat. "Sadie and Abigail shouldn't be left alone."

Sol grabbed his arm and jerked him back. His brother had a considerable amount of strength, honed from spending the past six years working as a carpenter and delivering large pieces of furniture to customers. "You take one more step and I'll make sure you won't walk right for the next six months."

Aden met Sol's intense glare. He knew his brother meant what he said and that he was capable of delivering on his threat. He also knew he couldn't leave. "Then you'll have to stop me," he said, turning and heading toward the store.

Within seconds his body pitched to the ground as Sol tackled him. His cheek scraped against the gravel as Sol yanked him up by the back of his shirt. Aden spun around. Years of suppressed anger from being at his brother's mercy threatened to push through the surface. For the first time in his life he cocked his fist, ready to plant it against his brother's elongated jaw.

But Sol easily grabbed Aden's arm and twisted it behind him. "Don't you know better than to test me, Aden?"

Aden winced as Sol thrust his bent arm farther up his back. He heard and felt his shoulder crack.

"Now, are you going to *geh* with me, or do I have to drag you out of here?" Sol spoke low in Aden's ear. "You wouldn't want the *maed* or the sheriff to come outside and see us like this." He jerked Aden's arm up again. "Fighting isn't our way, *ya*?"

Aden could feel the ligaments in his shoulder start to stretch. Fighting wasn't the Amish way, but that had never stopped Sol. "Fine," he muttered, making sure to keep the pain out of his voice. He wouldn't give his brother the satisfaction of knowing how much he'd hurt him. He was also ashamed of how easily his brother could render him defenseless.

Sol gave him a shove as he released Aden's arm. "Now, get in the buggy like you were told."

Aden followed his brother, a fury he couldn't express driving each step. Before he climbed into the buggy, he glanced over his sore shoulder at the store, wishing he wasn't such a coward. That he wasn't so weak. That he could offer Sadie comfort or at least be there so she wouldn't be alone. Instead he clenched his fists as he and Sol left.

• • •

"I know it's difficult for you to understand, Sadie. But this is God's will."

Sadie sat in the surgery waiting room of Langdon Hospital, staring at the huge abstract painting on the wall in front of her. It was a riot of color, the bright reds, blues, and yellows practically screaming at her, taunting her, doing the exact opposite of calming her down. Her hands curled around the arms of the chair as Bishop Troyer droned on.

"We will pray that Joanna makes it through the surgery." He paused, but she didn't look at him. "However, you must be prepared to accept God's will if she doesn't."

Pain shot through her hands as she squeezed the arms of the chair. "Joanna will make it."

"You cannot be sure about that."

She turned to him, her steady voice belying her quaking insides. *"Mei schwester* is going to live."

Bishop Troyer looked at her, pity in his eyes, the pale green shade so similar to Aden's. It was about the only physical characteristic the two men shared. With the exception of the bishop's gray beard, Sol was the mirror image of his father. Her skin crawled as she turned from the bishop, trying to push Sol and Aden from her mind. Why wouldn't Bishop Troyer leave her alone?

Then she heard Abigail sniffling and saw *Frau*

Troyer put her arm around Abigail's shoulders. Abigail leaned against her, and Sadie was glad she could find comfort from the bishop's wife, who was also grieving the loss of her friend. If Sadie had to suffer through Bishop Troyer's painful attempts at reassurance to help Abigail, so be it.

"Sadie, I know the time isn't *gut* right now." Bishop Troyer crossed one leg over the other. "But we must discuss *yer* parents' viewing and funeral . . . and possibly Joanna's, if that is God's plan."

I'm going to scream. I'm going to turn and scream right in his face.

"We can hold the viewing at *yer* home, or ours if you wish."

Shut up. Just shut up.

"I'll ask the ladies of the community to prepare a meal, of course. I can also pen an appropriate obituary for the local paper—"

"Fine," Sadie said, her teeth clenched so hard pain spiked through her jaw.

"You can look over it before I send it. The community will absorb the cost of the notice. You won't have to worry about that."

She nodded, still staring at the ugly painting, still wishing she could turn back the clock to this morning, before her mother and father and Joanna had left to pick apples. A simple task, something they did every fall. For years they had picked apples. She'd gone with *Mamm* and *Daed* last year. She should have been with them today. Maybe if she had—

"Then there is the issue of the store and the *haus*."

Sadie turned to him. "What did you say?"

"Many things concerning *yer* parents' property need to be settled. We can talk about it after the burial."

She jumped up from the chair, ignoring the curious looks from the other people waiting to hear about their own loved ones. She wrapped her arms around her waist and walked to the front desk. "Can you tell me when Joanna Schrock will be out of surgery?"

The short-haired woman looked up from her computer screen. "I'm sorry. We don't have that information."

"But it's been three hours."

"I'm sorry," she repeated, her voice monotone. "Please have a seat. As soon as the doctor is able, he'll come out and talk to you."

Sadie fisted her hand and planted it on top of the counter. The woman peered over her black square-framed glasses at Sadie's fist. Sadie withdrew her hand and turned around.

Bishop Troyer was now sitting next to Abigail, who was still leaning on *Frau* Troyer's shoulder. At least he wasn't talking anymore. Sadie sighed. Abigail didn't need to hear about obituaries and funerals and property discussions. She needed comfort. She needed hope.

Sadie was quickly losing hers.

"Ms. Schrock?"

She turned at the sound of the male voice. A tall, thin man wearing light blue clothing and a paper cap looked at her. "*Ya?*" she said, as she heard Abigail come up behind her.

"I'm Dr. Parr. Your sister is out of surgery."

"Thank God," Abigail said, threading her arm through Sadie's. "How is she?"

"Stable."

"What does that mean?" Sadie demanded.

"It means your sister is alive and in no immediate danger." He rested his hands on his narrow hips. "Though there is not the internal injury we had feared, her injuries are still extensive. Three of her ribs and her pelvis are broken, and she had a deep gash on her right cheek that we stitched closed."

Abigail sucked in a breath, her grip on Sadie tightening.

"She also suffered a concussion when she was thrown from the buggy. We've done a CAT scan on her brain, and the swelling is minimal." At Sadie's frown he added, "We don't think she has any brain damage."

The room began to spin. *Brain damage?*

"She's in recovery right now," the doctor continued. "When she comes to, we'll have more answers. There is one thing I can tell you now—she'll need extensive rehabilitation. One of our rehabilitation coordinators will contact you to discuss what that entails." He looked beyond Sadie's shoulder. "Are these your parents?"

Sadie turned to see Bishop and *Frau* Troyer standing behind her.

"*Nee*," Abigail whispered. "Our parents died in the accident."

The doctor paused. "I'm so sorry. I didn't know." He shook his head, looking slightly embarrassed. "I need to check on my patient. If anything changes, one of the nurses will let you know."

"When can we see her?" Sadie asked.

"Not for a couple of hours. It will be a while before she'll come out of the anesthesia. If she's still in stable condition, you can visit her briefly before we move her to intensive care."

After the doctor left, Sadie turned to Abigail. Tears were streaming down her sister's face. Sadie touched Abigail's cheek, wiping the tears away. "You heard the doctor," she said firmly. "Joanna is all right."

"But—"

"She's all right." Sadie hugged her sister, choking back her own tears. "Don't worry, Abby. The three of us will be all right."

The next afternoon, Sadie stood in the basement of her home, the bodies of her parents lying out on two tables side by side. For the past hour members of the community had filed by, offering their prayers and condolences. But she barely heard them, nodding numbly when she thought it was appropriate, saying thank you when someone paused during conversation, as if expecting her to respond.

The bishop and his wife made sure the viewing ran smoothly. Bishop Troyer stood at the basement door, solemnly greeting everyone as they came in, making quiet small talk with the ones who were waiting for their chance to speak to Sadie and Abigail. *Frau* Troyer was upstairs with some of the women, preparing simple fare for the guests after they were finished paying their respects.

Sadie wanted them all to go home.

"Sadie?"

She stiffened at the low, familiar voice. She met Aden's gaze with a steely one of her own. She knew he was here to keep up appearances. Sol had even walked by, barely acknowledging her and Abigail. She'd been grateful that she didn't have to pretend to be polite to him. Why didn't Aden ignore her too? It would be so much easier if he did.

Instead he remained in front of her, sorrow and sympathy punctuating each word he spoke. "I'm sorry about *yer* parents." He glanced down at his feet before looking at her again. "How is Joanna?"

"She's fine."

"Will she be coming home soon?"

Bile rose in Sadie's throat. Didn't he know the extent of Joanna's injuries? Or was he as deliberately cruel as his brother, only in a different way? "*Nee*," Sadie said firmly. "She's not."

"Oh." He took a step back. "I will keep praying for her then." He walked away, said a few words to Abigail, and went upstairs.

Surprised, Sadie didn't know what to think. He seemed genuine. Then again, he would have to be completely heartless not to be affected by what had happened to her family. He'd have to be like . . . Sol.

She put Aden and his brother out of her mind as she saw her friend Patience Glick approach.

"I'm so sorry," Patience said, hugging Sadie. Her husband, Timothy, stood behind her, his hands folded together, his gaze darting to Sadie's parents' lifeless bodies. "I wanted to *geh* to the hospital yesterday, but I was worried I'd be in the way."

"You're never in the way, Patience."

"Then I should have been there."

"It's all right that you weren't." For the first time since the sheriff's deputy walked into the store, Sadie felt something break inside. She and Patience had been best friends since childhood. She had been Patience's maid of honor at her and Timothy's wedding last year. She was like a sister to Sadie, and she felt warmth and love from her friend's embrace. Tears burned at the base of her throat.

"What can I do to help?" Patience asked.

Before answering, Sadie looked at Abigail, who was wiping her eyes for the hundredth time that day.

Sadie forced down her own sorrow. She needed to be strong for Abigail. "*Nix*," she said, giving Patience an even look. "We're okay."

"Are you sure?" Patience peered into Sadie's eyes.

She nodded. "I'm sure."

Patience took Sadie's hand. "If you need me, I'm here. Don't forget that, Sadie."

Sadie squeezed her hand and nodded but didn't say anything else.

Finally, everyone left, with the exception of two older women who insisted on staying to clean up the kitchen and living room. They were also going to spend the night, saying she and Abigail shouldn't be alone. Sadie was too tired to argue. Exhausted, Abigail had gone upstairs to her bedroom. But Sadie couldn't bring herself to leave her parents. Not yet.

She walked over to them. Both were dressed in their Sunday clothing. Their eyes were closed, their hands folded across their bodies, their skin a grayish color that made Sadie's stomach churn.

"I'll take care of everything," she said, her voice sounding thick, unreal to her ears. "The store, the *haus*, Abigail . . . Joanna." She touched her mother's shoulder, then her father's, saying good-bye the only way she knew how. "I won't let either of you down. I promise."

CHAPTER 3

Sadie sat beside Joanna's bed, brushing back a strand of mahogany hair from her forehead. It had slipped from beneath her bright pink kerchief, which Abigail had put on her this morning after carefully brushing Joanna's waist-length hair. Three days had passed since the accident, and Joanna had been moved out of intensive care and into her own hospital room. A small vase of pink geraniums was on her nightstand, courtesy of Patience and Timothy. Joanna's favorite color. It was typical of her friend to be so thoughtful.

"Sadie?"

She stilled her movements as Joanna's eyes, the tender skin around them black and blue from the accident, fluttered open. A white bandage covered her right cheek. Sadie had seen the stitches, which ran from the top of Joanna's cheek to the midpoint of her jaw line. Her heart ached for her sister's lovely face, which would be forever scarred. But the skin would heal, as would her pelvis and her ribs. Joanna was alive. That was all that mattered. "I'm here," she said, making sure to keep her tone as light as possible.

"Abigail?"

"She's getting a cup of *kaffee*. Do you need anything?"

Joanna started to shake her head, then grimaced. "Hurts."

Sadie took her hand. "I know. I'm sorry."

"Very . . . tired."

"*Geh* back to sleep, then. You don't have to stay awake for me." An IV tube trailed from Joanna's arm to what the nurse had called a medicine pump, which gave Joanna morphine on a regular basis. Sadie couldn't imagine her sister's pain. She also didn't know how much Joanna had understood when they told her yesterday about *Mamm* and *Daed*. Abigail had wanted to wait, but Sadie didn't see the point. They had to come to grips with the reality of the situation so they could face it head-on.

As Joanna drifted off, Abigail came into the room carrying two cups of coffee. The strings of her white *kapp* lay limply against her plum-colored dress. She gestured with her head to Sadie, whispering that they needed to leave the room.

Sadie glanced at Joanna, who was already asleep. She quietly rose from the chair next to the bed and joined Abigail in the hallway.

Her sister handed her one of the warm Styrofoam cups. "I ran into the rehabilitation coordinator as I was going to get the *kaffee*," Abigail said. "She was at the nurse's station."

"What did she say?"

"That Joanna should be going to rehabilitation by the end of next week."

"So soon? She can barely stay awake."

Abigail nodded. "But they think she'll be ready. It's a *gut* thing, Sadie. There's only so much they can do for her here. When she's at the rehabilitation facility, she'll get the care and therapy she needs to help her heal as fast as possible."

Sadie nodded, both hands circling her coffee cup. "Where is the facility?"

"There's one in Middlefield."

Her heart dropped. "That's the closest?"

"*Ya.*" Abigail took a sip of the coffee.

After their parents' burial she'd managed to pull herself together a little bit more. Sadie knew how difficult it was for her sister. She was the most carefree of the three of them, but she also had the biggest heart.

"Middlefield is far." Sadie mentally calculated the cost of hiring a taxi to travel the nearly hour's drive to the city. Even without one of them visiting Joanna every day, it would be expensive. That plus the cost of the facility, the hospital bills . . . her temples started to throb.

"I have an idea, Sadie." Abigail leaned her hip against the wall. "You might not agree with it, but I think it's our best option." She paused. "I want to call Mary Shetler."

Surprised by the suggestion, Sadie asked, "*Mamm*'s cousin?"

Abigail nodded. "I'm sure once I explain the situation I can stay with her. I already looked up the facility's address, and it's a short taxi ride from Mary's *haus*."

"I don't know . . ."

"I realize it will leave you shorthanded at the store." Abigail's lower lip started to tremble. "I don't want to leave Joanna alone, Sadie. She needs one of us with her."

She touched Abigail's shoulder. "It's okay," she said softly and was pleased to see Abigail steady again. Remembering her friend's offer of help, she added, "I can ask Patience to work with me at the store for a little while. I'm sure Timothy won't mind." She paused. "But what if Mary won't let you stay? We're not close to *Mamm*'s side of the *familye*." Her cousin had come to the funeral but hadn't stayed long. Sadie barely remembered speaking with her.

"We have to try," Abigail said. "If that doesn't work, I'm sure God will provide another way for me to be with Joanna."

"*Ya*," Sadie said, her voice barely above a whisper. "I'm sure he will." She looked at the small placard beneath the room number. *J Schrock*. Her heart lurched as she thought of her sister's long recovery. She and Abigail wouldn't let Joanna go through the healing process alone. She needed family with her, even if it was only one sister and a cousin they didn't know.

"I'll *geh* make the call," Abigail said.

As Abigail walked away, Sadie leaned against

the wall and closed her eyes. "Make a way for her, Lord," she whispered. "Please, make a way for all of us."

On Friday of the following week, Sadie stood in front of Schrock Grocery and Tools holding the key to the door in her hand. The store had been closed since the day the sheriff's deputy had arrived, almost two weeks ago. The day her life had changed forever.

She paused before unlocking the door, biting her bottom lip and steeling her determination. She couldn't let her emotions overcome her, not now. Joanna and Abigail were on their way to Middlefield. Mary had agreed to let Abigail stay with her as long as she needed to. With her sisters somewhat settled, Sadie needed to make good on her promise to her parents, and that included making sure Schrock Grocery and Tools would be open for business on Monday. With a deep breath, she put the key in the lock and turned it.

She walked inside, memories immediately washing over her with so much force she had to use the counter for support. Every inch of the store reminded her of her parents. She picked up a yellow pencil off the counter and put it in the plastic cup next to the simple cash register, one her parents had purchased last year after Sadie had begged them to buy it. Despite acquiring the little bit of technology Bishop Troyer had approved for their business, her mother had still used a calculator, a scrap of paper, and her favorite yellow pencil to tally up customer purchases. "This way is easier for me," she'd said more than once when Sadie asked why she wasn't using the register.

Sadie stared at the cup of yellow pencils, the memories dissolving into anger. She hit the cup, knocking it over and spilling the pencils. They tumbled off the counter and rolled on the concrete floor. She didn't bother to pick them up.

She opened the door to the office and sat down in her father's old emerald green desk chair, one he'd bought at an auction when Sadie was a little girl. She turned on the small battery-operated lantern on the desk. Light flooded the room. She stared straight ahead at the plain cork bulletin board her father had used to tack up his scribbled notes and reminders. Every inch of the board was covered, and some of the notes overlapped other notes. She couldn't bring herself to look around the office, with its stacks of catalogs, order forms, and invoices shoved wherever space allowed. *Daed* had never been organized with his paper-work, yet he claimed to know where everything was. "I got a system," he'd said time and time again, and sure enough, he was able to produce any document or catalog without hesitation.

Rubbing her left temple, she opened the top drawer of the desk, and after rummaging for a bit, pulled out a pad of paper. She began writing down expenses—first the taxi fares she and Abigail had incurred since the accident, then the taxi fare to send Abigail to Middlefield. She wrote down the words *ambulance, hospital,* and *rehabilitation center,* but left the amounts blank. She'd get the bills soon enough for those. Then she estimated how much money the store had lost from being closed for two weeks. When she finished writing down the amount, she tossed the pencil onto the desk.

She spent the next few hours looking at invoices and bank account statements, finding bills that were either due soon or hadn't been paid and were overdue. She was shocked to discover how far in the red—a term she'd read about in that accounting book—the store's finances were. She propped her elbows on the desk and put her hands on either side of her head. How could her father have been so irresponsible with money? Did her mother know? She couldn't imagine her parents had any secrets from each other. Then again, she never would have imagined they would have been this deeply in debt.

She sighed and lifted her head. Abigail couldn't know about this. Neither could Joanna. And she couldn't continue to let the store bleed out money. She and her sisters had no income without the store. They'd have nowhere to go if she had to sell their property to pay their debts.

Every muscle in her body tensed. She needed help, and there was only one person she could turn to. The community had established a fund for any member in need. All the families that could contribute did so yearly, and Bishop Troyer managed the money. He was in charge of disbursing the emergency funds, and this certainly qualified as an emergency.

The idea of going to him and admitting her father's mismanagement not only galled, it felt like a betrayal. Like she was tainting her father's memory. The bishop would be discreet—Sadie had never heard of anyone receiving the money, even though she knew that over the years there must have been times when the fund was needed. She pushed back from the desk and stood. She'd only ask for enough to cover the expenses from the accident. Somehow she'd figure out the rest. She locked up the store and headed for her buggy. It was suppertime, but this couldn't wait.

As she put on Apple's harness, it slipped through her fumbling hands and fell to the ground. She picked up the harness and tried again. Maybe Sol wouldn't be home. Maybe Aden would be far in the backyard with his bees. Maybe she wouldn't have to explain too much to the bishop about her father's mismanagement. Maybe he would write her a check from the fund on the spot.

Maybe a miracle would happen.

But as she headed toward the Troyers', she had the feeling she wouldn't see a miracle anytime soon.

The clink of silverware against plain white dishes was the only sound in the Troyers' dining room. Aden held a fork in his hand, but he could barely bring himself to eat the open-faced meat loaf sandwich his mother had prepared for supper that night. He was still concerned about Sadie, even though he hadn't seen her since her parents' burial. He glanced at Sol, who was shoveling the food into his mouth as if he couldn't get it down his gullet fast enough. His brother had always eaten that way, polishing off a meal in record time, then excusing himself as soon as possible. Which was fine by Aden. The less time he spent with Sol, the better.

"I gotta *geh*," Sol said, shoving back from the table, barely giving a glance to his mother as he stood. He hurried out of the room. He never explained where he went, although Aden suspected whatever he was going to do most likely would involve booze and trouble. He set down his fork in disgust.

"Delicious supper, Rhoda. As always." *Daed* wiped the corner of his mouth with a paper napkin and gave her a small smile. Then he looked at Aden, his expression frosty. "Is there something wrong with *yer* food?"

"*Nee.*" He quickly shoveled a forkful of meat loaf into his mouth. He swallowed, barely chewing it. Of course his father would ignore Sol's rude behavior and focus on nitpicking Aden's every move.

A sharp rapping sound came from the front door. *Mamm* quickly stood. "I'll get it," she said and hurried from the kitchen.

Aden turned to his *daed*, who was finishing off the last bit of tea from his glass, and fought the deep-seated resentment that never wavered. How many sermons had his father preached on the Ten Commandments over the years—the commandment to *honor thy father and mother* in particular? Aden loved his mother. He honored her. But he had to scrape the bottom of his soul to find a shred of respect for his father.

"We have company."

Aden looked up as *Mamm* came into the kitchen, followed by Sadie. His heart stilled at the mix of emotions passing over her face. Sorrow, exhaustion, grief . . . and shame? Her rosy cheeks shone with it, and her gaze never strayed to his. She barely glanced at his father when he started to speak.

"What can we do for you, Sadie?"

She held a black leather purse and rubbed

her thumb back and forth on the strap. The black bonnet that covered her white *kapp* framed her face, and Aden couldn't pull his gaze from her. He wished he could erase the past and ease her pain. But there was nothing he could do.

"I was wondering . . ." Her thumb moved faster across her purse strap until Aden thought she might rub the color right off the leather. "Could I talk to you for a minute?"

The bishop nodded and stood. "We can *geh* into *mei* office." He didn't say anything else, and Sadie followed him out of the kitchen.

His mother began to clear the table. Aden stood and started to help, but she shook her head. "I'll take care of it," she said. She always declined his offers of help, especially when it came to doing anything in the house.

"I'll check on the hives then," he said, pushing his chair up to the table. The bees were fine, but he couldn't stay in this house. Not when he wanted to know what was going on with Sadie. The urge to listen in on her conversation with his father overwhelmed him. He fought against it and went outside. But instead of going to his hives, he looked up at the sky, taking in the streaks of pale pinks, purples, and oranges. A beautiful sunset. He briefly wondered if Sadie appreciated sunsets as much as he did. Then he shrugged. It didn't matter what she appreciated. He would never find out. He sighed and headed toward his hives, one of the few things in his life that brought him peace.

Sol made his way along a dark, almost empty road. He wasn't quite sure how he'd strayed in this direction after leaving his house, and he didn't care. He brought the whiskey bottle to his lips and took a long drink, letting the amber liquid burn his throat. He had a couple of bottles stashed away in the top loft of the barn, where his father would never find them. A few more deep gulps from the bottle and he wouldn't have to think. Or feel. He would be numb, if only for a little while.

He tipped up the bottle and took another long pull. His father knew he drank spirits, but for some reason he looked the other way when it came to Sol's drinking habits. As long as he didn't do anything to publicly embarrass his old man, nothing was off limits. But it hadn't always been that way. There was a time when his father had held a tight rein on Sol, measuring what seemed to be his every waking breath and comparing it to some unattainable standard of what a real "man" was. When Sol fell short his father took action . . . and Sol had permanent scars to remind him of his failure.

He blew out a breath, his brain already fuzzy and his legs starting to wobble as he was transported to the past. He had just turned twelve, and his father's discipline had changed. Even now, years later and through a whiskey-induced haze, Sol could remember the first time his father had told him to punish his brother, under the guise of turning his sons into men. Aden had been eight and had been late bringing the four cows they owned back into the barn. That deserved correction, and his father instructed Sol not to touch Aden's face or any other part of his body that would show a bruise.

Sol hadn't wanted to do it. But he chose self-preservation over his little brother, and it wasn't long before taking out his frustration on Aden became routine. Eventually his brother had stopped crying. He'd stopped trying to dodge the blows. He started looking Sol straight in the eye and taking whatever Sol gave him.

And every day, Sol had to live with that.

When he'd twisted Aden's arm behind his back the day the Schrocks died to get him to leave the store, it had been nearly two years since he'd touched his brother. But Sol had seen the pain and shock on Sadie's and Abigail's faces, and he couldn't handle it. He had to get out of there. But Aden wouldn't listen to words. So, like his father had said dozens of times over the years, sometimes physical force was required.

He took the last drink from the bottle and let out a bitter chuckle. What would the community say about their bishop if they knew the way he treated his sons? His father would justify it, of course. He always did to their mother, though Sol doubted she truly knew the extent of *Daed*'s disciplinary methods. Never sparing the rod wasn't a proverb in the Troyer house; it was the law. No one ever questioned Emmanuel Troyer—not as a bishop, and definitely not as a father.

He threw down the bottle. It smashed into dozens of sparkling shards that littered the street. He meandered farther, his drunken steps zigzagging from the asphalt to the soft ground at the shoulder of the road, then back again.

A few minutes later he tripped over his own feet and landed facedown on the street. His cheek stung as he levered himself up to an unsteady standing position. He needed to find a place to lie down, to sleep off the whiskey so he could get up in the morning and go to work. Lately he'd been drinking too much and had missed work a couple of days over the past two months. He'd also shown up to work hung over. At the rate he was going, he knew he would lose his job.

But at that moment, Sol didn't care. He walked into an empty field, collapsed to the ground, and passed out.

CHAPTER 4

Sadie sat on the hard wooden chair across from Bishop Troyer. He was behind a simple small desk. The surface was neat and tidy, with only a short stack of papers, a Bible, and a pen in sight. Such a stark contrast to her father's jumbled desktop. Sadie opened her purse and pulled out the legal pad she'd been writing on earlier. She kept her gaze averted as she handed it to him.

He perused the figures before carefully placing the pad on his desk. "This is all so tragic, Sadie. So . . . senseless."

"I thought you said it was God's will."

"Oh, it is. I have *nee* doubt about that. But knowing that it's God's will that *yer* parents departed this earth and left behind three daughters and an extraordinary amount of debt doesn't make it any less unfortunate."

Sadie cringed, wishing she hadn't come. She'd never understood the bishop's tendency toward such formal speech. He sounded almost like he was from another time when he talked, especially when he preached. Since their district had been so small for so long, he wasn't just the bishop, but also minister and deacon. He filled all the roles in the church, although she recalled her father saying a few weeks ago that since their numbers had grown, it might be the right time to select a minister or two. But as far as she knew, nothing ever came of that.

Tonight his words weren't just overly formal. They cut her deeply.

"I understand *yer* sisters are in Middlefield." Bishop Troyer looked at Sadie, a slight frown tugging at his lips above his gray beard. "I wish you would have consulted me before making the decision to send Joanna there."

"Middlefield has the closest rehabilitation center. There really wasn't much of a decision to make."

"Still, it would have been nice to have been informed. Since *yer* father is *nee* longer here, I'd like you to consider me a *vatter* figure in his absence."

Sadie stilled. "That's . . . kind of you, Bishop Troyer." No one would ever, *ever* replace her father. She ignored his offer and got down to the real reason she was here. "I need some help. I plan on opening the store on Monday, but it will take time to get enough money to pay the expenses from the"—she swallowed the hard lump that had jumped to her throat—"accident."

"I see." He stared at her for a long moment.

She started to shrink beneath his gaze. His eyes were on her, but he seemed to be looking right through her. Why couldn't he give her what she needed so she could be on her way? The only good thing was that Sol didn't seem to be home. Seeing Aden had been bad enough.

Then the bishop's eyes seemed to focus, a spark of light glimmering from them. "I have the utmost sympathy for you, Sadie. You've lost *yer* parents, *yer* youngest sister is gravely injured, and *yer* other sister is away from home. You're alone, Sadie. All alone. That is a desperate place to be."

"But I'm not alone," she said. "God is with me."

The bishop cleared his throat. "That is true. He is a Father to the fatherless."

She lifted her chin. "I also have *mei* friends—"

"But it's not the same, is it?" He leaned forward in the chair. "Having friends who drop by, who pat you on the back and bring you casseroles and tell you everything will be all right, isn't what you want. It isn't what you need."

"I don't understand."

The bishop clasped his hands together. "So many responsibilities are being thrust upon you." He started ticking off a list on his fingers. "The hospital bills. Running the store. Maintaining a household. Keeping up with the seven acres of property *yer* parents owned. It's too much for one person to handle. While God is *yer* spiritual Father, you also need someone to help you make the decisions you're incapable of making yourself."

She popped up from the chair, indignant. She

might be young, but she wasn't stupid. She could make any decision necessary, with prayer . . . and some financial help. "All I need is some money from the community fund. Which I will pay back as soon as possible."

The bishop shook his head. "Really, now, Sadie. If you were a *mann* . . . maybe."

A mann? She had to force herself not to snap at him. Yes, she understood that her father had been the head of their household and that her future husband—which she did *not* intend to have— would be the head of hers. That was biblical. However, to assume that she couldn't manage a house and a store because she was female—that wasn't fair.

She could see now that he wasn't going to give her any money. With the weird look in his eyes, she didn't want anything except to leave. "I need to get back home," she said, moving toward the door.

"*Ya*," he said, standing. "You do need to *geh* home." He moved toward her and put his hand on her arm, causing her to flinch. "Rest assured, there is a solution. I'll be in touch." He opened the door and held it open for her. She didn't have any choice but to leave.

When she walked into the living room, it was empty. From his office doorway, the bishop nodded in the direction of the front door. Sadie let herself out.

Confusion stunned her as she traveled back home. Fortunately her horse knew the way because she was having trouble concentrating. What did he mean by a solution? Why couldn't he have given her the money she asked for? She even offered to pay it back, but it was like he'd never heard her request.

She pulled into the driveway and put up her horse. The barn needed cleaning. The laundry needed to be done. Winter would be here before she knew it, and there was still firewood to be cut, split, and laid. Her stomach lurched as she thought of everything she had to take care of. The bishop had been right about all the responsibility she had to carry. She knew all she had to do was say the word and members of her community would help.

But she had asked for help, from the leader of the community, and he hadn't given her what she asked for. *I'll be in touch.* What did that even mean? Maybe he would change his mind after some time to think about it. He had to know she had nowhere else to turn.

She readied herself for bed, the house eerily quiet. She'd never felt so alone. Even God seemed distant. A couple of women had offered to stay with her for a few days, but she didn't want to take anyone away from their own families, including Patience.

Sadie pulled the covers up to her chin and

closed her eyes, praying for help. God would provide, she kept reminding herself over and over. Yet it was hours before she was able to fall into a fitful sleep.

The next morning, Aden finished up the chores in the barn, making sure their two horses had their breakfast hay. They didn't keep any other animals now, and Aden didn't count his bees as part of the family assets. They were his alone.

He went back into the house, and even though he was hungry, he thought about skipping breakfast. Sometime during the night he'd heard his brother stumble into his room, which was next door to Aden's. Over the past couple of years they had formed a sort of truce—or at least Sol got drunk to release his frustration instead of pounding on Aden. He could almost feel sorry for his brother . . . and then he'd remember all the times Sol had never shown him mercy. And as for himself . . . he could never let himself be angry, much less allow it to show. Keeping up appearances. Showing strength at all times. That was part of being a man.

Secrets and shame were also part of being a *Troyer* man.

He bypassed the kitchen for the stairs. The smoky scent of cooked bacon and freshly toasted bread almost made him change his mind about breakfast. But sitting through the

77

evening meal with his family was torturous enough.

Then he heard his father say Sadie's name. Aden stopped, then he crept nearer to the open doorway. He'd wondered what had happened between *Daed* and Sadie when she was in his office last night, but he hadn't dared ask. He hadn't seen Sadie leave, so he had no idea if their conversation had gone the way she'd wanted it to. For her sake, he hoped so.

"It's the only practical solution for her," his father continued.

Aden peeked around the corner and saw his father standing at the end of the table, his coffee cup in hand. A platter of bacon, a dish of eggs, and a stack of toast were on the table, but he wasn't eating. Neither was *Mamm*. She sat on the opposite end, darning a black sock.

"It must be soon. There is *nee* time to tarry."

Aden's brow lifted. What was his father talking about?

"Emmanuel." *Mamm*'s voice sounded small, but there was a tiny bit of force behind it. She laid the sock on the table and lifted her gaze to his. "Why not give Sadie the money she needs?"

His father shook his head. "Because her situation isn't one that will be solved with a check."

"And you think it will be solved with a marriage?"

Aden sucked in a breath. Marriage? Surely

not to Sol. Even his father wouldn't be that controlling . . . or cruel. *Not to someone who wasn't his son.*

"I have always done what is best for the members of this community," *Daed* continued. "Sacrifices must be made, sometimes, for the betterment of all."

Sacrifices? How would Sadie marrying Sol be better for *anyone?*

"Do you trust me, Rhoda?" his father asked.

Aden peeked farther into the room to see his *daed* looking at *Mamm*, his profile intent and expectant. Was he asking for approval? Aden doubted it. More likely, he expected her compliance.

She lifted her eyes to him and nodded. "I always trust you will do the right thing, Emmanuel."

Clenching his teeth, Aden pulled away. His father was *not* doing the right thing, and either his mother was blind to that fact or she was agreeing to avoid conflict. She was completely devoted to him, something Aden found difficult to understand as he got older.

But even though his mother would go along with *Daed*'s plan, Aden refused to. He hurried upstairs and barged into Sol's room. The smell of stale alcohol immediately hit him as he saw the lump that was his brother underneath a pile of quilts. He hadn't woken up yet. Aden pushed against Sol's shoulder, not caring if he drew the man's anger.

Sol opened his eyes. They were glassy and red-rimmed. Aden didn't drink, and after seeing his brother hung over like this a few times before, he wouldn't touch the stuff. "What?" Sol snarled.

"Did you know?"

"Know what?" Sol sat up, his forehead falling into his hands. He groaned, keeping his head down.

"About *Daed*'s plan."

Sol looked up and glared at him. "You sound *ab im kopp*. Get out of *mei* room before I throw you out."

Aden held his ground. "Did you know *Daed* wants you to marry Sadie Schrock?"

Sol didn't move. "What?" he finally said after giving Aden a blank stare.

Aden filled his brother in on what he heard downstairs. As he talked, Sol scrambled out of the bed, now at attention. "He's crafty," Sol mumbled. "I'll give him that."

Now it was Aden's turn to be confused. "What are you talking about?"

Sol shrugged. "I suppose there are worse women I could be stuck with."

He's still drunk. That was the only explanation for his casual acceptance of his father's life-altering plans and backhanded compliment to

80

Sadie. Sol would be lucky to have her. Any man would.

Aden ground his back teeth. His father, and now his brother, were both deciding her future. Did they even have the right to do this?

Then again, who dared defy Bishop Troyer?

Before Sol could say anything else, Aden fled the room. He had to warn Sadie. He had no idea what he would say, but he couldn't stand by and do nothing.

He couldn't allow Sadie's worst nightmare to come true.

Sol's head pounded as he pulled on his trousers, barely noticing as Aden ran out the door. Marriage to Sadie Schrock. He had to let that sink into his hangover-addled brain. He was having a hard time comprehending it. He had liked her at one time—a lot, more than he'd liked any girl in their district. She had a unique beauty that he'd found irresistible when he was eighteen. Yet anytime he tried to show her the slightest bit of friendliness, she'd barely acknowledged him. When she did, she always cut him with irritated glances and caustic frowns. He could have any girl he wanted, and more than a couple had definitely let him know they were willing. But unlike those other girls, Sadie had acted like she was above him. Like his existence on earth annoyed her.

He'd wanted to teach her a lesson that day in the cornfield. He'd been drinking that afternoon too. Homemade beer, which had been easy to get from his friend Jalon, whose father had been making his own beer for years. When he saw Sadie walking on the side of the road, alone, he reacted. He had only wanted a kiss, but once his lips had touched hers, something shifted in his mind and body, and he suddenly wanted more.

He'd sensed her repulsion as he kissed her. Felt her fighting against him. She didn't want him even though he was the bishop's son. She looked down on him like he was horse manure on the sole of her shoe. And when she kneed him and left him curled up in agony on the ground, any romantic interest in her disappeared.

He shook his aching head at the irony that his father thought marriage between him and Sadie Schrock was a good idea. The only person who would benefit would be *Daed*. He knew exactly what his father's true reasons were for arranging a marriage with Sadie. He was the only one who knew.

Sol let out a long breath. This wasn't what he'd envisioned for his future. Then again, his future had been bleak for so long, he didn't dare look very far ahead. Getting through each day was an accomplishment.

A thought occurred to him, making him pause in the middle of slipping on a black sock.

Marrying Sadie meant he would be *free*. At least somewhat free—until his father got what he wanted out of the arrangement. Even after that he would still owe loyalty to his father, but as a member of the congregation. Not as a son trapped in a situation—in a family—he was desperate to escape.

He finished putting on his socks as he heard his father's approaching footsteps on the stairs. He couldn't afford to think about Sadie except as a means to an end—and he refused to feel guilty about it. When the door opened, he stood and met his father's steady gaze, ignoring the pulsing throb in his head. He smoothed his hands over his hair and tried to look presentable and not like he'd been on a night-long bender and slept part of it off in a grassy field.

"Solomon," his father said as he entered the room. He closed the door and faced him, his nose wrinkling as he took an audible breath. His look traveled from Sol's head down to his feet, then back up again.

He didn't say anything. He didn't have to. Sol could see every thought in his eyes. The disappointment. The derision. The repulsion. What he'd never seen from his father was caring, or compassion, or love. He used to crave that from him and would do anything *Daed* asked to try to gain it—even if it meant destroying his relationship with his brother. But he'd never succeeded in earning it, and he'd given up trying.

Except now he had another chance, not only to be free, but to gain his father's respect.

Daed set his stony eyes on Sol. "*Sohn*, we need to talk."

After his father explained his plan and Sol's part in it, Sol nodded. "I'll marry her," he said, his breath held as he waited for his father to respond.

His father didn't say anything, only nodded and opened the door.

"*Daed*," Sol said, unable to stop himself. When his father turned, Sol asked, "What if I'd said *nee*?"

His father regarded him for a long moment, his eyes as flat as they usually were when they dealt with each other. "You wouldn't have."

Sol sank down onto the bed after his father left. He rubbed his aching head and leaned forward, his elbows on his knees. This wasn't sitting well with him. Then again, not much in his life had. He sat up, straightening his shoulders and steeling his nerve. Now he had a chance to change his future, and he would grab the opportunity and run. Sadie Schrock would just have to go along for the ride.

Still exhausted from lack of sleep and a preponderance of worry, Sadie walked into the store office and sank into her father's chair. She didn't know what she was going to do, and she was troubled by her visit to the bishop. She had needed his help, and he refused to give it. He'd lost her trust at that moment, and some of her respect.

Earlier that morning she'd skipped breakfast and gone outside for a walk. She needed to pray, to clear her head, to get away from the house that held so many memories that it was becoming difficult to be there alone. She missed Abigail and Joanna so much it ached. She didn't dare think about her parents for any length of time. That pain was more than she could bear. Focusing on her financial problems was stressful, but also a distraction.

Sadie didn't know how long she was gone, but by the time she returned she was hungry. She'd opened the door to the store and taken a snack package of donuts off the shelf, snatching a bottle of pop off another shelf as she made her way to the office. Not the best breakfast, but she didn't care. She needed something to stave off her hunger.

She stared at the powdered donuts on the desk and sighed. She had the thin plastic packaging halfway open when she heard the knob to the office door turn. She froze. She'd forgotten to lock the store door behind her. She'd never had a reason to be afraid of being alone in the store before, but for some reason a cold shiver shook her spine.

"Hello, Sadie." Bishop Troyer walked into the office, not waiting for an invitation. He closed the door behind him and sat down on a metal chair beside the desk, the one her mother used to sit on when she and her father shared their lunch in the office.

"Bishop Troyer," Sadie said, her eyebrows lifting. "I'm surprised to see you so soon."

He looked around the small room with intense curiosity before shifting his gaze back to her. "I told you I would be in touch." He smiled.

"Then you've brought me a check?" she asked, hope igniting within. It was extinguished with the bishop's next words.

"*Nee.* But there is a way to resolve *yer* situation that will be best for everyone concerned."

He was looking at her with complete surety and confidence. What she felt was the exact opposite, and she didn't want to hear what he had to say. "I've solved the problem myself," she lied. "You don't have to be concerned about it anymore."

He held up his hand. "Sadie, of course I'm concerned. How can I not be? I'm not only here for spiritual guidance, but for practical assistance as well. I'm sure *yer vatter* would be pleased to know that you and *yer* sisters will be well cared for." He leaned closer to her. "I came here to offer you comfort, Sadie. A future and a hope."

Her distrust of him grew with each word he

spoke. "*Danki*, Bishop," she said, struggling to keep her tone even. "But really, I'm okay. I had a moment of panic, but it's passed now." She lifted her chin, hoping she showed a self-assurance she didn't feel.

"*Yer* reaction to *yer* situation has proved *mei* point." The bishop stood. "You shouldn't be alone, Sadie." He opened the door and Sol came striding in.

Sudden fear propelled Sadie from the chair. "What is he doing here?"

Bishop Troyer motioned for Sol to stand beside him. "Solomon has offered to marry you."

"*What?*" She looked from the bishop to Sol, trying to judge if they were serious. One glance at each of them told her they were. The bishop's lips formed a satisfied smile above his gray beard, and Sol was steadfast in his posture and expression. He looked almost . . . blank, but also determined.

This can't be happening . . . She stumbled back, falling against the chair. "*Nee*. I'm not marrying *him*."

"Sadie." Bishop Troyer admonished as if he were addressing a five-year-old. "Surely you can see the practicality of having a husband to help you and *yer* sisters."

"I don't care about being practical!"

The bishop's smile disappeared. "There's *nee* need to raise *yer* voice." He turned to Sol, whose lips had tightened into a thin line. "Perhaps I should have a word alone with *yer* future bride."

"I'm not his bride—not in the future, not ever."

Bishop Troyer shifted his focus back on her. The coldness in his eyes chilled her blood.

Aden jerked the buggy to a stop outside Schrock Grocery and Tools. He'd been by earlier, but Sadie hadn't been home, and he'd spent the past hour driving to any place he could think of in Birch Creek where she might be. Finally he gave up and decided to check her house one last desperate time. Maybe she had gone to see Joanna in the hospital. For her sake, he hoped so. He saw his father's buggy in the driveway and panicked, knowing Sadie had to be inside and fearing he was too late.

He hurried out of the buggy and ran into the store. Light shined from the back of the building, where the office was located. He headed there, stopping in front of the office door when he heard Sadie's trembling, angry voice.

"I'm not his bride—not in the future, not ever."

Once he heard those words, he rushed into the room, knocking into his brother.

"Hey!" Sol snapped.

But Aden ignored him. "*Daed*, stop." He took a deep breath, his pulse hammering through his body, his chest rising up and down. "Sadie can't marry Sol."

"Shut up, Aden," Sol said. "This doesn't concern you."

"*Ya*, it does." He scrambled, his mind frenzied. "Sol can't marry Sadie," he repeated, grasping for something else to say, for the words to put a stop to this.

Sol was about to say something else, but their father held up his hand. "Why not, Aden?"

The words flew out of his mouth before they were fully formed in his brain. "Because . . . I'm marrying her."

Chapter 5

Sadie's mouth dropped open. Had she heard Aden correctly? She grabbed the side of the desk to steady herself. None of this made any sense. Turning to him, her mouth clamped shut when she saw he was absolutely serious.

Aden's eyes searched hers, sending an unspoken message she couldn't decipher. He moved to stand next to her, staying close, and looking at her with a warmth she'd never seen from him before. "I want to marry you."

He sounded convincing. As if the words were true. Her breath unexpectedly caught in her throat.

"Aden," the bishop said, his voice composed amid the turmoil in the room. "I must say, *yer* proclamation is a surprise."

"*Ya.*" Sol took a step toward Aden, his eyes flaring. "It is."

Bishop Troyer put out his arm, holding Sol back. "There's *nee* need for anyone to get upset, Solomon. Let *yer bruder* explain himself."

Aden grasped her hand. She flinched but didn't pull back even though she wanted to. She didn't understand what he was doing, but she knew she needed to play along for both their sakes. He looked at her, his lips forming a pinched, awkward smile. The silent plea in his eyes was still there.

"We didn't want you to find out this way," Aden said, facing his father. "I wanted to tell you when the time was right."

"Tell me what?"

He let out a long breath. "Sadie and I have been courting in secret."

She flushed. His declaration shocked her, along with the unqualified certainty with which he'd said the words. If she didn't know the truth, she would have believed him.

The bishop's intense gaze landed on her. "Is this true, Sadie? Have you been seeing *mei sohn*?"

Sadie swallowed. She yearned to tell him no, to send all of them away so she could be left alone to try to piece her life back together, to stop it from shattering even more. Yet slowly she was realizing her life wasn't hers anymore. "*Y-ya*," she whispered, forcing out the lie, almost choking on the falsehood. She clung to Aden as black dots swarmed her vision. *God, forgive me . . .*

Aden squeezed her hand, the gentle gesture adding to her confusion and shock.

The bishop stroked his beard. "Why did you feel the need to keep this from me, Aden?"

He squared his shoulders and released Sadie's hand. "I didn't realize I had to tell you. We wanted to keep our relationship private. We

91

wouldn't be the first couple to do that in our community."

Sadie's legs started to tremble. She felt like a spectator despite knowing the conversation concerned her future. She was observing some sort of personal struggle between father and son. Even Sol seemed to be left out, although he kept his stunned stare fully targeted at Aden.

Bishop Troyer turned to Sadie again. "If what you say is true, that you and Aden have been seeing each other behind *mei* back—"

"In private," Aden insisted.

"Then you must have feelings for him. Tell me, Sadie . . . do you love him?"

"*Ya*," Aden said.

His father raised his hand. "I want to hear it from you, Sadie. If you love *mei sohn*, truly love him, then I will allow the marriage."

Her head spun. She didn't understand Bishop Troyer's quick change of mind. Moments ago he'd been ready to insist she marry Sol, whom she definitely did *not* love. Now he wanted her to admit a lie.

Either way, she realized now that he was never going to help her with money from the community fund. He didn't think she was capable of taking care of her own family. She'd have to marry one brother or the other to survive, to care for her sisters. There was no one else to turn to. She was trapped.

"*Daed*," Sol said, his voice growing sharp. "I said I would marry her."

"The situation has changed, Solomon." He dismissed him with another wave of his hand. "It is up to Sadie to make her choice."

A choice. She choked back a bitter laugh. This wasn't a choice. It was coercion. If she admitted she didn't love Aden, that they had never exchanged more than a few strained words, she would default to being Sol's bride. The bishop wouldn't take no for an answer. Even if she refused today, he would find a way in the near future. She could tell how determined he was for her to marry one of his sons. Clearly, the only thing he didn't care about was which one.

But why? Why was she being forced into a loveless marriage by a man who was the absolute spiritual authority in her community?

Lord . . . what am I supposed to do?

Her frantic gaze darted to each of the men in the room, all of them waiting for her answer.

Aden forced down the bile climbing up his throat. He couldn't believe she was going along with the farce he'd set in motion. An idea he'd thrown out in desperation was now being seriously contemplated not only by her but by his father.

He watched as her eyes jerked from his eyes to Sol's, to their father's. He could put an end to this and admit he'd lied. He could walk away, go back to his bees and his empty life. Sadie Schrock wasn't his problem. She didn't even *like* him.

But he couldn't leave her at the mercy of his father and Sol. Even though he could take back the proposal . . . he realized he didn't want to. When he told Sadie he wanted to marry her, he meant it.

He could sense her body trembling beside him. He saw the stark fear in her deep brown eyes. Knowing their past, he wasn't sure who she was more afraid of—his brother or him.

"Sadie?" His father's voice pierced his thoughts. "You need to make a decision. Which one of *mei sohns* do you choose?"

"This isn't fair," Sol muttered.

Aden refused to look at his brother. This morning he'd been so blasé about their father's plan, but now he was furious about possibly being denied. If Sol had feelings for Sadie all these years, Aden never knew it. He only knew about the time in the cornfield—and he didn't know what really happened. Whatever was going on here, Sol's reasons for agreeing to marry had nothing to do with love.

And mine do?

He gave himself a mental shake. He was protecting Sadie. He had to. He'd failed her once. He wouldn't do it again.

For her encouragement as much as his own,

he took her hand once more, expecting her to pull away. To his relief, she gripped his fingers.

"With everything that's happened in the past weeks," she said, lifting her chin, her words sounding measured, "I would hope that I could have time to think about it."

"What's to think about?" Sol said, his tone sharp. "If you two are courting, if you are both in *love*"—he spat out the word—"then the decision should be easy." He took a threatening step forward. "Unless you're both lying." He looked at Aden, then at her. "I think you are." His eyes lingered on Sadie, challenging her.

Aden felt Sadie tighten her hold on his hand, pinching his fingers as if they were in a vise. She looked up at him, her pale skin the shade of freshly fallen snow. "I . . ." She cleared her throat. "I love him." Somehow she managed a smile. A sickly, halfhearted one, but her voice was strong when she turned and spoke to his father. "I love Aden . . . and I will marry him."

Out of the corner of his eye, Aden saw Sol leap toward him. He let go of Sadie's hand and shoved her out of the way.

Sadie yelped as Aden pushed her against the desk, her hip ramming into the edge of the metal furniture. She was about to protest when she realized why he'd shoved her so hard.

Sol lunged at him.

Fear gripped her as Sol reared back to strike. But Aden barely flinched, as if he'd expected the reaction. He also didn't do anything to protect himself.

Fortunately his father did. "Solomon!" His voice boomed through the office, bringing Sol to a halt.

The two brothers faced off, their eyes locked—Sol's look hateful and challenging, Aden's stoic and strong.

"Outside, Solomon," Bishop Troyer said, his voice lower, but still edged with steel. "You need to gain control of *yer* temper."

Sol glowered at Aden, then stormed out of the office, the door slamming hard behind him.

Sadie's heart jumped to her throat. She'd never witnessed such a violent reaction from someone before. But Aden didn't move, and his expression became vacant. How could he be so unaffected in the face of Sol's physical threat?

Unable to stop herself, she moved closer to him. It was then she realized his outward composure was only pretense. She could feel his body shaking as he stood his ground.

"I'm sorry about that, Sadie." The bishop calmly looked at her, as if the explosive exchange had never happened. "You can be certain Solomon will be disciplined accordingly."

But Sadie didn't think she was the one who deserved the apology.

"If I had been aware that you and Aden were a couple," the bishop continued, leveling a blame-filled gaze at Aden, "we could have avoided this misunderstanding and the ensuing unpleasant-ness." He turned to Sadie. "The marriage will take place next week."

"So soon?" Sadie squeaked.

"If you love *mei sohn*, there's no need to wait, is there?"

She swallowed, forcing herself to nod. She felt trapped, like a rabbit in a cramped cage.

"We'll have the ceremony at *mei haus*. It will be small. Private, just like *yer* courtship. You may invite one attendant." Bishop Troyer kept his attention on Sadie. "I am sure this is what *yer vatter* would have wanted, to know that his daughters and his possessions will be well cared for. You have *mei* word on that." He finally looked at Aden. "I will leave you two alone for a short while. Do not linger, Aden. You are expected home within the hour."

Aden nodded but didn't say anything.

Sadie frowned, troubled by the condescending way the bishop spoke to Aden. She knew he was a stern man, but this went beyond sternness. There were no congratulations, no handshake. No smiles. No happiness.

Then he cast both of them a long look, one that seemed to penetrate straight through them. Her pulse seemed to stop. He had seen through her and Aden's lies, like Sol had. Yet that didn't deter him from approving the marriage and wanting it to take place as soon as possible.

After the bishop left Sadie put her palms on the desk, her head hanging, her breathing quickening.

"Sadie?" Aden moved close to her—he had the right to, she realized, now that they were officially betrothed. "Are you all right?" His voice was soft and surprisingly kind.

She shook her head, the full force of what had just happened hitting her. Somewhere inside her mind she knew Aden had saved her and that she owed him. But all she could think about was how she'd been forced to make a choice, one she resented having to make at all. "Why is he doing this?" she whispered, her voice splintering.

She heard him suck in a deep breath. "I don't know."

"How can you not know?" She turned to him, everything tightening inside her. "He's *yer vatter*. He's the bishop!"

But his eyes looked hollow. She knew he was telling the truth.

I have to spend the rest of my life with him.

The realization slammed into her like a bitter winter wind. She would make that sacrifice, and somehow she would come to terms with it. But not now. Now she had to fight to keep from breaking down in front of him.

She took a deep breath and turned to Aden, digging deep inside herself to keep her tone neutral. "You should *geh*."

"We need to talk," he said. But even as he spoke, he started to back away.

"There's *nix* to say." She bit the inside of her cheek, suppressing the urge to lash out at him. Of everyone involved, he was the least to blame. Yet she resented him with equal fervor. "You and *yer* family have decided *mei* fate."

"I didn't mean for this to happen, Sadie. I hope you believe that."

She turned her back to him. "Just *geh*."

"All right."

After he left she collapsed in the chair and bit her bottom lip, drawing blood. *Why, Lord? Haven't I suffered enough?*

Her life was in pieces, her emotions in tatters. She was being punished, but she had no idea what she had done to deserve such harsh correction. And the sentence was beyond cruel—a lifetime married to a man she would never trust and could never love.

But he saved me from Sol.

She shoved the thought away and wiped the blood from her mouth. Her pulse pounded as she reminded herself why she had agreed to the marriage—her promise to her parents. If marrying Aden meant she could keep her business and property and keep what was left of her family intact, she would do it. Abigail and Joanna would have a home to return to and a business that would support all of them—one she vowed Aden would never be a part of. Her sisters were her family—the only family she had left. And she would do anything for them . . . even give up her own future.

But she would never give up her heart.

Emmanuel Troyer walked into the barn to see his oldest son pacing back and forth. He approached him with measured steps. The *bu* had always had a temper, one he struggled to keep in check and seemed to worsen over time. Another weakness Emmanuel had tried to correct. He wanted his sons to be strong men. To be respected and, yes, slightly feared. Fear, like all emotions, was a useful tool if used properly.

But over the last couple of years, he'd started to wonder if Solomon was worth the trouble. The drinking, the fits of temper, his sheer inability to be a man of strength and character . . . Emmanuel shook his head. He'd stopped questioning why God had given him two difficult sons. Everyone had a cross to bear, and his children were his.

Solomon was hardheaded and impulsive, while Aden was too sensitive and weak. He had tried to rectify these problems by giving Solomon disciplinary responsibility over his brother and Aden the opportunity to stand up for himself, a method his own father had used with Emmanuel and his younger brother, John. One that had kept them both in line.

Yet Solomon's anger had increased and Aden had passively taken the blows. Neither son had learned his lesson. They were as different as dark and light, but they had one common denominator: they were both cowards, and that was something Emmanuel couldn't fix.

But he had to admit Aden had surprised him. Emmanuel had seen the fear in Sadie's eyes when he'd told her Solomon would marry her. She was afraid of his eldest and Aden knew the reason. Emmanuel wasn't concerned with Aden's motivations, however. He could get what he wanted through his youngest son. Possibly more easily, considering Solomon's unpredictable temperament.

Solomon continued to pace the length of their barn, his huge hands opening and closing into meaty fists. He stopped when he saw Emmanuel. "How could you let that happen?" Solomon glared at him.

Emmanuel met Solomon's furious gaze evenly. "Do I need to remind you of *yer* place?"

Those simple words caused Solomon to stop pacing. He inhaled a deep breath, unclenching his fists. "I had already agreed to marry her," he said, sounding slightly more conciliatory. "I had agreed to go along with *yer* plan."

"Plans change."

"Does Aden know? Is he aware of the real reason you're forcing Sadie into marriage?"

Emmanuel's jaw twitched. "What *yer* brother knows or doesn't know isn't *yer* concern."

Solomon looked away from him and grunted. "Which means he doesn't have a clue."

"This worked to *yer* advantage," Emmanuel said, ignoring Solomon's bitter remark. His son was taking Sadie's rejection harder than Emmanuel would have predicted. "She is a hardened, ungrateful woman. She would strive against you. Let Aden deal with her."

"Because you think I can't."

He shrugged. "Why would you want to?"

Solomon paused, as if he were considering what Emmanuel said. "So what does this *change of plans* mean for me?"

Emmanuel looked at his son's large hands, which were balled into fists again. He was growing weary of being questioned. Solomon was fortunate he was showing restraint. His own father would have laid him out on the barn floor at the first spark of disrespect.

Yes, Aden would be much easier to deal with.

But he couldn't afford to alienate Solomon, not during this precarious time. He went to his son and put his hands on his shoulders. "Remember what I promised you," he said, looking him in the eye. "Aden's marriage doesn't change that."

Solomon looked away, but didn't shake off Emmanuel's hands. That gave Emmanuel the opportunity to squeeze them. Hard, so Solomon understood his meaning.

"You must focus on managing *yer* temper. And *yer* drinking." That got Solomon's attention. "I've turned the other way, hoping you would come to *yer* senses, that you would use *yer* God-given sense to realize how stupid you've been."

Solomon swallowed and tried to step away. Emmanuel kept him pinned in place. His son was strong, but Emmanuel was stronger.

"*Yer* foolishness," he continued, speaking in a low and steely tone, "will *nee* longer be tolerated." He released Solomon's shoulders, then patted Solomon's cheek, hard enough to leave a red mark. "Now, I must tell *yer mamm* to prepare for the wedding. There is much to do." He started to leave the barn, only to stop and look at Solomon. "Be a *mann* and accept God's will for *yer bruder*. Sadie made her choice . . . and it wasn't you."

Sol's temples pulsed as he watched his father calmly walk away, as if he hadn't hurled a verbal jab that struck Sol directly in the heart. Of course Sadie wouldn't have chosen him. She hated him.

What outraged him was knowing she wouldn't have chosen Aden either. They had both lied about being in love, and his father knew it. Yet he had accepted their explanation and had made Sadie choose. Sol hadn't stood a chance.

Bitterness twisted inside him, ugly and foul. What was he supposed to do now? Stand by and watch Aden not only get the girl, but get his freedom? *And the money . . . don't forget the money.* But money didn't matter to him, not the way it did to his father. Solomon was required to pay a good chunk of his earnings every two weeks to *Daed*, without fail. The irony was that if his father simply asked for the money, Sol would willingly hand it over. But he demanded payment . . . and that rubbed Sol raw.

Only one thing between Sol and his father still connected them. *The plan.* Sol had found out about it accidentally and had felt a little bit of happiness when his *daed* had included him. But now that had changed. And despite the assurance that Sol wouldn't be left out, Sol didn't trust his father. Not anymore.

He'd tried to suppress his anger, but he was failing. The roomy barn suddenly felt too small, his skin hot and taut. He had to get out of there.

He had to get a drink.

He stormed out of the barn and cursed his father's warnings. He intended to get as drunk as he possibly could.

CHAPTER 6

"Sadie, are you sure about this?"

Sadie swallowed and faced Patience. Worry creased her friend's forehead as they stood in Aden's room, dressing for the wedding. She had tried not to pay attention to her surroundings, but curiosity had gotten the best of her. She was surprised to see how tidy his room was. And extremely plain, even by Amish standards. His single bed was low to the ground and covered with a thin, worn quilt. He had only one other piece of furniture in the room, a small bureau with two drawers. That was it. Not a single personal item in view. It was hard to believe he'd spent almost his entire life here in such a sterile place.

"Sadie? Did you hear me?"

She looked back at Patience, who at the moment wasn't living up to her name. "*Ya*," she said, entwining her fingers together and forcing herself to sound convincing. "I'm sure."

"I was hoping for a different answer." She handed over Sadie's *kapp*. "I don't understand what the big hurry is. Can't you and Aden wait a couple of months?"

"*Nee*," Sadie mumbled.

"But so much has happened in a short time . . .

with the accident and everything. I'm wondering if . . ."

"If what?" Sadie asked, more out of politeness than wanting to hear the answer. She knew Patience meant well, but her questioning wasn't helping.

"If maybe you're rushing into things."

"I'm not." Aden didn't have a mirror in his room, so she put on her *kapp* the best she could, using bobby pins to fasten it in place. One of the pins slipped from her shaking hand and fell to the floor.

"I'll get it." Patience picked up the pin and slid it smoothly through Sadie's hair, securing the *kapp*. She tilted her head and frowned.

"I wish you could be happy for me." *I wish I could be happy for myself.* But happiness was a distant memory now.

Patience curled her mouth into a half-smile. "How's this?"

Sadie couldn't help but return it. "A little better." She moved away from Patience and, without thinking, sat on Aden's bed. She grimaced. His mattress was as hard as stone.

"I'm sorry," Patience said. "I want to be supportive. I really do. I'm just so confused. Why didn't you tell me you and Aden were a couple?"

"I already explained—we wanted to keep it a secret."

"But from me?" Hurt crossed her features. "I'm

yer best friend. You know I wouldn't have said anything."

Sadie pressed her lips together, the guilt almost overwhelming. She hadn't meant to hurt her friend. But she didn't have a choice. "It was all very sudden. Like a whirlwind romance." She cringed at the idea of anything romantic between her and Aden. "We haven't been together that long," she added. Finally, a truth she could tell.

"I didn't even know you liked Aden. I've never seen you two talking."

"He's shy."

Patience nodded. "Very shy. He doesn't say much when he drops honey off at *Mamm*'s."

Sadie looked at her, surprised. "How long has he been doing that?"

"Since last year. I think he said he overheard Timothy saying how honey helped her allergies. Since then he gives her a small jar every week. Doesn't even charge her for it."

Sadie tugged on one of her *kapp* strings. She really didn't want to hear about Aden's good attributes. It was easier to stoke her resentment than to acknowledge his positive qualities. Like how he had left her alone since Saturday, at her request, with the exception of a moment yesterday. She had not attended church service on Sunday, not wanting to see anyone. But on Monday he stopped by the store, handed her an envelope, then left without saying a word. She

107

opened it, gasping at the stack of twenty-dollar bills inside. When she counted the money, she nearly dropped it on the floor. He had given her five hundred dollars, close to the amount she and Abigail had spent on taxi rides to visit Joanna at the hospital.

She wanted to chase after him and give the cash back. She didn't know what to make of it, what his reasoning was for giving her so much money. Had his father told him about her financial difficulties? For some reason she didn't think so. After seeing how he and his father had interacted that day in her father's office, she didn't think they had a good relationship.

And his reason didn't matter. She needed the money. She just didn't want to be more beholden to him than she already was.

"I'm surprised you're not waiting until Joanna comes home. I thought you'd want her and Abigail here."

Sadie jumped up from the bed. "What I want is to get this over with." She smoothed her dark blue dress. *Mamm*'s wedding dress. She took in a deep breath. "I'm sorry. I'm nervous."

"I understand." Patience hugged Sadie. When she pulled back, she said, "Remember how I was right before I married Timothy? A complete wreck."

"You were excited." And happy. Joy had radiated from Patience that day, and it had been mirrored in her groom's eyes when they exchanged vows. All Sadie felt was misery. She didn't want to guess at what Aden was feeling. She didn't want to make the effort to care.

"But it was the most wonderful day of *mei* life." Patience peered at Sadie. "It will be for you too."

Sadie was tired. Tired of pretending. Tired of acting like this was all okay, that getting married to Aden Troyer while wearing her dead mother's wedding dress was perfectly normal. Yet there was nothing she could do but get it over with. "We should *geh* downstairs," she said, picking up her black bonnet from the bed. "We've kept everyone waiting long enough." Sadie started for the door, but Patience stopped her.

"I don't know what's going on," Patience said, grasping Sadie's arm fully. "But I know this isn't right."

Sadie turned around, unable to force the barest of smiles. "It's right for me, Patience. That's all that matters."

She put on her bonnet and walked downstairs.

When she reached the bottom of the stairs, she wanted to weep. Although she'd always said she never wanted to marry, a tiny part of her had thought that *if* she ever married, her wedding would be perfect. She and her groom would be surrounded by family and friends. Everyone would be laughing, except for her mother, who would of course be crying tears of joy that her stubborn daughter had finally found a *mann* to put up with her.

She touched the cuff of her long-sleeved dress, brushing her fingertips over her wrist. *Oh, Mamm, how much I miss you and Daed.* If they were here she would be at the store working beside them. She would be bickering with Abigail and encouraging Joanna. She wouldn't feel the dread and emptiness.

She wouldn't be marrying Aden.

Somehow she found the strength to keep her tears at bay and put one foot in front of the other.

The gathering in the bishop's living room was pathetic. The only people there were Aden, his mother, Timothy, and Bishop Troyer. Sol was nowhere in sight. At least she had something to be grateful for.

The bishop stood by the front window, the dark blue curtains closed tight behind him. He held his Bible in his hand and faced her. Aden stood in front of him, dressed in his Sunday clothing—a white shirt, black vest, and slim black pants. Timothy's gaze was everywhere except on Sadie and Patience, and Aden's mother stood mutely to the side, almost seeming to shrink in on herself.

As Sadie took her place next to Aden, she saw him stick his finger beneath the neckline of his crisp shirt, his Adam's apple bobbing up and down, his forehead glistening with a sheen of perspiration.

"Are we ready to proceed with the ceremony?" Bishop Troyer said, looking from his son to Sadie, a smile on his thin lips.

Sadie had to keep herself from walking out of the room. How could the bishop be okay with this sham of a marriage? She'd been raised to believe marriage was for life, and that a husband should be chosen carefully. Yet Bishop Troyer, a man chosen by God to be the spiritual leader of their community, was eager to marry off his son to someone he didn't love.

How is any of this right?

"We're ready," Aden said, his voice pitched higher than normal. He cleared his throat and faced his father.

Sadie had no other choice but to do the same.

Aden went through the motions of the wedding ceremony, his focus more on Sadie's pain than on the words his father spoke. Sweat poured down his back, even though the living room was cool. What was he doing? What were *they* doing? There was no turning back from this. Once he and Sadie accepted the vows, they would be husband and wife for the rest of their lives. He wiped his drenched forehead with his fingers.

Glancing at Sadie, he couldn't help but admire her. She stood next to him, her eyes dry, her chin lifted in resoluteness. She should be marrying the man she loves, not him. Yet she was handling the ceremony with grace and courage.

And beauty. *She is so beautiful . . .*

At that moment he promised himself he would do whatever it took to be the man she deserved.

His father hurried through the ceremony, as if he was concerned that either Aden or Sadie—or both—would abandon the wedding and flee. Aden had tried to avoid *Daed* as much as he could during the week, spending most of his time with the bees and praying he was doing the right thing. Concern for his mother also had him tied up in knots. Would she be safe once he was gone? Whenever he considered backing out of the wedding, he thought about Sol and Sadie together. The idea of her marrying his brother made his stomach turn inside out. He ultimately decided that for Sadie's sake, he had to go through with the marriage, and he promised himself that he would check on his mother as much as he could. Sadie was the innocent in all this, and he had to put her before his mother . . . and himself.

She was facing him now, her brown eyes meeting his for a brief moment, but long enough for him to see the flicker of despair in her eyes. It made him want to take her in his arms. To tell her everything would be all right. That their future was bright and happy and full of hope.

Instead he wiped his damp palms on his pant legs as he and Sadie were joined in marriage.

"We have cake!" his mother said as soon as the ceremony was over, speaking in that tinny, bright voice she used when she was under stress. He turned to see her gesturing to a small round cake covered in fluffy white icing. His gut lurched.

"Congratulations." Timothy grabbed his hand and shook it, his expression a mix of confusion and encouragement.

"*Danki.*" Aden glanced at Sadie, who was with Patience, Timothy's *frau*. Patience was talking, but Sadie stared straight ahead, not responding. It was as if she was in shock.

"Who wants a piece?" his mother asked, brandishing a serrated cake knife. No one answered, but his mother cut the cake anyway, slopping pieces on small plastic plates.

Patience stepped forward and picked up a plate. She tasted a piece and smiled. "Delicious," she said, looking at Sadie. "Do you want some?"

Sadie shook her head. "Excuse me," she said, then ran upstairs.

The room was quiet. Aden's feet felt like concrete. He was unsure what to do.

His father came up beside him. "As it says in Ephesians, 'The husband is the head of the wife.' This is an opportunity to help her understand her place."

"Her place?"

"See to *yer frau*, Aden." He leaned closer. "Be a *mann* for once."

The insult would have stung if Aden hadn't heard it so many times over the years. And while he was unsure what "seeing to" his wife meant, he did know that now that he was married, he wouldn't have to suffer his father's insults—and wrath—anymore.

That brought a smile to his face.

"*Gut.* I see you understand me."

But you never understood me.

Eagerness to get away from his father surmounted his trepidation over checking on Sadie. When he reached the top of the stairs, he asked God to give him the right words to say.

Sadie burst into Aden's room—the only room she was familiar with in the Troyer household—and yanked on her bonnet ties. Downstairs the room had suddenly become too confining, too suffocating. Watching Aden's mother pass out cake as if they had something to celebrate was the breaking point. She sat down on his rock-hard mattress and buried her head in her hands.

She wanted to cry. She *needed* to cry. But her eyes remained dry, her sobs staying trapped in her chest, squeezing her heart so hard the room started to spin.

"Sadie?" A soft knock sounded on the door.

She looked up. Aden. His voice was tentative.

Fearful, almost. She wanted to yell at him to go away. But she couldn't do that, not while she was in *his* room. Not when his parents, particularly his father, expected nothing less than for his son and daughter-in-law to keep up appearances. She clenched her bonnet in her hand, stood, and answered the door.

"May I come in?" he asked quietly.

His reddish hair was damp on the ends and his cheeks were still ruddy from his profuse sweating. She almost felt sorry for him—almost. She shrugged and stepped away, allowing him to walk inside the room. He closed the door quietly behind him, but made no move toward her.

Unable to take the silence, she snapped, "What?"

He tilted his head to the side, his green eyes taking her in. Not in the leering, offensive way Sol had looked at her in the cornfield. Instead, his gaze was almost reverential. Which didn't make any sense to her at all.

He walked past her. She watched as he opened up his small closet and pulled out a duffel bag. He put it on the floor next to his bed and then sat down, not saying a word.

She crossed her arms and stared at him. "What?" she asked again, unable to take the silence engulfing the room.

"When you're ready, I'll take you home." He didn't move. He didn't say anything else. He sat on the edge of his pitiful mattress, his hands resting on his knees, and continued waiting. No pressure. No cajoling. Just calm patience.

He continued to confuse her, which stoked her animosity. She didn't want him to be *nice*. She didn't want his kindness. She didn't want to think about how she knew, for some unknown reason, that she could take his hand and find comfort from his touch.

She didn't want that to be possible.

Uncrossing her arms, she threw the door open. "I'm ready," she said and went downstairs, not bothering to wait for him. Patience and Timothy were still there, talking with the Troyers. Sadie didn't want to stay in their house a minute longer.

She gave Patience a quick hug, unable to speak. She didn't even look at Timothy or the bishop and his wife as she hurried out the front door to the end of the driveway to wait for Aden. For her *husband*.

Now she had to fight to keep from crying.

Patience peeked out of the bishop's four-paned window and saw Sadie standing at the end of the driveway. She longed to go to her friend and try to talk to her again, but she knew it would be pointless. Sadie Schrock was the most stubborn person she knew, and when she didn't want to discuss something, she wouldn't. But Patience's heart ached for her friend. After Sadie got into Aden's buggy and left for her home, Patience couldn't stem the niggling feeling that Sadie had made a huge mistake.

She let the curtain fall and turned to see Bishop Troyer speaking in hushed tones to Timothy in the corner of the room. As if he felt her gaze on him, her husband glanced at her and inclined his head toward the front door. Patience understood his meaning, and after she said good-bye to *Frau* Troyer, she went outside and waited for him in their buggy.

It wasn't long before Timothy joined her. When he climbed inside the buggy, he didn't look at her. She frowned as he turned onto the road, waiting for him to speak. After several moments her curiosity got the best of her. "What did the bishop want?" she asked.

Rain pelted the buggy. Timothy glanced at her, his brows knit above his pale blue eyes. Recognizing his worried look, she scooted closer to him. He reached for her hand, giving it a quick squeeze before saying, "I love you."

Worry kicked into gear. "Timothy, what's wrong?"

"Everything is okay. With us," he added quickly. He looked at her again. "After today . . . I just wanted you to know how much I love you."

She nodded as she said, "I love you too."

He released her hand and held on to the reins. "The bishop asked me about the natural gas rights papers again. He wanted to know if I'd signed them yet. When I told him I was still thinking about it, he seemed a little . . . upset."

"Upset? Like mad?" She couldn't imagine Bishop Troyer showing anger. He was an even-keeled man, if a little emotionally detached. His strictness, as he often reminded the congregation during his sermons, was for the best interests of the church members—and their souls. Being the spiritual leader of their community was a solemn and hefty responsibility, one she wouldn't want for herself or for her husband.

Yet during the wedding ceremony, she had watched Sadie and Aden carefully. Neither of them had made eye contact with Aden's father. There was no warmth or love coming from anyone, including the father of the groom. Aden's brother hadn't even attended, and his mother seemed on the verge of tears, and not happy ones. It was the strangest wedding she'd ever been to. Seeing the lack of emotion involved made her more unsettled.

"He wasn't mad, exactly," Timothy said, breaking into her thoughts. "More like irritated. I don't know why he's so bent on me signing those rights over to him."

"But you wouldn't be signing them over to him, right? I thought the money belongs to everyone."

"It's supposed to."

The rain started to ease up, but Patience stayed close to Timothy. "But?"

"I was talking to Freemont Yoder last week. Saw him walking down Burton Road and offered him a ride. He had to sell his dairy cow, and his horse is on the verge of going lame."

"Oh, *nee.*"

"He's having a hard time financially. Seven mouths to feed and a failed feed corn crop last year set him back. I asked him if he'd talked to the bishop about it, knowing there should be plenty of funds to help Freemont get on his feet." Timothy looked at Patience, his frown deepening. "He said the bishop told him the church wasn't in the position to give him the money he needs. He arranged for a few women to bring over food for the family, but that was all the help he got."

Patience frowned. "I don't understand."

"Me neither. We're not the only ones with natural gas rights on our property. I know the bishop has told me not to discuss it with anyone, but I did a little asking around. Carefully. At least three other families have signed over their rights. I'm not going to say who."

"You don't have to." She knew defying the bishop's request for secrecy would get him in trouble.

"If their rights are worth anywhere near what we have, then there should be a lot of money in the community fund. So why would he tell Freemont there wasn't any?"

She sat back in the seat, confused. "I don't know."

"And now he's eager for me to sign those documents." He shook his head. "I'm sorry, Patience, but I can't do that. Not yet. I need to pray about it more."

She took his hand. "We both need to pray."

"I feel guilty," he said in a low voice. "I don't want to be selfish. But I have to be practical. The money we would get from those rights will give us and our family a secure future."

"*Ya*, it would."

"I trust in God's provision, I truly do. And if he leads us to sign the rights over to the church, I will happily do it. But I would feel better if I knew for sure the funds would be used for the community. After talking to Freemont, I'm having *mei* doubts."

Patience heard the pain in his voice, plus the unspoken concern over doubting their bishop. Certainly there was a reasonable explanation for why Bishop Troyer had told Freemont there wasn't money available to help him. Both she and Timothy had been taught to have complete trust in the church bishop, along with complete obedience. Doubting was akin to showing a lack of faith—something she and Timothy took very seriously.

But after the wedding and what her husband had just revealed . . . Patience couldn't shake the thought that Bishop Troyer wasn't as infallible as he seemed.

"Anyway," Timothy said, interrupting her thoughts. "We'll put the matter to prayer." A pause. "And we'll add Sadie and Aden to the list." He looked at her again. "I know it's not *mei* place to say this, since she's *yer* friend, but something isn't right between the two of them."

"I know. I'm concerned too. It's not like Sadie to be secretive. Not with me, anyway."

"I should get to know Aden better," Timothy said as they turned onto their road. "We've only said hello in passing since you and I got married."

"He's difficult to get close to. Aden has always kept to himself. Come to think of it, I'm not sure if he has any friends."

"He's a loner, then."

"*Ya.*" She paused as a car sped by them. "But that doesn't mean he couldn't use a friend."

"Especially now," Timothy added.

Patience rubbed her thumb over the top of her husband's hand, once again thankful God had brought him into her life. She remembered when they met, almost three years ago when she had gone to a relative's wedding in Lancaster. The moment she'd seen him, it was love at first sight. Six months and dozens of letters later, he came to Birch Creek and asked her to marry him. She didn't hesitate to say yes. He had been glad to move to their small community, finding Lancaster too crowded and competitive. Their life together, while not perfect, was filled with love.

She wanted her best friend to be as happy, as wholly in love as she was. Yet if today was any indication, Sadie was despondent. As Patience held her husband's hand, she said a quick prayer for Sadie and Aden, knowing they would need as much help from God as they could get. And someday, very soon, she would find out the real reason Sadie married Aden Troyer.

As Aden steered his buggy down Pinton Road, a crack of lightning streaked the sky, followed by a loud thunder boom that made his horse slightly jumpy. Spatters of heavy raindrops beat on the top of the buggy, and within a minute it began to pour. It figured. Even the weather was against them today.

He glanced at Sadie, who hadn't said a word since they'd left the Troyers' house. She was angled away from him and seated as close to the opening of the buggy as she could be without falling out. When the wind kicked up, he looked at the skirt of her dress and saw that it was damp. He started to tell her she could scoot closer to him, but changed his mind. If she wanted a drier seat, she knew she could move.

After about fifteen minutes, the rain eased to a light drizzle. He tugged on the reins and guided his horse to turn right on Macon Creek Road, where her house was located. When he pulled into the driveway and stopped in front of the house, a decent-sized home painted the typical white with a slate gray roof, she started to get out of the vehicle.

"Sadie, wait," he said.

She paused before turning to him. She looked completely miserable.

And he felt completely helpless. "I have these beehives," he said. It wasn't the best time to bring them up, but timing hadn't been in either of their favors lately.

"I know," she said dully.

Of course she knew, and he felt stupid for stating the obvious. "I . . . I was thinking it would be easier if I moved them here. To *yer* house." He sounded like a blabbering idiot, but he wanted to make sure his bees were taken care of. He also wanted to sever as many ties with his father as he could. The money from the bees would be Aden's now—his and Sadie's. He'd already given her some of his savings to help cover expenses he knew she had to be buckling under. "They'll be in the backyard—"

"You don't have to ask." She got out of the buggy and looked over her shoulder. "It's *yer* house now."

He watched her, expecting her to go straight to the house. Instead she ran to the store, unlocked the door, and disappeared inside.

CHAPTER 7

Aden settled his horse in the empty stall near Sadie's horse. A third stall remained unoccupied. Aden sighed, saddened at the reminder that the Schrocks' other horse hadn't survived the accident. Once he was finished taking care of Rusty, he checked on Sadie's horse. He didn't know the mare's name, driving home again how little he knew about his wife.

The barn needed cleaning, and Sadie needed her space. He spent the next three hours working in the barn, scraping out the stalls, removing old manure and straw and laying down fresh bedding for the horses. He climbed the ladder leading to the small loft where the hay was stored and checked the supply. There wasn't enough to last the winter, and he made a note to purchase more next week.

When he finished cleaning, he looked down at his clothes, realizing he'd forgotten he'd been wearing his Sunday best. The black pants were covered with dust, dirt, and manure, his shoes were coated with muck, and his white shirt was so stained it was basically ruined. He briefly wondered if Sadie could sew, then knew he wouldn't ask her to make him a new shirt even if she did.

He made one last check on the horses. They were content. If only he felt the same. He pulled his duffel bag out of his buggy, then looked down when he felt something brush against his lower leg. "Where did you come from?"

The dog lifted its head, his long tail thumping against the buggy wheel. He didn't know Sadie had a dog. Aden crouched down and scratched the animal behind his ear. He was an oddly colored dog, with solid light brown ears, a honey-colored tail, and a sprinkling of tan spots all over his white coat. His large dark brown eyes were soft and happy, and his long pink tongue lolled out of the side of his mouth as Aden continued to scratch.

"What's *yer* name?" Yeah, he was talking to a dog. Then again, he talked to his bees, so why not add another animal to his list of conversation companions. He'd always wanted a dog, but his father had refused to let them have pets of any kind. Only horses and farm animals, and now they were just down to horses.

He moved his hand down the side of the dog's flanks, frowning as he felt the ribs protruding. He was hungry, and on closer examination, dirty and possibly flea ridden. This couldn't be Sadie's dog. The Schrocks wouldn't allow a dog to get in this condition. "Want something to eat, boy?"

The dog suddenly pulled away and ran off into the woods. Aden's frown deepened, and he considered going after the mutt. But he figured the dog would run away again. He went inside instead. After he entered the side door, he walked into a small foyer and slipped off his dirty shoes. Then he stepped to the kitchen doorway.

This was his new home, but other than the times the Schrocks held church service here, he'd rarely been in the house, and never farther than the kitchen. The Schrocks had either held church in the barn or in their large basement. For the past six years, out of respect for Sadie, he had never stayed for fellowship after service, always leaving as soon as church was over. As he stood there, he realized he had no idea where anything was.

The fading light of evening peeked through the thin opening between the kitchen curtains. Not bothering to find where the lamp was in the kitchen, Aden opened cabinet doors until he found what he needed: two plastic bowls. He opened a door, which he hoped was the pantry, and was glad to see he'd been right. He searched the shelves, saw a mason jar filled with what he recognized as canned meat, and dumped it into one of the bowls. He filled the other one with water and set both bowls on the back patio.

He fumbled his way through the house and managed to find the stairs, his body suddenly consumed with weariness.

A sliver of light shined underneath the door at the end of the upstairs hall. His nerves tightening, he headed toward it, knowing it had to be Sadie's room. The door was cracked open enough for him to see inside. He paused, thinking he should leave her alone. But he needed to know she was all right. He peeked inside the room, making sure he didn't touch the door.

She was curled on her bed, still in her wedding dress, her cheek resting on the palm of her hand. Her eyes were closed. He held his breath until he saw the rise and fall of her chest, indicating she was asleep. Relieved, he stepped back into the hallway.

He found the bathroom and took a shower, the hot water giving him the only comfort he'd had during the past week. After he slipped on his long white nightshirt, he gathered his bag and stepped into the hallway.

Aden paused and looked at Sadie's bedroom door. As her husband, he had as much right to her bed as she did. And although his father had never discussed the intimate relationship between a man and a woman, Aden knew what happened between them. He shoved his hand through his hair, gripping the ends. He wasn't without feelings and desires. God help him, he wanted to go to her.

But knowing he could . . . didn't mean he should.

He turned and walked away.

Sadie held her breath as she heard Aden outside her door. She'd been awake when he first came to her room, but feigned sleep, hoping he would go away. She'd listened as he took a shower, her hands clutching the quilt she was lying on. With every minute that passed, her nerves grew more rattled. He would be within his rights to sleep with her. She knew that, just as she knew what happened when a marriage was consummated. The thought of being with Aden that way terrified her.

The shower ended. She closed her eyes and lay as still as she could, waiting for him to come in, praying that he wouldn't.

But the door never opened. When she heard him walk away, she expelled a breath of relief. She remained still for a moment, wondering if he would come back. When he didn't, she sat up. *Thank God.*

Sadie removed the pins from her *kapp* and took off the head covering, but she kept her hair bound. She didn't change into her nightclothes either. She switched off the light and climbed underneath the quilt, hoping sleep would come quickly. Maybe she'd wake up and discover this was all a horrible dream. In the morning she would smell her mother's delicious banana pancakes, smothered with pure maple syrup. She'd see her father reading the morning paper and hear her sisters arguing over which was better, bacon or sausage. She closed her eyes, clinging to the memories. How she'd taken all those simple, silly moments for granted. She'd do anything to have them back now.

Her eyes flew open and she turned flat on her back. She put her arm over her forehead, struggling with the pain of the memories and the desire to hang on to every last mental image of her parents. Even now she could feel some of those memories slipping away, replaced by the terror of reality.

She was married, but she was completely alone.

Sadie didn't know how much time had passed before she got up to go to the bathroom. When she finished, she stopped in the hallway. Despite herself, she wondered where Aden was. The hallway was dark. The doors to all the bedrooms were closed. She should go downstairs like she intended to, to warm up a small pan of milk in the hopes that drinking it would help bring the sleep she desperately wanted.

Instead she crept to the room across from hers, her heart stilling, her fingertips on the doorknob. This was her parents' bedroom. Surely he hadn't dared claim that room for his own. Slowly she turned the knob. The last thing she wanted to do was wake Aden—if he was in there.

Her heart resumed its rhythm when she saw the bed was empty.

She looked inside Joanna's room. Aden wasn't there either. That left Abigail's room, unless he had decided to sleep downstairs. She felt an unexpected stab of guilt at the idea of him spending the night on the couch. It was an old, dilapidated piece of furniture that was comfortable to lie on for an hour or so but not for a good night's sleep.

Abigail's bedroom was at the opposite end of the hall, near the top of the stairs. It was also the farthest away from Sadie's bedroom.

The door was closed, but not completely. She quietly pushed on the solid wood and peeked inside. Abigail's curtains were open, letting in the dim moonlight. She made out an unfamiliar lump on her sister's bed. She was about to close the door when she saw Aden flip over on his back, the quilt slipping from his shoulders, his profile outlined in the faint, silvery light.

She knew she should leave, but she couldn't resist looking at him. She'd never seen such ease in his expression before. His forehead, often furrowed just under the hank of russet bangs that hung above his eyes, was smooth, the normal tension around his lips nonexistent. She saw the shadow of his lashes as they rested against the top of his cheek. She hadn't noticed how long they were before. And at that moment she realized she had never seen him truly smile.

She stepped back from the door and hurried down the hall, switching off the bathroom lamp on her way to her bedroom. She shut the door and sat on the edge of the bed, relieved that Aden was a safe distance away and confused by the path her thoughts traveled. Sadie was often accused of being too serious, but even she knew how to smile. How to laugh. Surely Aden did, too, but as she searched her mind, she couldn't think of a single instant when he looked happy. She'd seen him resigned, like he was today at the wedding. She'd also seen him concerned, tense, shy, fearful . . .

But never happy.

Her warm milk forgotten, she climbed into bed and tried to focus on anything but Aden—and how little she knew about the man with whom she would be spending the rest of her life.

When Aden walked into the kitchen the next morning, Sadie was nowhere in sight. Since it was early he thought she might still be asleep, but he nixed that idea when he caught the scent of freshly brewed coffee from the percolator on the stove and saw a plate of cinnamon rolls covered in plastic wrap in the center of the table. He lifted up the plastic, and the sweet, yeasty scent made his stomach growl. He wondered if Sadie had made the rolls, realizing it was just as likely they were given to her by friends in the community after her parents' funeral. Was Sadie a good cook? He had no idea.

He did discover that she made excellent coffee. After drinking two cups and downing three cinnamon rolls—they were too good to resist—he gathered up his beekeeper clothing and went outside, intending to go to his parents' house and prepare his hives for removal. He peeked out the window of the kitchen door to see if the dog had visited during the night. The food and water were still in the two bowls on the patio. He decided to leave them out there until he got back.

He stopped at the store and wasn't surprised to find the front door wasn't locked. He went inside, past the long shelves of nonperishable food and the separate area that contained a decent selection of tools, and stopped in front of the office door. Last time he was here he had told his father he would marry Sadie. The memory of that day was never far from his mind.

He hesitated to knock on the door, not wanting to disturb her. Yet he didn't feel right leaving without seeing her. He quietly knocked on the door and waited for a response. When he didn't get one right away, he lifted his hand to knock again, only to lower it when she opened the door.

"*Ya?*" she said, her tone cross, the shadows under her eyes prominent. Whatever sleep she'd gotten last night wasn't enough. Strangely, he had slept better than he had in months.

"I'm heading out. Going to pack up *mei* hives." He flinched at her cranky gaze.

"You don't have to check in with me."

"I know." He stared at the tip of his dusty work

boots. "But I want to." When he looked up at her, she was eyeing him oddly. "Do you have a dog?"

She shook her head. *"Nee."*

"Have you seen one around here lately? He's brown and white . . . nice dog. I gave him some food last night."

"I haven't seen any dogs."

He bristled a bit at her tone. "I'll see you later," he said, backing away.

She didn't respond, but she didn't close the door either. He could feel her gaze almost boring into his back as he walked away from the office.

He stepped out into the chilly morning air. The sun had hidden behind layers of flat, grayish clouds. The season was changing, shifting from summer to fall. He'd have to winterize the bee-hives soon. He walked toward the backyard and surveyed the area, searching for the right place to put the hives. They couldn't be too near the house or the barn. The Schrocks' property was bordered with thick woods along the back, in a semicircle configuration. He spotted a large oak tree, the gigantic branches thick with green leaves that were starting to show spots of vibrant orange and crimson. He walked to the tree, paced out the space where he could put his hives, and looked at the area with satisfaction. Yes, his bees would be happy here.

Aden turned toward the barn, intent on hitching Rusty to the buggy, but he stopped mid-stride. He listened to the birds twittering, recognizing a robin, blue jay, cardinal, and finch. His boots rested on a carpet of too-tall but lush green grass. He'd have to mow it soon. The property contained a sturdy barn, a small but weedy garden, a tool shed, the house, and of course, the store. Was it wrong that he already felt at home here? It had to be, since the only reason he was here was because Sadie's parents had died. The thought sobered him.

A short while later, Aden arrived at his parents' house, carrying his beekeeper clothes. He planned to slip into the backyard, get the hives, and leave before he was noticed. But he couldn't do that to his mother, remembering the strained look on her face when he told her good-bye yesterday. He started to open the door and walk inside, then realized he didn't live here anymore. Out of respect he knocked instead.

His father answered, his gaze narrowing slightly. "Aden. I didn't expect to see you here so soon. I thought you'd want to spend time with *yer* new bride."

"Sadie is working in the store today."

"I see."

Aden stood on the porch, waiting to be invited inside. But instead his father stepped outside and shut the door. He pulled out his pipe, already filled with tobacco.

"Is *Mamm* home?" Aden asked.

Daed lit the pipe and blew out a few puffs of smoke before answering. "She's busy in the kitchen." He glanced at Aden's clothes. "Are you here to gather honey? I noticed our supplies were low."

"I'm moving the hives."

Daed blew out another puff of smoke. "Why?"

Because they're mine. "It will be easier to take care of them at . . . at *mei haus*."

"How will disturbing them be easier?"

"They'll acclimate to their new home. It won't take me long to move them."

His father put his hand on his arm. He squeezed, his fingers digging into Aden's flesh. "And what of the honey sales?"

"I don't understand."

"I assume our arrangement will still stand? That you will keep the commandment to honor *yer* mother and father? That you will still contribute to the care of *yer* parents who have given you so much?" Before Aden could answer, his father spoke again. "Although you are to cleave to *yer* wife now, do not forget *yer* loyalty to *yer familye*."

"Sol is still here."

"What does Solomon have to do with *yer* duty?"

Aden squared his shoulders. Something about knowing he wasn't stuck living under the same roof as his father bolstered his courage. "He makes a *gut* living as a carpenter. I'm sure he can replace the small income I provided you."

"*Yer* brother's financial affairs aren't *yer* business." He let *geh* of Aden's arm and blew a puff of smoke close to his face. "I'm disappointed, Aden. You would be so selfish with the bounty our heavenly Father has provided you? Not only the honey, but the gift of a wife who comes with vast financial resources?"

"What?"

"A family business. One that you will be expected to take over."

Not if Sadie has her say. Aden could run the store and delegate Sadie to taking care of the house and garden. He was experienced in sales and simple accounting, and he knew he could easily learn how to manage other aspects of the grocery and tool store. But he also knew how much the business meant to her, and he wouldn't cross that line, not when she had already lost so much.

"I will be more than willing to guide you in *yer* new business venture." His father took another puff of the pipe and blew out two perfect smoke rings. "Perhaps you won't have to deal with the bees for much longer."

"I didn't start beekeeping to make money."

"I know." *Daed* waved his pipe. "It was a hobby. But hobbies must be useful. They must serve a purpose. Otherwise you're wasting time."

"Beekeeping isn't a waste of time." Aden could feel the familiar squeezing of his chest. His father had never respected his line of work, even though he had no problem taking the profits.

"*Nee*, it isn't, now that you're able to earn a real income." He waved his pipe in front of him. "Enough of this conversation. You have work to tend to. Make haste with the bees, Aden. You need to get started on *yer* new job as store-keeper."

"That won't be happening anytime soon."

His father moved closer. They were nearly the same size, with Aden less than an inch taller. "Is that *yer* decision or Sadie's?"

"We've been married less than a day." Aden shifted his feet. "I'm not going to upset her life any more than it already is."

"You are the head of the relationship," his father said in the same tone he used during his sermons. "It is *yer* responsibility to put *yer frau* in her place."

Aden bit the inside of his cheek, the familiar pound of anxiety reverberating in his head. Sadie's place was fine as far as Aden was concerned. He didn't see any reason why she shouldn't run the store. But his father always had a different view of a woman's role in the community. Aden's mother was a prime example. She was quiet. Meek. Never raised her voice, rarely questioned her husband and never in public. Never ventured beyond the accepted female role of housekeeper and caretaker. And never, ever interfered with the bishop's decisions.

"Do we have an understanding, *sohn*?"

Aden looked at his father. What choice did he have but to agree? "*Ya*. You'll get the money you deserve."

His father smiled, his grin so similar to Sol's it was unnerving. "To worry is to give in to the devil's schemes, Aden. That is something I never do." He lowered his voice. "I'm pleased we have kept our agreement concerning the honey sales. I didn't want to have to explain to *yer mudder* the selfish nature of her youngest *sohn*."

Aden didn't see how keeping the money he made from his bees was selfish. If his parents were experiencing financial hardship, he wasn't aware of it. And if they were, he'd do whatever he could to help.

Daed took one long puff on his pipe, then opened the front door. "I'll let you get to *yer* bees." He stepped inside, the door closing behind him.

Aden's shoulders slumped. No invitation for coffee, no offer to see his mother. When would he stop expecting more from his family? Every time he did, the disappointment chipped away at him.

He hurried and put on his beekeeper clothes over his regular clothing, eager to be done with the task. It would take two trips to get all the bees to the Schrocks'. He'd have to unhitch his buggy and hitch the horse to an old cart he'd used in the past, which he would use to transport the bees. Then he would return and retrieve his buggy. Hopefully by this evening the bees would be introduced to their new home. With careful attention they would acclimate to their new surroundings and possibly even vary the flavor of their current output since they would be pollinating different flowers at the Schrocks'. He was enthusiastic about seeing the changes, enough so to make him forget about yet another disheartening conversation with his father.

He was putting on his protective headgear as he rounded the corner of the house and entered the backyard. He was halfway to his hives when he looked up, then froze.

The hives were in pieces.

He ran toward them. A few disoriented bees buzzed around the crushed hives, as if lost. Aden knelt in front of the wooden frames that looked like someone had taken a sledgehammer to them. He noticed the screens had been scraped clean before they were shredded.

Anger brewed inside as he thought of the hours he'd spent constructing the hives, cultivating the honey, caring for the bees. How many books he'd read on beekeeping techniques and pollination, hoping one day he would have his own garden with a variety of flowers and vegetables, possibly even some new varieties he would create himself.

A dream that had seemed possible moments ago.

Now a crushed dream, and he knew who was to blame.

He rose, kicked at a broken frame, and tore off his head covering. He stormed back to the house, plowing through the back door, where his mother was kneading a ball of bread dough. By the way she jumped he knew he'd scared her, but he was too furious to apologize.

"Where is *Daed*?" he demanded.

"Aden, I didn't know you were here." His mother started to stand, but Aden's glare pinned her in place.

"I need to see him. Now."

His father came into the room, his face calm but his lips set in a tight line. "Aden, why are you upsetting *yer mudder*—"

"The hives," he said, approaching his father until he stood only inches from him. He was crossing the line of respect, but his fury cleared all rational thought. "Someone destroyed them."

Daed's graying brows shot up. "What?"

"You don't know anything about this?" He fisted his hands, the urge to physically lash out at his father almost overwhelming him. "Don't tell me you didn't know!"

"Aden."

He felt his mother's small, steadying hand on his shoulder. It brought him back to reality, but didn't soothe his rage. He took a step back. She positioned herself between him and his father.

"I *didn't* know," *Daed* said. A flicker passed across his eyes so quickly Aden barely saw it—and it confirmed his suspicions.

He scrubbed his hands over his face. "Sol."

"Solomon wouldn't have done such a thing," his father said.

Aden looked at his mother, who glanced away. He knew she was thinking the same thing he was.

"Solomon knew not to touch the hives. I told him to leave them alone," his father said.

Aden scowled. "Perhaps you don't control him like you think you do."

His father's face pinched. "You will not talk to me that way—"

Aden walked out, not waiting around to hear another word about how disrespectful he was . . . what a lousy *sohn* he'd always been . . . how weak and worthless he would always be.

He climbed into the buggy without taking off his beekeeping clothes. Only then did he realize he'd been stung several times by the bees that were out of sorts now that their home was gone. Slapping the reins on the flanks of his horse, he urged him on, wanting to get as far away from his father, and his broken dreams, as possible.

Sadie finished counting the tool supplies on the shelves in the back of the store. The grocery was divided into two separate areas—one for food and household goods, the other strictly for a variety of garden and farm tools—all *Ordnung* approved, of course. She wrote down how many screwdrivers were in the last bin on the bottom shelf, then went back into the office and sat down, exhausted from stress, lack of sleep, suppressed grief, a marriage she didn't want—the list of things dragging at her seemed endless.

She went through the inventory and made a separate list of what she needed to order. That task finished, she sat back in the chair and looked at the desk, knowing she had to tackle the paperwork sooner rather than later. She'd already started a pile for the bills from the accident. She pulled open the bottom drawer of the desk and sighed. What a mess.

Needing a change of scenery, Sadie stood and arched her aching back. She turned off the lamp and locked the office, then the front door of the store. Even though the sign on the door showed Closed, she didn't want any customers who might show up to try to get into the store.

She headed for the house, glad that Aden would be busy for most of the day. At least she assumed he would—she really had no idea how long it took to transfer beehives. She wasn't ready to face him for more than a few minutes, which was why she'd gotten up so early. That and the fact that she couldn't sleep knowing he was only a hallway away. They would have to talk to each other sometime soon, but she would put that off as long as possible.

She thought about the bills and invoices in her father's office. Maybe he did have a plan for getting his business out of debt and she hadn't found it yet. Even though Bishop Troyer thought she needed a husband to handle the store, she didn't, and a part of her wanted to prove it. It wouldn't change her marital status, but she would feel more competent again. Other than her sisters, her confidence in herself as a businesswoman was all she had left.

Sadie decided to search her parents' bedroom, which on the surface was more organized than the mess in the office. But as she neared the back door that led to the kitchen, her stomach twisted in knots. She hadn't gone near her parents' bedroom, other than last night. Still, she trudged on, determined to put her grief aside.

But when she opened the back door, she froze, her mouth falling open at the sight of Aden standing by the kitchen table, his shirt halfway over his head, the lower part of his body clad in a pair of strange-looking white pants. Her face reddened at seeing him in the middle of undressing, and she was about to chastise him for stripping down in her kitchen. Yet the words stuck in her throat when she got a better look at his torso . . . and saw the array of purplish bruises covering his skin.

CHAPTER 8

Aden didn't move, and Sadie saw his eyes widening by the second. "Sadie, I . . . uh . . ."

She barely heard his stammering as she took in the bright purple, yellow, and green blotch covering his ribs on his left side. On the right was another darker spot above the waistband of his pants. There were smaller, more faded bruises, but he grabbed his shirt and threw it on again before she could see anything else.

He pulled the shirt front closed. "I thought I was alone . . . I got stung a couple of times." He let out an awkward chuckle. "The suit doesn't always give the best protection."

"Does that always happen when you get stung?" she asked. "The purple marks?" she added at his confused look. She was a little relieved by the possibility that the marks were a reaction to bee stings, which she knew very little about. She'd been stung once, and that was enough for her. But she'd heard about people having allergies. Maybe that's what the marks were, not the bruises they looked like.

She could almost convince herself of that, despite realizing it didn't make sense that he would be around insects he was allergic to. Yet a nonsensical explanation was preferable to what she suspected was the truth.

His mouth moved as if he was answering, but no sound came out. Then he snatched the rest of his clothes from the table and rushed out of the room. She heard the heavy tread of his footsteps as he ran up the stairs. She blinked at the sound of Abigail's door slamming shut.

An unexpected sense of concern washed over her as she remembered that day in the office, when Sol had lunged at him. He hadn't made a move to protect himself. It was as if he'd expected Sol's reaction and was prepared to accept whatever his brother would literally throw at him.

She left the kitchen and went to the stairs, pausing at the bottom, unsure if she should continue. She didn't love Aden. She didn't care about him. He was a grown man and could handle his own problems.

But her heart gave a tiny squeeze after seeing how painful the bruises looked. And she couldn't ignore the fleeting shame in his eyes before he disappeared from the kitchen. She walked up the stairs, slowly, then lifted her hand to knock on Abigail's door. She stopped. If she knocked, he would send her away. It's what she would do.

With a deep breath she opened the door. She found him folding the white clothing, his shirt completely fastened and tucked into his broadfall pants. He didn't look at her as she walked into the room.

"Those are bruises, aren't they?" she asked, her voice nearly a whisper.

He continued to fold the clothes.

Undaunted, she pressed on. "Did someone punch you?"

His long fingers pressed against the creases of the white clothing so hard she thought they would remain there permanently.

"Aden—"

"Leave it be, Sadie." He put the pants on the bed and looked at her, his light-green eyes haunted. "Forget about what you saw."

"How can I do that?"

"By ignoring me," he said, his tone holding a sharp edge. He moved past her. "Like you always do."

As he went downstairs, a chill went through her.

Aden pounded his fist against the barn door. He pulled away, seeing the blood on his knuckles. But he'd barely felt the pain. Shame and anger filled him. He hadn't meant for Sadie to see the bruises. No one ever saw them except his father and Sol. They were always in places where no one would find them.

Except his wife. He leaned his forehead against the wall, ignoring the rough wood scraping against his skin. What she must think of him. She already couldn't stand to be around him. Now she saw his secret humiliation.

The night after Aden had proposed, Sol had come home, more drunk than Aden had ever seen him—and more angry. Without warning he hoisted Aden out of bed and worked out his frustration on him. After the initial shock, Aden had taken every blow without uttering a sound. He'd had enough practice over the years, although it had been a long while since Sol had hit him like this. Unwilling to fight back, he allowed himself to be beaten while his mother and father slept in their bedroom down the hall.

But after a few minutes, Sol had stumbled away, muttering incoherently as he left Aden's room. Breathing hard, Aden had grabbed his side and sat on the edge of his bed. As far as beatings went, this one had been mild. But it had left its marks. After it was over he crawled back into bed, ignoring the pain and putting what had just happened out of his mind—the way he'd always done.

Sadie's horse whinnied in the background. He went to the animal. She was beautiful, like her owner. He touched her soft nose, stroked it gently, swallowing the tears that swelled his throat, not only for what happened last week, but for all the beatings he'd taken in the past. Tasting the burn angered him. Why couldn't he be strong? Why was he always so weak, like his father had told him he was over and over and over?

A mann *doesn't cry.* A fist to the kidney.

A mann *doesn't show weakness.* A hit to the back.

A mann *never brings shame to his father.* A crack of the ribs.

Aden stepped away from the horse, his body shaking. Now Sadie knew. Then again, she always had. She knew he was weak. A coward. The one thing he could have brought to the marriage—his beehives—had been destroyed.

How could he expect her to ever respect him when he was so much less than she deserved?

Sadie kept looking at the back door as she prepared a late lunch. She wasn't the best cook around, but she could make a passable meal, unlike Joanna, who could whip up miracles in the kitchen, especially when it came to pies.

After Aden left, her emotions were raw. She couldn't face going into her parents' bedroom to search for any papers or plans her father might have kept that would help with the bills. Not when she couldn't stop thinking about what had happened to Aden. Despite his refusal to confirm, she knew Sol had caused the bruises. He was the one person Sadie could see ignoring the bishop's dictate for turning the other cheek.

butter. Sliced bread rounded out the meal. She took a step back from the table. She'd made too much food for two people.

Aden entered the room, his long hair combed, but still wild looking and in need of a cut. He pulled out the chair at the end of the table. She unwittingly sucked in a sharp breath.

He stilled. "I shouldn't sit here?"

"It's not that." She hugged her arms around her waist. *"Mei daed . . ."*

Aden nodded. "This was his seat." He pushed the chair back under the table. "Where would you like me to sit?"

Another kind gesture. Focusing on supper instead of how he continually destroyed her expectations of him, she pointed to Abigail's chair, then sat down across from him.

Aden bowed his head and she followed suit for prayer, struggling to maintain focus. When she heard Aden helping himself to the food, she looked up.

He pierced a pork chop with his fork. He eyed the five other chops on the plate, but didn't say anything. She took a small spoonful of potatoes, her appetite still gone.

The silence in the kitchen was punctuated with the sound of silverware scraping against dishes. Aden kept his head down as he ate. For some strange reason she couldn't stop watching him, thinking about the bruises, about the past, about the secrets he held that were possibly more painful than she'd ever imagined.

As if he knew she was staring, he lifted his head. His lips twisted in what she thought might be an attempt at a smile but looked more like a grimace.

"I hope it's okay," she blurted. "The food, I mean."

"It is. I like pork chops." He pushed his fork around a few bites of potatoes still on his plate.

"So did *mei daed*." She pushed her plate away. "They were his favorite." She looked at him, and this time he held her gaze. His fern-colored eyes seemed to turn hazel in the light from the propane lamp suspended above the table. She didn't like what she saw in them—compassion, sincerity, and the worst emotion of all—pity.

Sadie pushed back from the table and started clearing the dishes. She turned on the hot water tap. Soon steaming water poured into the sink.

Aden came up behind her and set his plate on the counter next to the sink. "Can I help you?"

She couldn't look at him. She didn't want these feelings that were bubbling to the surface so fast they threatened to take her breath away. She didn't want to let go of the resentment she'd held on to for six years. She didn't want to wonder about his life, to be concerned about his pain, to feel the strange and foreign warmth coming over her at his nearness.

"I'll check on the horses," he said when she didn't answer.

She nodded and turned off the hot water tap, resisting the urge to watch him leave. She thrust her fingers into the scalding water. They burned, but she didn't pull them out right away. The physical pain shoved everything else out of her mind, and she was grateful for it. When she removed her hands, they were red and hurting—but she'd take that over the way she felt when Aden stood next to her.

After she finished cleaning the kitchen, she went upstairs to her room and shut the door. It was barely dark, but she was exhausted. She undressed, changed into her nightclothes, and got into bed. Despite her fatigue, her body tensed as she lay there, waiting, wondering for the second night in a row if Aden would come to her, and praying as hard as she could that he wouldn't.

Time seemed to slide to a stop as she listened for the now-familiar sound of his footsteps. Finally, she heard him come up the stairs. But when she heard the door to Abigail's room close, she didn't feel any peace.

CHAPTER 9

The next morning Aden managed to avoid Sadie as much as possible. She took a cup of coffee and went to the store, which he presumed was becoming a refuge for her. More than anything, he was glad she had dropped the subject of his bruises.

Since Sadie didn't want him involved in anything that had to do with the store, Aden decided to explore the Schrocks' property. The backyard was about an acre in size and surrounded by woods. He didn't know how far the woods extended or where the Schrocks' property line was, so he didn't stray far. From what he could tell, it was a nice piece of land.

He glanced at the spot he'd marked off for his hives. The new hives, he corrected himself. He'd have to order them soon, and his plans for expanding the business would have to wait. Losing the hives was a deeper setback than he'd initially realized because of the money he'd given Sadie. Still, he wasn't giving up on his plans, and he didn't regret giving Sadie the cash. Eventually he would have a thriving beekeeping business that would rival his previous one.

Aden spent the rest of the afternoon picking out a place for the garden, discovering several spots in the barn that needed repair, and then mowing the lawn with a reel mower that required some oil. He was raking the grass clippings into a neat row when he heard a buggy pull into the driveway. Since the store was still closed, he expected the driver to see the sign on the front door and turn around. Instead the buggy rolled past the store and parked near the house. Aden paused to see Timothy and Patience exit. Patience waved at him before walking to the store while Timothy tied the horse to the hitching rail.

Aden was surprised when Timothy didn't follow his wife. Instead he headed toward Aden. They hadn't had company since the wedding, in contrast to most Amish weddings when the couple either visit family and friends or they visit the couple. There was nothing normal about his and Sadie's marriage, and it wouldn't surprise him if his father had spread the word to leave the young couple alone. Which was fine by Aden. Still, he wouldn't be rude. He picked up the rake and walked in Timothy's direction.

"Patience wanted to check on Sadie," Timothy said after he and Aden had greeted each other.

Aden nodded. "I'm sure Sadie's been missing her friend."

"I know Patience misses her." Timothy smiled a little. "From what I heard, those two used to be inseparable. Before Patience and I got married, that is."

"They were."

"Almost like sisters."

"I guess." Now Aden had his guard up. He wasn't used to people engaging him in small talk, and he didn't know Timothy very well. From what he'd observed at church, the Amish man from Lancaster had fit in with the Birch Creek community just fine. But Aden couldn't shake the thought that Timothy wasn't here to chitchat. "Is there something you need?"

"Direct and to the point. Patience says Sadie is the same way."

"She is."

"I was thinking, since our wives are *gut* friends and all . . . we should have supper together soon. You and Sadie could come over to our place."

"I'll talk it over with her." Aden tilted his head, trying to discern if Timothy had another agenda.

"*Gut, gut.*"

When Timothy glanced away, Aden knew a friendly supper wasn't the only thing on his mind. "Anything else you wanted to talk about?"

Timothy's gaze snapped back to him. "What?" Then he scratched his beard. "Maybe." The man was struggling with something, that much was clear. After a moment he spoke again. "Do you know anything about the church's community fund?"

Aden measured his next words. "*Nee*. Why?"

"Just wondering. Since *yer vatter* is the bishop . . . I thought you might . . . I don't know . . ." He sighed. "I shouldn't have said anything."

"But you did." Aden's wariness turned to apprehension, along with a good dose of defensiveness, which surprised him. Why would he be compelled to defend his father from anything? He set the feelings aside to discern what Timothy really wanted.

Was something wrong? Patience was Sadie's best friend. Did they need money? Sadie had been hit with enough challenges and grief lately. She didn't need to add worry over Patience to the list. "Are you in trouble?" he asked Timothy.

Timothy shook his head. "*Nee.* Everything is fine. But I was curious . . . if something were to happen and we needed a little help, how that kind of thing worked here. Me being from another district, I'm discovering things here are a little different."

"If someone needed money, *mei daed* would make sure he got it. All the church members contribute to the fund."

"How long have they been contributing?"

"As long as I can remember."

"So there should be plenty of money available?"

"It's a small community. *Nee* one here is rich. But we help out the best we can. God has always provided."

"*Ya*. He always does." His troubled expression seemed to ease. "I better get Patience. We only stopped by for a short visit. Looking forward to having you and Sadie over for supper."

Aden nodded as Timothy walked away. He frowned. Timothy's questions didn't stem from idle curiosity. Maybe he'd lied about not needing money. They wouldn't be the first family who needed help. It was the reason the community fund existed. Being new to the district, maybe Timothy didn't feel comfortable asking Aden's father for help directly.

He went back to raking. Whatever was going on with Timothy and Patience wasn't his business. He had enough worries of his own to think about.

"So you don't mind helping while Abigail and Joanna are in Middlefield?" Sadie asked. She'd been surprised and relieved when she saw Patience walk into the store. The unexpected visit gave her a chance to take Patience up on her offer to help. Plus, she missed her friend.

"Of course not. I'd be happy to." Patience smiled. "When are you planning to reopen?"

"Monday."

The frown slipped from Patience's face. "So soon?"

"*Ya*. We will have been closed for three weeks." Sadie dusted the top of the cash register with a soft cloth. She'd restocked the shelves and cleaned the store from top to bottom, with the exception of the office. The work was tiring, but it kept her mind off what had happened with Aden the day before.

"No one would blame you if you were closed for a few more days," Patience said. "You could *geh* visit Joanna."

Sadie paused. She'd talked to Abigail on the phone yesterday, and while her sister had assured her that Joanna was improving, there had been underlying strain in her voice. She would love to visit her sisters, but that wasn't financially feasible. She also didn't feel comfortable leaving Aden here alone. She still didn't trust him.

There was also another reason she wanted to put off the visit. Although she'd had the opportunity during her call with Abigail, she hadn't told her about her marriage. Avoiding the subject was easier than trying to explain what had happened.

"Sadie?"

She turned around. "Sorry. The window is really dirty."

"Looks spotless to me." Patience took the cloth from Sadie's hand. "Can we sit down and talk?"

"I've got a lot to do," Sadie said. She should have expected this from Patience. Her friend was not only caring but tenacious.

"It can wait."

Sadie folded her hands and rested them on the counter, preparing herself for the onslaught of questions.

Patience set the cloth to the side. "Tell me how you're really doing."

"I'm doing fine."

"You're not fine. You can't be."

Sadie stiffened. "What do you mean by that?"

"I know you're handling things. I know you're strong." Her mouth turned up in an encouraging, yet not quite complete, smile. "But how can you pretend everything is fine when you're married to someone you don't love?"

The bell rang above the store door. Timothy started to come inside, then left after Patience gave him a look.

When the door shut, Sadie said, "You have no idea how I feel about Aden."

"Then tell me." She leaned forward. "Tell me you love him."

Sadie sighed. "There are more important things to base a marriage on than love." She snatched the cloth and began scrubbing the already shining counter. "There's respect." Which she was realizing she did have for Aden, especially since he hadn't said a single word about consummating the marriage. In fact, he didn't intrude or push her at all. He was just . . . there. And for some reason that was what she needed from him more than anything else.

"True, but without love—"

"Patience, *mei* life isn't like yours. Not everyone can live a fairy tale." She stopped wiping the counter and looked at her, frustrated that she was hurting her friend and couldn't tell her the truth. There was no one she could talk to about her conflicted feelings toward Aden, how she fought against breaking down with grief every day, how much she missed her sisters, and how she was afraid that the lonely ache in her soul would never go away.

Somehow she found the strength to keep her voice from collapsing. "Can you help me on Monday or not?"

Patience's eyes widened before she slowly nodded. "I'm sorry. I didn't mean to upset you." When Sadie looked away, Patience went to the door. "Just so you know, *mei* marriage isn't perfect either," Patience said. "No one's is. See you on Monday." She walked out of the store.

Sadie pressed the heel of her hand against her forehead, hoping she hadn't ruined their friendship. She couldn't bear to lose anyone else.

The door opened again, and this time Aden walked in. "The phone was ringing in the shanty."

Sadie didn't answer, and was questioning whether she should go after Patience and apologize when Aden added, "It's Abigail." He paused. "She sounded surprised that I answered the phone."

She steeled herself, waiting for Aden to ask why she hadn't told Abigail they were married.

"I told her you would be there in a minute." Then he left, shutting the door behind him.

Sadie looked at the closed door. Didn't he wonder why she hadn't told Abigail? Even if he did, he wouldn't pry. Unlike she had when she saw his bruises. She rubbed her nose with the tips of her fingers, trying to gain her composure. She also tried to stem the worry that her sister was calling two days in a row.

As she walked to the phone shanty at the end of the driveway, she saw Aden out of the corner of her eye. He was pulling weeds out of the flower bed in the front of the house. She hadn't asked him to do it; the task was something her mother and sisters had normally done. Sadie preferred working in the store to dealing with the garden. Then she noticed how trim and tidy the yard was, the scent of freshly mown grass hanging in the air. She breathed it in. She loved the smell of cut grass, and for the briefest of moments she felt the heaviness in her chest ease a little.

She stepped into the shanty and lifted the receiver of the landline telephone. "Hello?"

"Sadie, is everything all right?" Abigail asked.

"*Ya.*" She gripped the receiver, steeling herself for the inevitable question.

"Who answered the phone?"

"Aden." She squeezed her eyes shut. "He's . . .

helping. Helping . . . with the yard work." At least it wasn't a complete lie.

"Oh. That's nice of him. The lawn must be in bad shape if you let him come over."

"What do you mean by that?"

"*Nix.* You normally don't like to accept help, that's all." She paused. "Are you sure everything is all right?"

Sadie kept her voice calm. "Everything is fine. We're opening the store on Monday. Patience agreed to help out for a little while."

"Oh." Abigail's voice took on a melancholy tone.

"Now it's *mei* turn to interrogate you." Sadie's voice softened. "Are you okay? How is Joanna?"

"The same as yesterday. She's very sweet and cooperative and tries to please everyone. Typical Joanna." Abigail sighed. "At least I think she's being typical."

"What do you mean?"

"I don't know . . . it's a feeling I have. She seems so . . . overeager, if that's possible. And she's working so hard on her therapy that she collapses at night with exhaustion. Even her therapists are a little concerned."

A knot of tension appeared in the middle of Sadie's back. "I would think they would want her to work hard."

"They do. I guess I'm not explaining it right." Abigail sighed again. "I miss you, Sadie. I know

Joanna does too. I was hoping you could come for a visit soon. Maybe delay the opening of the store for a couple of days? Wait, hang on for a minute."

Sadie picked at the splintered wood in the shanty. The tiny building had been there since Sadie could remember. It needed stripping and sanding and probably a good coat of white paint. Yet another thing that needed to be done.

"I've got to *geh*," Abigail said when she returned. "Joanna's therapist wants to talk to me. Come soon, Sadie. Please?"

"I'll . . . try."

Abigail hung up the phone and Sadie stared at the receiver. How could she deny her sister? Just hearing her voice made her yearn to be with her and Joanna. Still, she couldn't leave. Not right now. And she had no idea how to explain that to Abigail without telling her about Aden or about their family's huge debt.

She left the shanty and walked up the driveway. She could see Aden a few yards away, putting grass clippings into the wheelbarrow, probably to add to the pile of debris behind the barn. Sadie paused for a moment, watching his methodical, unhurried movements. He was slender but tightly compact, with broad shoulders and a torso that tapered to a narrow waist. Although it was nearly fall, the hot summer weather had hung on longer than usual. He paused and pushed his hat back from his face, his cheeks red from the heat. Then he gripped the handles of the wheelbarrow, and she could see the outline of his lower bicep grow taut underneath the edge of his shirtsleeve.

Shaking her head, she trudged back to the store, annoyed with herself. She didn't want to notice Aden that way. Keeping that mental separation between Aden the interloper and Aden the man was the only way she could maintain her sanity.

She went back to the office and plopped into the desk chair. The short stack of mail she'd brought in earlier was on the desk. With a heavy sigh she picked up the first envelope and looked at the return address. Langdon Hospital. She tossed the letter to the side, not wanting to look at the bill.

Desperate to do something, she yanked open a drawer and emptied it, sifting through the huge stack of expired catalogs. Why had her father kept all these useless things? She set the catalogs on the growing pile of trash she needed to get rid of. She'd burn it in the next couple of days. The thought triggered another memory—bonfires with her parents, her sisters, and occasionally friends. Patience had come to a few. They would have popcorn and cider in the fall and ice cream in the summer.

She slammed the drawer shut, her frustration rising. She heard something fall inside the desk. She pulled out the drawer and reached her hand inside. Her fingers touched the corner of a small box. Sadie withdrew it and placed it on the desktop.

She'd never seen the simple brown cardboard box before. It was the type of container that might have held large Christmas cards or thank-you notes. Two rubber bands were wrapped around it and on the top was her mother's name, written in her father's handwriting.

Carefully she took off the rubber bands and lifted the lid. Her throat constricted as she picked up several letters, still in their envelopes, all addressed to her father from her mother.

The tears she tried so hard to hold back for so long started to slip down her cheeks as she read the first letter.

Dear Matthew,

By the time you read this we will have been married. Oh, how I have waited for this day! I've thanked God every day for you, since you asked me to marry you six months ago. I love you, and I can't wait to start our lives together as husband and wife. You are my best friend, the love of my life, the man of my prayers . . .

Sadie continued to read several letters, each one dated the day of their anniversary, each one declaring her mother's love for her father. She'd had no idea how romantic their marriage was. As she continued to read, it was as if the words brought her parents alive again.

Their marriage had been everything a marriage should be—the union of friends who loved each other deeply.

Her parents' marriage had been everything her marriage wasn't.

When Aden walked into the kitchen that evening, part of him hoped Sadie was preparing supper. He found himself looking forward to the evening meal, even though they hadn't said much to each other last night and had exchanged even fewer words today. Sadie was a decent cook, and he appreciated the effort she'd put into making last night's meal, although it was too much food. Clearly she was used to making meals for a family of five. When he didn't see her, he went upstairs to wash up, assuming she would come in shortly.

He returned to the kitchen and waited for her. He'd fix supper himself, but he didn't know where anything was in the kitchen, and he felt awkward about rummaging through the cabinets again. When it was nearly seven o'clock, he decided to check on her. First he went to the pantry, found a loaf of bread and a jar of peanut butter, and made her a sandwich. He poured her a glass of cold tea and went outside. Not much of a supper, but he figured she had to be hungry.

The store was still unlocked, and he walked inside. The grocery area was dark, with only a little light shining through the windows from the setting sun outside. The days were growing shorter, and tomorrow he planned to start laying in more firewood. Before long they'd have to light up the wood stove in the living room.

An image of Sadie and him sitting in front of the warm stove passed through his mind. Drinking cups of coffee, talking about their day, sharing their dreams . . .

He shook his head, stopping himself from wishing for something that would never happen. He saw the light on in the office and walked toward it.

Aden knocked on the door and waited. When she didn't answer, he knocked again. Again, no answer. He opened the door a tiny crack and heard the sound of her sniffling. "Sadie?" he said, opening the door wider.

She was sitting in front of the desk, a paper in her hand. She didn't seem to realize he was there. At first he didn't know what to do. Should he set the sandwich down and leave? Should he ask her what's wrong?

He set the sandwich and tea down on the desk and knelt beside her. He glanced at the paper she was reading and realized it was a letter. Several more lay in her lap.

She turned to him, her beautiful brown eyes red-rimmed and liquid with tears. She stared at him for a moment, as if she didn't recognize him. Then she turned. "*Geh* away," she muttered, gathering letters and shoving them into a small box.

Her sharp tone smarted, but he didn't move. "I brought you something to eat," he said, as if food would solve everything.

"I'm not hungry." She shut the lid on the box and threw it into the desk drawer.

"But—"

She slammed the drawer shut and glared at him. "Leave me alone!"

"I don't think that's a *gut* idea right now."

She shoved her chair back and jumped up. He rose and stepped back before she bumped into him. To his surprise, she faced him. Sadie was only a couple inches shorter, and they could look each other in the eye. What he saw in her gaze made him draw back.

"Stop it!" she yelled. "Just . . . stop."

He flinched. He started to speak again, but she held up her hand, shutting him down.

"Stop trying to help me. Stop being *nice*." Her chin trembled. "It was easier when I hated you," she said in a harsh whisper.

He stiffened. She might as well have plunged a knife in his back. His jaw tensed as he turned and went back to the house.

He climbed the stairs and entered Abigail's room, shutting the door behind him. He leaned against it, the darkness of the room enveloping him. What was he supposed to do now? His marriage was rooted in deceit, and from Sadie's point of view, hate. How could they move past that?

A knock sounded at the door, making him jump away. He opened it. Sadie's silhouette was outlined in the shadows of the hallway.

CHAPTER 10

Sadie stepped into the room when Aden moved aside to let her in. With unsteady legs she took a few more steps, still wondering what brought her here. She'd told Aden the truth—that she hated him. Yet when she saw his stricken look, the way he walked out of the office as if she'd physically wounded him, her heart had compressed in her chest.

What had he done to deserve her anger? Brought her a sandwich? Asked if she was okay? *Saved me from Sol?*

She wrestled with her thoughts as she turned on the lamp in Abigail's room. The first thing she saw was her sister's childhood doll sitting on the side table near her bed. It was a faceless Amish doll. Her mother had made one for each of her daughters for Christmas when they were little girls. Abigail's was dressed in light blue, Sadie's in light green, and Joanna's in light pink. Sadie touched the top of the doll's little black *kapp*, then she turned around.

Aden stood by the door, which was still open. He looked out of place in this room, which reflected Abigail's girly tastes. Two of Abigail's cross-stitched samplers were framed on the wall, both full of flowers and pastel colors. Her sister had picked up weaving a couple of years ago, and one of her muted-colored rag rugs covered the middle of the room. The sweet scent of Abigail's favorite vanilla candles, ones she lit almost every night, still permeated the room.

Aden wasn't a large man, yet his presence almost overwhelmed the delicate and feminine bedroom. His strong jaw was unmoving, his lips set in a cold line that reflected the ice in his green eyes. He didn't belong in her sister's bedroom. But he stayed for Sadie's benefit. He spent his nights next to an Amish doll instead of claiming his right as her husband. That unsettled her. But the idea of sleeping with Aden plain scared her.

She crossed the room and sat on the floor, leaning her back against the closet door. She pulled her knees up to her chin, her toes touching the edge of Abigail's woven rug, the skirt of her dress shrouding her legs.

Aden didn't move. He didn't say anything. She glanced at him, saw the pain in his eyes . . . and looked away.

"I'm sorry," she finally whispered.

"It's okay."

She looked at him. "*Nee*, it's not. I was rude." *More than rude.* "I don't hate you."

He kept his gaze on hers. "I wouldn't blame you if you did."

Sadie stared at him until the question that had

burrowed deep inside her all these years came to the surface. "Aden . . . why did you leave me with Sol?"

Looking away, he leaned his shoulder against the door frame. He didn't speak for a long time. Finally he said, "Because I was scared."

"So was I."

"I know." When he turned to her, his expression was raw. "It's not an excuse . . . or even a *gut* reason. It's just the truth."

She thought about the bruises on his body. "Are you afraid of him now?"

He paused, then shook his head. "Not anymore. I feel sorry for him."

She frowned, not expecting that answer. "I don't understand."

"It's complicated, Sadie."

"Everything is complicated."

He shifted on his feet, and she thought he would walk out the door. Instead he walked over and sat down on the floor next to her, leaving plenty of space between them.

"Bees are complicated," he said after a long stretch of silence.

"What?"

"They have a complex hierarchy. All the bees have to work together for the colony to survive. But there's also a beautiful simplicity to them."

"They sting, Aden," she said, confused by the sudden change of subject.

"Only when they feel threatened. Can you really blame them for that?"

She shook her head. "*Nee.*"

"Once their hives are established, they follow a routine. They don't deviate from it. It allows them to produce honey, honeycomb, beeswax, royal jelly . . . they are amazing creatures."

Sadie watched him as he explained the bees, oddly pleased to see the pain slip from his expression, replaced by a spark of excitement in his eyes and a twitch of a smile on his lips. Now she knew why he had shifted from talking about his brother to discussing bees. The tiny creatures somehow helped him cope.

She could see the light freckles on his face, the small cleft in his chin covered with a light shading of stubble, the fullness of his bottom lip . . . they all combined to make Aden Troyer a rather handsome man.

Feeling her cheeks heat, she dropped her gaze, rubbing her big toe against the rug.

"I'm sorry I intruded on you in the office," he said, shifting the conversation again.

"You didn't. I mean, you did, sort of . . ." She sighed and looked at him. "The timing was bad, that's all."

"I seem to have a knack for that."

She thought about how he'd kept her from having to marry Sol, and thought his timing was pretty perfect. "*Danki* for taking care of the yard. I haven't had time to do it, with everything that's been going on. And the money you gave me—"

"Sadie, you don't have to shoulder everything alone." He angled himself toward her. "I know the circumstances of our marriage are less than ideal—"

"No kidding," she couldn't help saying, then felt bad for being sarcastic.

He gave her a wry smile. "I guess that was a big understatement. What I'm trying to say is that I can help. With the yard, the store, the *haus*—anything you need me to do, I'll do it. Anything I have is yours."

"Why?" The question flew out of her mouth, but she couldn't stop herself. "Why are you so willing to help me?"

He faced her fully now. "Because you deserve to be happy."

For a moment she was lost in his eyes, letting his sincerity and kindness wash over her. But in the next breath she raised her guard. There had to be a catch. "What do you want in return?"

Hurt flashed across his face, then his expression quickly turned to stone. "*Nix*," he said, rising to his feet. "I don't want anything from you, Sadie. One day I hope you'll believe that." He turned his back to her and walked out of the room.

Sadie stared at the empty doorway, trying to grasp his words. He wanted nothing from her?

How was that possible? Yes, their Amish upbringing taught them to help their neighbors, but this went further than helping out a friend—and they weren't even friends.

She skipped supper, troubled that it was becoming harder to be unaffected by him. The anger and hatred had felt safe. Comfortable. Easier to handle than the fleeting moment of trust and connection she'd felt when they were talking in Abigail's room.

She washed up quickly for the night and hurried to her room. She removed her *kapp*, but as she had done on her wedding night, she kept her clothes on. Maybe that was his angle—he thought he'd softened her up. That she would welcome him in her bed tonight. She clutched at the edge of the quilt. If he tried anything, she knew how to stop him—the same way she'd stopped Sol.

Sadie waited for Aden to come. And waited. And waited, until she couldn't stay awake any longer.

When she woke the next morning, she was still alone, as she had been the entire night.

She changed into a fresh dress and went downstairs, the scent of brewing coffee in the air. She entered the kitchen and saw he'd prepared a simple breakfast—two boiled eggs with sliced bread and butter. A coffee mug was near the place setting, along with a cloth napkin and silverware. But he wasn't there.

She spotted a folded piece of paper near her plate and picked it up. Opening it, she read the few sentences, written in small, neat handwriting.

Sadie,
I went to town to order supplies for the beehives. I didn't want to wake you. I'll be back this afternoon. Hope breakfast is okay.
Aden

PS—we should talk about you going to visit your sisters. You must miss them.

She folded the note and put it back on the table, not knowing what to think. Another act of kindness. Two, if she counted him making her breakfast.

Sadie took her mug and poured the coffee. She took a sip and nearly choked. She picked up the pot and dumped the liquid into the sink, noticing that it wasn't a nice, rich brown but a deep black color. She put a fresh pot on the stove.

While she waited for it to percolate, she sat down, said a quick silent prayer, and tapped one of the eggs with her spoon. The shell broke, and instead of a firm, hard-boiled egg, a gooey mess ran out of the shell. She put down her spoon. Aden was probably the worst cook she'd ever encountered.

And for the first time since her parents died, she smiled.

He'd tried to make her a good breakfast, and that meant more to her than if he'd prepared perfect coffee and eggs. To top it off, he'd realized without her saying a word that she needed to see Abigail and Joanna.

Her smile dimmed as she tried to tell herself yet again that she couldn't trust him. But the words rang false, and a little part of her started to hope that while she and Aden would never love each other, they could come to some kind of understanding. Perhaps there could be peace in her life after all.

A knock sounded at the back door. She stood up, wondering who would be visiting her this early. She opened the door, and her legs buckled at the sight of Sol.

CHAPTER 11

Emmanuel slid his finger under the flap of the sealed envelope. He pulled out the document and perused it. He'd expected this counteroffer from one of the gas companies bidding for the natural gas rights he possessed. And as he expected, the amount wasn't enough. But he wasn't worried, and he put the letter back in the envelope. Other companies were interested in the rights, and once Timothy Glick signed over what he owned, Emmanuel would have more to bargain with.

Other than Timothy's claim, there was only one more claim he needed to acquire, one that made the other properties pale in comparison.

He leaned back in the stiff chair in his office and tapped the wood desk with his fingers. Now that Aden technically owned everything that belonged to Sadie, it was time for Emmanuel to make his move. Aden would have to do what Matthew Schrock hadn't done before he died— turn over his natural gas rights to the community. And as the steward of the community fund, the rights would have to be transferred into Emmanuel's name.

Emmanuel frowned as he remembered the excuses Matthew had given him for not signing over the rights, the latest one being that he couldn't find the paperwork. After visiting Matthew's chaotic office, Emmanuel understood why. But he still suspected Matthew had been stalling. However, that didn't matter, now that his son controlled the rights in question.

He stood, clasped his hands behind his back, and walked to the window. No curtains covered the glass panes, and he stared at his front yard, contemplating his next move. Aden wasn't the only wild card involved. Instead of Solomon heeding Emmanuel's warning to get his act together, he had done the opposite. Emmanuel had heard his son stumble home the past three nights, probably full to the gills with liquor. Yesterday Tobias Chupp, Solomon's boss and owner of Chupp's Carpentry, had stopped by and told Emmanuel he would have to let Solomon go since he hadn't shown up for work the past two days, and his attendance had been spotty recently.

Emmanuel sighed. Even the promise of a secure future had done nothing to curb Solomon's bad behavior. He would have to be dealt with, and soon.

The door opened and he turned to see Rhoda enter with a cup of tea. He smiled his thanks as she set it on the desk, expecting her to leave right away, as she always did when he was working.

But for some reason she stayed. Her hands were folded in front of her apron, her head bent slightly so he could see the neat part of her graying hair. He knew when he married her she would be the perfect wife, and after twenty-seven years together, that hadn't changed. She knew her place, knew how important it was to support him as a bishop and a husband. She didn't question him or pressure him to make her privy to his private dealings, both personal and business. Whatever she needed to say must be weighing on her mind. "What is it, *frau*?" he asked.

She lifted her head slightly, the creases on her forehead and around her eyes visible in the morning light filling the room. She'd been a beauty in her day, yet over the years he held her deference to him in higher esteem.

"I was hoping we could stop by and see Aden and . . . Sadie," she said, pausing. "Perhaps today, if you aren't too busy."

He didn't let on that he had been entertaining a similar idea. "Don't you think they deserve some time alone together?"

"*Ya*." She lifted her head a little more, now looking him in the eye. "I just thought they might like the company."

"You want to check up on them." He picked up his tea and took a sip.

"I want to see how they're doing, *ya*. When Aden left the other day, he was so angry. And Sol." She cast her gaze down again. "I'm concerned about them both."

"I understand." Emmanuel looked down at his

wife. "We'll *geh* see them today. I have a few items to take care of here and then we can leave."

Her pale lips formed a smile. "I'll package up the raisin oatmeal cookies I made last night."

"I'm sure Sadie and Aden will appreciate the treat."

When she left the room, Emmanuel sat back down. He couldn't deny the love in his wife's blue eyes when she talked about her sons. She viewed them through a rosy lens, only seeing the good and never the bad. When they were younger, she had been the one they sought out to fill their empty bellies and patch up their skinned knees. She had never disciplined them, seemingly content to leave that up to Emmanuel, since she never interfered. In her eyes her two boys were without flaw or blemish.

But they were men now, and both had pulled away from her over the years. Which was as it should be. He had left his home and family for a better life, one he had worked hard for. God had entrusted him with much, and he took that responsibility seriously.

Emmanuel opened the middle drawer of his desk and pulled out a small notebook. He laid it open and looked at the calculations. If only everyone knew how diligent he was with the community fund. How carefully he managed the money. He didn't trust banks, never had. And he weighed any request for help against the needs of the community as a whole.

He thought of Freemont Yoder, who had recently asked for a good-sized amount of the money. Emmanuel didn't see the point in giving him a handout, not when there were people in the community who could donate extra food to the family. Freemont would plant more crops next year, and if those failed, then they would talk about what could be done. Perhaps the failure of the crop was a spiritual issue. No one else's crops had been spoiled the way Freemont's had. Then again, Freemont also planted more than anyone else in their community.

Whatever the reason, Emmanuel couldn't entrust such a large sum of money in the hands of a man—or a woman, since Sadie had also asked for financial help—who didn't know how to handle it. He'd seen firsthand what happened when money was mismanaged, when not just a single family but an entire group of people lived in poverty due to the mistakes of one man. He wouldn't allow that in Birch Creek.

He looked at Timothy's name, saw the blank in the column beside it, and frowned. He'd been suspicious of the man since he'd first visited Birch Creek. When Patience's family had privately told Emmanuel that their daughter was marrying someone from another district, Emmanuel wanted to put a stop to it right away.

But he had to be realistic—the women in their church outnumbered the men. It was only a matter of time before outsiders would have to be a part of the community or it would fade away. That, or they would have to join with another church—something Emmanuel would never allow.

He had established this settlement, and he was determined to see it thrive.

Sadie stared in shock as Sol staggered toward her, the stench of alcohol coming off him in fumes. "Sol, *nee!*" She tried to shut the door against him, but even drunk—or hung over, she had no idea which—he was too strong for her. He shoved her aside and almost tumbled into the kitchen.

"Is that any way to greet your brother-in-law?" His gaze clumsily roamed around the kitchen before landing on the table. "Breakfast for one?" He swung his unsteady frame and faced her. "How sad. Guess the honeymoon's over."

"Leave, Sol."

"I think I'll stay a while." He yanked out a chair.

If he was staying, then *she* was leaving. She started for the door, but Sol was suddenly behind her, grabbing her by the arm and jerking her back into the room.

He slammed the door and turned the lock. "You don't want to do that again."

His dank breath was heavy in her face, his

bloodshot eyes staring her down with alarming clarity. "What do you want?" she said, pulling out of his grasp.

"To talk." He lifted both his hands and stepped back. "Just . . . talk."

"I have *nix* to say to you."

He plunked down on the edge of the table, his thigh less than an inch from her arm. "But I have something to say to you." He leaned over and whispered, "I know *yer* marriage is fake."

Her lips trembled, and she was too slow to deny his accusation.

He let out a bitter-smelling chuckle and moved back from her. His head lolled a bit before he leveled his gaze at her again. "He loves you."

Sadie's eyes widened. "What?"

"That's why he married you." Sol pushed up from the table and closed the space between them. "But he's weak."

"Aden is not weak," Sadie snapped.

He moved closer to her, his stronger, taller body crowding hers, filling her with fear—and making her feel like a terrified sixteen-year-old all over again. "I can take care of you, Sadie," he said, his voice low. "Like a *mann* should."

"Sol," she begged. "Please . . ."

"Please what?" He inched closer. "Aden isn't here." He gave her a crooked smirk. "Even if he was . . . he wouldn't stand up to me. He never has."

• • •

As Aden neared Sadie's house—his house, he had to remind himself—he tried to stem his frustration. What had started out as a trip to Miller's hardware to order new hives ended up being a waste of time. Zeb Miller had stopped ordering from the company Aden usually used, and the company he did work with that had bees and beehive supplies not only had outrageous prices, they couldn't guarantee the bees would be delivered before November, which meant he might as well wait until spring to start the hives. His other alternative was to hire a taxi to take him to the local library in Langston, a small town outside of Birch Creek, so he could use the Internet to order the bees. If he got caught doing that he'd be in big trouble. They'd require him to confess in front of the congregation for his sin and to promise he would stay away from "evil" technology for the rest of his life.

The thing was, he didn't find technology evil. He did think it was superfluous, except in cases like this. But he didn't regard it with as much suspicion as most of the people in his community. Life was simple in Birch Creek . . . at least on the outside.

As he approached the driveway, he wasn't sure what to do about the hives. He missed the bees. He missed having something of his own. Yet his business had never truly been his own, since he had to give almost all the money to his father. But now that he was married, the business would be his. *Ours. It will be ours.* He smiled wryly to himself. Sadie didn't care about bees. What she cared about was her store and her sisters, and he respected that more than she would ever know. But eventually he hoped she would want to partner with him in his business, and she would let him be a part of hers.

A pipe dream, probably. Yet not one he was willing to give up.

Distracted by his thoughts, he didn't notice the buggy in the Schrocks' driveway until he had turned onto the gravel drive. Alarm hit him like a lightning strike. Sol was here.

Aden yelled for his horse to stop, then jumped out of his buggy. His eyes shot from the store to the house, unsure where to go first. He dashed to the store and tried opening the door. It was locked.

"Sadie!" He waited, listening for her to respond. When she didn't, he ran to the house. He looked through the back door window, saw Sol hovering over Sadie. Saw her paralyzed with fear. Aden turned the knob, but it didn't move . . . and he didn't have a key. Then he saw Sol touch his wife.

Something inside him exploded.

"Sol, please!" She couldn't believe she was trapped with Sol again. Her whole body shook, and she was more afraid than she'd been six years ago.

He was bigger now, stronger, more determined . . . and very drunk. Gripping her upper arm, his mouth moved closer to hers.

"I'm *yer bruder*'s wife," she managed to say.

He stopped, his mouth close to hers, his breath and nearness making the sip of Aden's coffee rebel in her stomach. Sol stared at her, the light green eyes that resembled Aden's searching her face, then becoming glazed over, as if he were struggling with something inside.

"Why are you doing this?" she whispered.

That seemed to pull him out of his stupor. His jaw jerked as his hold on her tightened. "Because I can."

Lord . . . nee . . .

The back door broke open. Sadie turned as Sol released her, relief shuddering through her when she saw Aden. He stood in the doorway, his freckled face blazing red, his eyes looking like dark green fire as the door slammed against the wall and fell off one hinge.

Sol straightened, only to lose his balance. He grabbed the edge of the table, but his defying gaze remained on Aden. "Breaking down a door. Didn't know you had it in you."

With a yell that resembled a roar, Aden charged at Sol, his straw hat hitting the floor. He seized the front of his brother's shirt and slammed Sol back against the table. Hovering over him, he growled, "Stay away from *mei frau*."

Sadie couldn't breathe. Veins were pulsing against the skin of Aden's neck as he continued to keep Sol pinned down.

Sol's drunken eyes widened and he lifted his hands. "Aden—"

Aden yanked Sol up, glaring at him.

Shock registered on Sol's face, which twisted into anger. He swung back and delivered a punch.

Sadie covered her face with her hands, expecting Aden to hit the ground. She peeked through her fingers. Aden had blocked his brother's blow and now had Sol's arms pinned behind his back. Aden shoved him toward the splintered doorway.

"If I see you near her again, you'll regret it," Aden said, his chin hovering above Sol's contorted shoulder.

Somehow Sol managed to pull out of Aden's grip, although Sadie suspected Aden had released him at the same time. He stumbled forward a few steps before turning around and shaking out his shoulders. "You'll be sorry you did that, Aden." But he still looked stunned and off-kilter by what had happened.

"*Nee*," Aden said evenly. "I won't."

Sadie moved her hands from her face. She gulped for air as she looked at Aden, who was also breathing heavily. His face was still red, his eyes still wild. The anger and violence she'd witnessed scared her to the core.

She dashed out of the kitchen and ran upstairs to her bedroom, locking the door behind her.

Aden leaned against the table, struggling for air, trying to regain his bearings. It was as if his mind had left his body the moment he saw Sol put his hand on Sadie, replaced with white hot, blinding rage. In that moment he hadn't been afraid of Sol or shocked by the intensity of his own anger. All he'd wanted was to keep Sadie safe.

That's not all I wanted.

He'd also wanted to pummel Sol unconscious, to unleash the years of pent-up fury he'd contained. And through the darkness of his rage, he saw the helplessness in Sol's eyes. That had brought him a moment of clarity, but it wasn't the only thing that held him back.

When he saw Sadie cowering from fear, he couldn't bring himself to hit Sol. Now she was upstairs, afraid, probably of him as much as she was of Sol. He rubbed his hand over his perspiring face. What was he supposed to do now?

Care for your wife.

The words scratched against his brain like a nail scraping a rusty tin can. He didn't know how to care for Sadie. He made terrible coffee, he had no idea if the eggs he'd boiled this morning were done when he put them on the plate, and last night when she was upset all he could talk about were his stupid bees. He was awkward, clueless. He thought she'd seen him at his worst when she found out about the bruises. He'd been wrong.

His breathing slowing, he wiped the sweat from his face, pushing his damp hair off his forehead. He picked up his hat off the floor and tossed it onto the table. Shame filled him as he walked up the stairs. He doubted she would even talk to him. But he had to try. He had to tell her that he'd never fought back before. He had to convince her that she didn't have to fear him the way she feared Sol.

But how could he do that when his anger had scared him?

He knocked on her bedroom door, prepared for her to send him away. She didn't answer and he was tempted to leave. But this wasn't something he could run from or pretend didn't happen. He waited a few seconds before knocking again. This time she opened the door, but didn't move to let him in.

"Sadie, I'm—"

"Sorry?" Her body was mostly hidden by the door, as if she were using it as a shield. "You scared me, Aden. You both did."

"I know. But that wasn't me. I mean, it was, but I've never . . . I . . ." The words stopped. How could he explain his past? Would she believe him if he did? He backed away, swallowing the fire in his throat, desperate to go somewhere and hide, like he had done so many times in his life. *You're weak,* his father always said. He hated that his *daed* was right.

"Wait."

She touched his arm. It was the first time she'd voluntarily reached out to him. He closed his eyes, savoring the gentle pressure of her fingers against his skin. It was nothing but a gesture, a way to get his attention. But it meant much more than that.

"Tell me, Aden."

He opened his eyes and saw she had opened her door to him. "Tell me about the bruises. The past. The secrets you're hiding. Tell me everything."

He shook his head. "You don't want to know."

"*Ya,*" she said, taking his hand. "I do."

CHAPTER 12

Sadie didn't know what caused her to reach out to Aden. When she heard his knock at the door, she hadn't intended to answer it. What if he was still angry? What if the man she saw downstairs, the one who had so much fury in his eyes it terrified her, was the real Aden Troyer? What kind of monster had she married?

But that wasn't true. Sol was the monster, not Aden. Her husband had saved her from his brother —again. How could she ignore him after that?

Then she saw the pain in his eyes when she opened the door. The shame. And she couldn't turn away.

He released her slightly shaky hand and walked inside. She closed the bedroom door, which was a foolish thing to do since they were alone. But she wanted to give him a sense of privacy. For him to feel safe.

She sat down on the edge of her bed while he hovered near the door. He shifted from one foot to the other, looking everywhere but in her direction. Sweat dripped down the sides of his freckled face. She went to her dresser and pulled out one of her kerchiefs. "Here," she said, handing it to him.

He wiped his face with the pale yellow cloth,

then gathered it into a ball in his hand. Finally he looked at her. "Sorry about the kitchen door."

She almost wanted to smile. After everything, he was apologizing for a stupid door. "It can be fixed."

"I'll take care of it right away."

She sat back down on the bed and met his eyes squarely. He was evading, and she wouldn't let him get away with it. "All right. After we've talked."

He looked away again. He didn't say anything for a long time, and she could hear his heavy breathing in the silence of the room.

"I have never hit *mei bruder*," he finally said. Then he turned to her with a desperate expression. "I need you to believe that."

She nodded. Because for some reason, she did.

"When I saw him here . . . when I saw how scared you were . . ." His voice cracked. "I lost it." His hand squeezed her kerchief. "I've never been that angry before. I promised myself I wouldn't let anything happen to you." He looked down at his feet. "It almost did."

"That wasn't *yer* fault. You didn't know Sol was going to be here."

He lifted his head to look at her, his smile off center. "Now look who's being nice."

Their gazes met, and something changed in Aden's eyes. There was a warmth there, a different emotion she hadn't seen before. It reached inside her, softening the hardness that had slowly consumed her since her parents died. She looked at the green-and-white quilt on her bed and smoothed the already straight fabric, needing to focus on something other than the perplexing emotions he was stirring inside her.

"Sol has a temper," Aden said after a long pause, his tone taking on an edge that hadn't been there before. "He has his own way of dealing with it."

She looked up as he moved closer to the bed. She saw the silent question in his eyes and scooted over, giving him room to sit down. As he lowered his lean frame next to her, she wondered how he found the strength not only to break down the back door but to overcome his bigger and stronger brother.

"I can't tell you any more than that." He faced her, his mouth tensing at the corners. "I won't speak ill of *mei familye*. Not to anyone."

"But—"

"Please, Sadie." He ran his palms over his thighs, staring straight ahead now. "Don't ask me about it again."

She looked at his hands, which were covering his knees. She hadn't realized how big his hands were. Noticing a raised scar that ran across the first two knuckles, she pointed to it. "Can I ask you how you got that?"

The corner of his mouth lifted. "By being

clumsy." He examined the scar. "I was about thirteen, and I'd been fishing at Birch Creek. The fish were biting, and I had a huge haul. I put some of them back, but saved the best ones and took them home. I was filleting one of them when . . ." He made a slicing motion across the scar with the opposite index finger. "The knife slipped. Bled like crazy. Fortunately *Mamm* was right there. A few stitches later I was *gut* to *geh*."

"That must have hurt."

"*Ya*, it did." He got up from the bed, but did not look at her. "I better take care of that door before the kitchen gets full of flies." He paused and glanced at her. "Are you okay?"

She looked up at him. His brow was furrowed, his eyes filled with concern. "*Ya*," she said quietly. "I am." She swallowed. "Thanks to you."

His ruddy complexion deepened a shade. "I mean to keep *mei* promise, Sadie. Sol won't hurt you. I'll make sure of it."

She watched him walk out of her bedroom, almost overcome by the respect she felt for him. He wasn't a coward, like she'd thought. He wasn't weak, like his brother had said. She had misjudged him, and the guilt settling over her was nearly suffocating.

Aden leaned the kitchen door against the door frame and frowned. He'd damaged it more than he realized. The bottom half of the door was splintered and there was a dent from the impact of his boot. By some miracle the hinges were intact so he could at least hang the door, but tomorrow he would have to get a new one. That meant hiring a taxi to go to the home improvement store, something that would take all day. If things were different he could ask Sol, an actual *carpenter,* to make him a new one. *How ironic.*

But Sadie was okay, and that's what mattered. He'd have destroyed the door, the hinges, the frame, even the house—anything to keep her safe from Sol.

He searched several drawers in the kitchen, hoping to find a screwdriver. Even a hammer would work as a temporary fix. But there were no tools in the kitchen, so he headed for the barn, remembering that he'd seen a rusty gray-colored toolbox somewhere in the building when he cleaned it up earlier that week.

When he walked outside he frowned. Sol's horse, Jasper, and his buggy were still parked in the driveway. Maybe he'd decided to walk off his anger, which was fine by Aden. Better he calm down than do something that might hurt himself or the horse.

Aden climbed into Sol's buggy and pulled it around to the back of the house, then unhitched Jasper and took him to the empty stall in the barn. He fed and watered him so he would be ready when Sol returned. Aden gave some extra oats to

Rusty, then to Sadie's horse, Apple, before searching for the toolbox. He found it on the ground on the other side of the barn and took it into the house. When he went inside the kitchen, Sadie was there washing the breakfast dishes.

"I have to *geh* to the store soon," she said. "We're opening on Monday."

He squatted in front of the toolbox, opened the lid, and searched for a regular screwdriver. "Do you need any help?"

A pause. "*Nee.*"

Aden shouldn't have been surprised that she refused his offer. Despite what happened this morning, nothing had changed between them. At least not for her. He couldn't say the same thing about himself.

He glanced up. She was standing at the sink, her back to him, and he couldn't keep his eyes off her. She continually amazed him. She'd been frightened for good reason, but she hadn't fallen to pieces. She could have pushed him further away, but instead she had offered comfort in her own way.

His gaze traveled the length of her, and he quickly averted his eyes. He was too much of a man not to admit her beauty affected him. While he'd always been attracted to her and admired her, something new shifted inside him when he thought about her now, especially when he was alone.

Last night he'd lain in bed, unable to stop thinking about her. Knowing she was a few feet away gnawed at him. But he couldn't—and wouldn't—do anything to make her uncomfortable. Yet that hadn't stopped him from dreaming about kissing her . . . and more. His arms ached to hold her . . . for her to hold him.

She turned, and he switched his gaze back to the toolbox. Somehow he'd have to find contentment in this one-sided relationship. Already he had a little bit of hope—they were talking, at least.

The screwdriver he needed was lying on top of the rest of the tools, which were a disorganized mess. He'd sort through them later. He concentrated on hanging the door the best he could.

"I thought I'd make stone soup for lunch," she said.

"Uh-mm." He stood back and regarded the hinges. They were a little damaged, although he could probably bend them back enough to support the door. He should get new ones when he picked up the door—

"Aden?"

Sadie's voice cut through his thoughts. He glanced over his shoulder, surprised she was looking at him.

"Stone soup?" she said, the corner of her mouth lifting in a tiny smile.

"What?"

"You want stone soup?"

He frowned. "What are you talking about?"

"You really do get involved in *yer* work, don't you?"

Aden caught the glint in her eyes. "Um, *ya*. Sometimes."

She turned back to the counter. "I'm making vegetable soup." She glanced at him. "Maybe with a couple of stones thrown in for *gut* measure."

Grinning, he smelled the sharp scent of onions cooking in the stockpot. "Sounds delicious." Aden marveled at the ease he felt. Like life was almost normal, and what had happened with Sol was a distant memory.

When he finished hanging the door, he put the tools away. He gripped the handle of the toolbox, then paused. He wasn't sure if this was a good time to broach the subject, which had been on his mind since Abigail had called, but since they were on relatively good terms right now, he might as well. "Sadie," he said tentatively.

"*Ya?*" She scraped a bit of diced celery into a tall metal stockpot.

"You should visit yer *schwesters* this weekend."

She froze, then looked at him and said, "I can't leave right now. The store—"

"Isn't opening until Monday." He went to her. "You need to see Abigail and Joanna." He longed to touch her. Instead he held on to the toolbox with both hands. "You need *yer* family."

She picked up a paring knife and began peeling the potatoes, not answering him.

"I can take care of things here," he added, hoping to reassure her.

Dropping the knife, she faced him, the guarded expression he was familiar with back in place. "Why are you so eager for me to leave?"

His brow shot up in surprise. "I'm not. I just thought—"

"You thought wrong." She picked up the knife again.

He rubbed his chin, feeling the scruff of his new beard, which was taking some getting used to as it grew in. He could tell by the furious way she hacked at the potatoes that he had struck a nerve, which made him think he was right to suggest she see her sisters. "I could *geh* with you," he said, fairly certain she'd balk. But maybe it would also push her to go anyway.

"*Nee*," she said quickly. "That's a terrible idea." Then she faced him, letting out a delicate sigh. "I didn't mean that the way it sounded." She put the knife down again. "I know I need to *geh* to Middlefield. It's just . . ."

He moved a step closer to her. "Just what?"

"I didn't tell them we got married."

"I figured."

"I couldn't . . ."

"It's all right." He gave her a half-smile. "It's

not exactly the kind of news you want to give over the phone."

She threaded her fingers together. "I don't know how to tell them. I have no idea how they'll react and what to say when they start asking questions." She looked at him, her eyes filled with concern. "I always said I'd never get married."

He tilted his head. He'd never thought much about marriage himself, mostly because of his family. "How does that saying *geh*? 'Never say never'?" He wished he knew how to give her the encouragement she needed to see her sisters. "Maybe I could talk to them."

She frowned. "Why would you want to do that?"

"To make it easier on you."

Sadie unclasped her hands and gave him an odd look. "I wonder if I'll ever understand you."

"There's not much to understand. I'm a simple *mann*."

"*Nee*." She shook her head. "You're anything but simple." She turned from him to finish cutting the potatoes. "I'll think about it."

He smiled. Getting her to think about something he suggested was a small victory, one he would eagerly accept.

Aden turned to take the toolbox to the shed. A knock on the back door stopped him, and he groaned when he saw his father through the window.

CHAPTER 13

Sadie poured piping hot coffee into two mugs and carried them to the table. She placed one of the mugs in front of Aden's mother, Rhoda, who was already seated. Aden and his father had gone outside shortly after his parents had arrived.

Rhoda nodded her thanks, but didn't pick up the mug. Wary, Sadie sat across from her. Rhoda and her mother had been friends, but Sadie hadn't had much interaction with her. Sadie realized that she was a lot like Aden, though—quiet, content to stay in the background, but friendly enough when approached. Rhoda's small hands rested on the table, her fingers clasped tightly together. Her gaze was angled down, and she hadn't said any-thing since she arrived.

"I apologize for the state of the kitchen," Sadie said, desperate to break the silence. "I was preparing vegetable soup for lunch today."

"Aden likes soup." She lifted her head a bit, revealing lines of worry around her eyes and mouth. But beneath the strain Sadie saw how much Aden resembled his mother. They had the same sloping nose and full lips. Like him, she was soft-spoken. But she looked worn, her shoulders slumped as if a heavy, invisible burden was permanently attached to them. "He also likes pineapple upside-down cake for dessert."

"I'll try to remember that."

Rhoda sat a little straighter. "The way to a man's heart is through his stomach. Aden has a healthy appetite. Some of his other favorite foods are liver and onions, cabbage casserole, chicken and noodles, peach cobbler, three-bean salad—"

"Would you mind making me a list?" Sadie managed to smile, feeling she needed to put Rhoda at ease. "I won't remember all of that."

"*Ya*," Rhoda said, her expression brightening a little. "I can give you the recipes, if you'd like."

"That would be great. I'm not a very *gut* cook, though."

"I could teach you." She unclasped her hands. "I have a notebook filled with recipes from *mei grossmutter* and great-*grossmutter*. We could make some of them together . . ." Her enthusiasm waned. "If you'd like. I don't want to intrude."

Sadie could see how Aden inherited his courteous nature. "You wouldn't be intruding. But I think you'd enjoy showing Joanna more than me. She is the cook in our family."

Rhoda nodded. "I remember *yer* mother saying the same thing. She'd mentioned how maybe Joanna should give her cooking lessons instead of the other way around." She put her hands around the coffee mug. "How is *yer schwester* doing?"

"She's . . . getting better." An ache appeared in her chest, and she thought about Aden's insistence that she see Joanna and Abigail.

Aden's mother smiled, and she transformed from dowdy to lovely with that one expression. "Would it be all right to send her a card? We've all been praying for her."

"I'm sure she would like that."

"I can't imagine how hard it is on her being away from home. Abigail too. Have you visited them yet? When will they return?"

Sadie took a sip of her coffee instead of answering Rhoda. Aden was right—she needed to see her sisters, and not only because she missed them. She wanted to see how Joanna was doing and to spend some time with Abigail. She also needed more information, so when she attended church service on Sunday she wouldn't be fighting for the right words to say when people asked after her. It was suspicious enough that she and Aden had such a quick wedding. Not knowing the condition of her youngest sister would raise more than a few eyebrows.

She set down the coffee mug, her decision made. "I'm not sure when she'll be well enough to come home. I'll find out when I *geh* to Middlefield tomorrow."

"Give her *mei* best." Rhoda glanced around the kitchen, and Sadie held her breath when her gaze landed on the battered door. She looked at Sadie again, and another long pause stretched between them.

"How is *mei sohn*?" she finally asked.

Another question Sadie wasn't sure how to answer. "We're getting used to being married." At least it was a partial truth.

"Are you both happy?"

"Marriage isn't what I . . . expected."

"It wasn't what I expected either." A small smile played on her lips and she moved her hand near Sadie's, almost close enough to touch her, but still maintaining distance. "The circumstances could have been better."

Sadie fought a sudden surge of resentment. Her parents dying and the bishop forcing her to marry one of his sons . . . yes, the circumstances could have been *a lot* better.

Rhoda leaned closer. "Please," she said, her voice growing low, shaded with a touch of pleading, "be a *gut frau* to *mei* Aden. Show him respect. Be kind and devoted to him. And maybe someday . . . show him the love he deserves."

Sadie blinked, oddly touched by Rhoda's plea on behalf of her son. "I will do *mei* best," Sadie answered. It was the only promise she could make.

Rhoda leaned back in her chair. She took in a breath. "The soup smells *gut*. Do you need some help preparing lunch?"

Sadie's heart twisted a little. She needed to

remember that Rhoda had not only lost a friend, but she had also seen her youngest son quickly married off, and her oldest son was turning into a drunkard, if he wasn't one already.

Then a thought occurred to her. Did Aden's mother know about the bruises? Did she realize how broken her sons' relationship was? Aden had refused to divulge anything about his family, and she could see him doing what he could to protect his mother, who now seemed to be a bit lost.

"*Ya*," Sadie said, trying not to speculate on the Troyer family secrets. Every family had their own mysteries. Right now she was keeping secrets from her sisters, so she didn't need to judge . . . or pry. "I'd like some help," she told Rhoda. "*Danki.*"

As Rhoda started on the biscuits, Sadie seasoned the soup, using her mother's special mix of spices. The hurt in her heart grew. Rhoda Troyer was fine company, but she couldn't replace *Mamm*. She held the small glass that contained the spices and looked at the worn label, her mother's handwriting faded to barely nothing. Is that what would happen to her memories of her parents? Would they end up being a faded impression in her mind, one that she could barely discern as the years went by?

"I always add a little bit of salt to *mei* dough."

Rhoda's voice interrupted Sadie's thoughts. She handed Rhoda the salt shaker. Aden's mother smiled in return, and to her surprise, Sadie was glad she was here.

"This is beautiful property, *sohn*." The bishop pushed up the brim of his hat with his index finger. "As is all of Birch Creek."

Aden's jaw tensed as he nodded. They were walking across the backyard to the edge of the grass, where the grove of trees stood. What was his father doing here? He almost didn't want to know. The bishop had a method and motive for everything. Eventually he would reveal it to Aden. In the meantime, he would keep up the ruse of small talk.

A flock of geese squawked above them. Aden glanced up, watching the birds, their long wings spread out, gracefully flapping against the blue, cloudless sky.

"They're heading south," the bishop said. "Winter is almost three months away, yet God gave them the instincts to know the exact time to leave." He looked at Aden. "God controls everything, *sohn*."

Aden knew this. He'd heard it all his life. More importantly, he believed it, even though he didn't always understand God's ways. Like why his father, an ultimate man of God, could be so cruel.

"Have you explored the woods, Aden?"

"*Ya*. I didn't *geh* too far. Wasn't sure where the property lines ended."

"It's seven acres, starting here." He tapped the toe of his boot against a sapling tree. "The line stops three acres west." He pointed to their left. "Two acres north, then two east. Orange painted marks on the trees show the boundaries."

"How do you know?"

The bishop nodded. "Matthew wanted *mei* opinion when he bought the place. I gave him *mei* approval." He turned to Aden. "That's part of the reason I'm here."

"Part?"

"That, and *yer mamm* wanted to see you." He shrugged. "She misses you."

And you don't? The freedom and confidence he'd felt the past few days away from his father quickly dwindled, replaced by an unexpected twinge of hurt. *Daed* didn't seem to care whether Aden was around or not.

"I need a *favor, sohn*." The bishop faced him, his gaze penetrating. Cold, even though his words could be construed as kind. "There is some paperwork you need to find."

"Paperwork?"

As his father described the papers, Aden frowned. "Sadie's family owns natural gas rights?"

"The rights don't belong to the Schrocks, Aden. They belong to the community. But according to the law, the paperwork needs to be in place."

"In place for what?"

The bishop narrowed his eyes. "That's not *yer*

concern. Find the papers and give them to me."

Aden was confused. He didn't know how natural gas rights worked. He was also surprised to discover that his father knew. His thoughts raced as he tried to piece the situation together. This had to do with money, he was sure of it.

But if Sadie's family had another source of income other than the store, why had his father still forced the marriage? And what did Sadie know—if anything—about the papers? "I'm not sure I can do that," he said slowly, still turning things over in his mind. "The papers belonged to her *vatter*. She needs to know about this."

The bishop's expression tightened into a familiar and unwelcome look. "You've been given *yer* instructions. You will not question me further."

Aden resisted fisting his hands together as his rage was triggered for the second time that day. His father was ordering him around the way he always had, speaking to him as if he were stupid. The only thing missing in this conversation was his *daed* calling him dumb, a word he'd heard more times than he could count while he was growing up.

But things were different now. He was married. He had his own house, technically, even though he still thought of it as Sadie's. He had more freedom than ever before. He was a grown man. He deserved to be treated like one.

His father turned away and started walking back to the house, so sure that Aden would do whatever he was told. Like he always had.

Maybe now was the time for him to take a stand. Maybe it was time for him to finally tell his father that he deserved respect.

"Oh, and Aden?" The bishop turned around and faced him. "If I don't have the papers by the middle of next week, there will be consequences."

Aden lifted his chin. He could take those consequences. He'd been taking them all his life.

"But they won't be for you," he added. "They'll be for Sadie."

Aden stilled.

"We have an understanding, I see."

Aden nodded slowly, pressing down the anger, fighting the desire to lash out at his father the way he had at Sol. It was one thing for his father to threaten him, but this was totally different. Not only did he have to protect his wife from Sol, but from his father. *How is this God's will?*

He caught up to his father, tamping down his frustration and bewilderment, pretending that he was unaffected, like he had done so many times in the past. When they walked by the barn, the bishop stopped. "Is that Solomon's buggy?"

"*Ya.*"

"What's it doing here?"

Aden ran his palm over the back of his aching

neck. His entire body was starting to pulse with painful tension. "He stopped by this morning."

The bishop peered at him. "What did he want?"

"To visit."

"And how was *yer* visit?"

Aden paused. "Fine."

"Strange," his father said, looking at the vehicle, "that he would leave his buggy here. Where did he *geh*?"

"He didn't say."

His father glanced at him, didn't say anything else, and walked toward the house.

Aden let out a long, relieved breath. As he followed his father to the broken back door, he steeled himself for another line of questioning. But *Daed* walked inside as if the house were his and not Aden's and Sadie's. Aden followed a few steps behind, ready for his father to leave.

When Aden crossed the threshold, he inhaled the savory scent of vegetable soup and the comforting smell of baking biscuits. His mother was washing her hands at the sink while Sadie set the table. Unfortunately there were four plates, Aden noticed.

His father noticed too. "We won't be staying," he said. "I have work to do at home."

Aden almost leaned against the wall with relief.

His mother turned around, and Aden saw the disappointment in her eyes. They hadn't had a chance to visit, and he could see she had wanted to. Sadie wisely didn't say anything and went back to the stove to stir the soup.

"I almost forgot, Aden." The bishop looked at him again. "Have you made plans to replace *yer* beehives?"

He felt Sadie's questioning gaze on him as he answered. "*Ya*. But it looks like I won't be able to until spring."

His father frowned. "That's too bad. I'm sure we'll all be glad when *yer* business is up and running again. *Kumme*, Rhoda. Let's leave the newlyweds to their lunch."

Aden's mother nodded. She started to go to the bishop when Aden put a hand on her arm. "I'll visit you soon," he said.

"That would be *gut*." His *mamm* smiled, and Aden felt a little better about letting her leave with his father. After they were gone, he felt the tension that had strained his shoulders start to lessen.

But when he looked at Sadie, the strain returned. She didn't say anything for a long moment. She only stared at him, her expression inscrutable, making him squirm beneath her gaze. What had she and *Mamm* talked about while he was gone? Surely his mother hadn't revealed anything. She, like him and Sol, had become masters at keeping family business private.

Sadie sat down at the table. She looked at him and said, "We need to talk."

CHAPTER 14

Emmanuel pulled out of Aden's and Sadie's driveway and onto the road, making sure to maintain his outward calm at seeing Solomon's buggy at the Schrocks'. He'd seen through Aden's evasive answers to his questions. Something had happened between his sons, and he had to find the truth.

"I will drop you off at Lydia Lapp's," he said, tapping the reins on the back of his horse's flanks so she would pick up her steps. Lydia lived down the street from the Schrocks, and she and Rhoda were good friends. It wouldn't look strange for his wife to drop in unannounced.

"Lydia's? But—"

"I'll pick you up as soon as I finish *mei* church business."

After a pause she said, "All right."

He relaxed slightly, grateful for the one person in his family who would obey without question —Rhoda. She'd never rebelled. Never gave him any trouble. He had to think, and he couldn't do that if he had to defend his decisions or come up with acceptable explanations. Even now she stared straight ahead and said nothing, which was what Emmanuel needed from her. She'd always known what he needed.

After he dropped off Rhoda at the Lapps' he headed to see Solomon. He knew where his son was. He fought for patience as he turned down a dirt road. On either side the stubble of harvested cornstalks pushed through the soil. Emmanuel couldn't fathom that despite naming his son after the wisest man who ever lived, that same son could be so reckless. So shortsighted. So stupid.

The road dead-ended at a grove of trees. He parked his buggy in the shade and walked into the woods. No one else in the community knew of this place, except for Solomon, who accidentally stumbled across it almost three years ago. Emmanuel found it years before when he was looking for the perfect place to start his new community after breaking away from his district in Holmes County. After leaving his family behind forever.

As it usually did when he was here, the past intruded on his thoughts. Sometimes he wondered how his brother, John, and their mother, Deborah, were faring. He hadn't had contact with them since he and Rhoda moved away. She had also left her family, and while it had been hard for her in the beginning, she understood why he had to leave. They had no future in Holmes . . . because of his father. Mahlon Troyer had destroyed almost everything in his family's life, and his actions had affected the community.

Emmanuel stepped over a fallen birch tree, his

teeth grinding. He'd asked John and their mother to come with him, but they wouldn't leave his father. They had been loyal to his drunken, worthless father, and nothing he said had changed their minds.

He halted his steps and took a deep breath, letting the cool air of the woods soothe him. He needed to focus on the present, not on a past he'd left far behind.

The copse of trees grew denser as he walked across the leaf-strewn ground, stepping over more fallen dead trees and other detritus. Fifteen minutes later he came upon a small shack, so old the wood was furled and decaying. He didn't know how long the shack had been there or who had built it. But it was serving an important purpose—and unfortunately, possibly as a hideout for his wayward son.

He opened the door and scowled. For once he wished he hadn't been right. Solomon was passed out in the center of the buckling wood floor, an empty whisky bottle beside him. A flashback to his father flickered through Emmanuel's mind, but he shoved it away, stepped over Solomon, and went to the back corner of the room. He crouched behind a rotting wooden chair, ignoring the creak of his knees, and pulled out the bottom slat of wood flooring. He removed the steel fireproof box from its hiding place and set it on the floor. Fortunately the lock didn't look tampered with.

His fingers pulled out the pin fastening the collar of his shirt, then he pulled out a thin leather cord that hung around his neck. A key dangled at the end, and he inserted it into the lock, which opened easily. Shuffling through the papers and stacks of money, he made sure nothing was missing. When the contents were accounted for, he sat back and let out a long breath of relief. This box was his bank, his security. Although the money belonged to the community, he was the one who had to keep it safe.

A million dollars was nothing to be trifled with.

He closed the lid, locked the box, and put it back where it belonged under the floorboard. After he tucked the key underneath his shirt, he stood and pinned the fabric closed at the neck. His gaze landed on Solomon and narrowed. His footsteps thudded against the warped wood as he walked over to his son and kicked him in the ribs.

"Oof." Solomon curled up like a baby and groaned. He opened one eye, then the other, his gaze widening as he looked up at Emmanuel.

Anger pulsed through him as Solomon's face morphed into Mahlon's. At times it was hard to look at Solomon without being assaulted by memories, especially when he smelled like a distillery. Emmanuel yanked him to his knees. "Get up."

Solomon didn't say anything as he complied. He stood on unsteady legs, his head lowered.

Emmanuel took in his son's matted hair and the streak of dirt on the side of his face where it had made contact with the floor. His shirt was half tucked into the waistband of his pants. He wasn't going to bother censuring him this time—it didn't work on his hard-nosed son. "What were you doing at Aden's this morning?"

Solomon wiped the spit that had slipped from the corner of his mouth. "He's *mei bruder*. Am I not allowed to see him anymore?"

"*Yer* sarcastic tone is not welcome." Emmanuel moved closer to Solomon until they were face-to-face. It was at that point Emmanuel realized his son wasn't drunk, but exceedingly hung over. "*Yer* presence here is also unwelcome. I thought you knew that."

"Yet you found me here anyway," Solomon scoffed, then winced. "Don't worry, I'm alone. I didn't break any of *yer* rules."

"You seem to have forgotten the most important one."

"Exactly which one is that? There are *so* many to remember."

Fed up with his insolence, Emmanuel's hand cracked against Solomon's cheek. "You are not to be here without *mei* permission." He slapped him again. "You are not to be here without me being present." He slapped him a third time. "You are never, ever, *ever* to touch the strongbox."

The strikes seemed to have knocked some

sobriety into Solomon. His eyes grew wide. "*Daed*, I didn't touch the box. I wouldn't do that." His shoulders dipped. "I just needed a place to lay low for a while. To clear *mei* head."

"With spirits?" Emmanuel reached up as if he were going to strike Solomon again. Fear flashed in his son's eyes. *Good.* Emmanuel gave Solomon's flaming cheek a pat. "Alcohol clouds the judgment and weakens the spirit. I believe that is what has happened to you, Solomon. Your imbibing has caused you to be reckless—*nee*, dangerous—to our *familye* and community."

Solomon paled, his bloodshot eyes standing out in the faint sunbeams shining through the weak wood. "I don't understand."

"Then let me make it perfectly clear for you. You have given in to the weaknesses of drink, which is a gateway to other deadly sins. By allowing evil into *yer* life, you have sinned against God and against our community. You must leave Birch Creek. Immediately."

"Wait, what?"

"You are in the *bann*." Emmanuel turned and walked away from Solomon, keeping his back to him. A dramatic, but necessary gesture.

"*Daed . . . nee!*" Solomon dashed in front of him. "I'll repent. I'll admit *mei* drinking . . . and then I'll stop. I promise." Tears filled his desperate eyes.

But Emmanuel wasn't moved. Mahlon Troyer

219

had been given more chances than he deserved, and nothing changed. Solomon was traveling down that same destructive path. This corrupt weed had to be dug out at the root and cast away—family or not. He put his back to Solomon again. "You are not allowed near members of this community. If you violate the *bann*, you will receive no pardon here. You will find no refuge with *yer mudder* or *bruder* or any other *familye* in Birch Creek. They will all be instructed to turn you away."

"*Daed*, you can't do this. You can't abandon me."

Emmanuel glanced over his shoulder. "It is you who have abandoned us. You have chosen drink over *yer* community. *Yer familye*." His eyes narrowed. "You've chosen sin over God." He started to leave when Solomon's tortured voice stopped him cold.

"Do you know why I drink?" Solomon's approaching footsteps scraped against the floor.

Emmanuel didn't move.

"Turn around and face me!" Solomon screamed. "Take a *gut* look at what you've done."

He couldn't stop himself from glancing over his shoulder. Solomon's arms were splayed wide, tears flowing down his cheeks. Emmanuel looked away, repulsed by the emotional display.

"I took *mei* first drink at twelve," Solomon said. "Did you know that? The exact day you told me to hit *mei bruder*."

Flinching, Emmanuel focused straight ahead again.

"You told me it would make me stronger. Just like you said the whippings you gave me would make me more of a *mann*." Solomon moved to stand in front of Emmanuel, blocking him from the door, his face red and raw with tears and pain. "I wanted to be a *mann* in *yer* eyes. I wanted *yer* respect." He let out a wounded laugh. "It took me a while before I knew I could never earn it."

Emmanuel's mouth flattened, his jaw jerking uncontrollably. "I didn't force the bottle to touch *yer* lips."

"You might as well have." He wiped his cheek with the back of his hand. "When I drink," he said, his voice lower, more in control, "I don't have to feel anything. I don't have to remember the past or think about the future. I can forget . . . even if it's only for a little while."

Emmanuel stared at his son. His pathetic, hung over, stench-ridden son. He'd tried so hard to guide Solomon, to give him the strength and character his eldest inwardly lacked. For the briefest of moments, a thought flitted through his mind. *Did I go too far?*

He quickly came to his senses. He'd endured beatings from his father. He had administered similar ones to John. Neither of them had succumbed to drink. No, Solomon's decision to imbibe was his alone. Emmanuel refused to shoulder that responsibility. "God will deal with you," he said to Solomon before shoving him aside.

"He'll deal with you, too, *auld mann*."

Emmanuel closed his ears to his son's warning . . . and walked out of his life forever.

Aden's nerves were stretched to the edge as he sat across from Sadie. First the talk with his father, now Sadie wanted to have a conversation. Maybe she was just curious about what he and his father had discussed. He hoped not, because if she asked he would have to lie to her, and that was the last thing he wanted to do. *I promised to keep her safe.* If anything, his father's threat made him realize how much he wanted to keep that promise.

He rubbed his hands together and took a dramatic sniff of the air. "Lunch smells *appeditlich*. I'm starving."

"You have a bad habit of changing the subject."

"Sorry." He sat down and braced himself.

To his surprise she gave him a small, shy smile as she sat across from him. Then she let out a sigh. "You were right."

Curious, he contemplated her words. "Right about what?"

"Telling me I needed to visit *mei schwesters*. I do miss them." She ran her finger against the top of the table. "I miss them very much."

The yearning in her voice touched him.

Strangely, he had been a little hurt when he found out she hadn't told her sisters about their marriage. He understood why she hadn't told them, but he couldn't help feeling as if she were ashamed of him. If she had married someone else, would she have already told them? He couldn't stop the nagging thought that she probably would have.

But this wasn't about him; it was about her reconnecting with her sisters. "When do you want to leave?"

"Tomorrow. I'll make the arrangements for a taxi. I won't be gone long, just for the day. I'll be back in the evening."

He glanced away. Unknowingly she had given him an opportunity to look for the papers his father wanted without her being suspicious. He still felt she needed to know about the natural gas rights, but he couldn't tell her. How many more secrets would he be forced to keep?

"So," she said, sounding more tentative than he'd ever heard her, "you're still okay with me going?"

Aden couldn't stop his smile. She was asking his opinion, including him in her decision. "*Ya*," he said, gently. "Enjoy *yer* visit. I'll take care of things here." His smile dimmed at the tiny prick of guilt that appeared.

She rose from the chair and went to the stove. She lifted the pot and carried it to the blue-and-white quilted trivet on the table. He continued to watch her as she pulled the biscuits out of the oven, the tops perfectly golden brown and smelling like heaven. As she put them on a plate, a feeling of contentment came over him. Not because he was watching her preparing lunch. That was something he'd seen his mother do hundreds of times.

No, the contented feeling stemmed from knowing she was serving lunch for the two of them, as if they were a normal married couple. Such a simple act, but it held so much meaning for him. She didn't have to make him a nice lunch or eat with him. She could have handed him a sandwich and gone to the store. She could have left him alone.

He was so tired of being alone.

She brought the biscuits to the table, and he smiled. She looked at him as she sat down, tilting her head to the side, the ribbons of her white *kapp* lying neatly against her pale blue dress.

"What?" he asked.

"You . . ." She cleared her throat. "You have a nice smile."

He had no idea how to react. Compliments weren't something he received.

Her gaze shot down to the table. "We should, uh, pray."

"*Ya,*" he said, still a little stunned. They prayed and she handed him the plate of biscuits.

"These look like *Mamm*'s," he said, taking two off the plate and trying to forget his pitiful response to the one compliment he'd gotten in years.

"They are." She set down the plate and looked at him, her earlier shyness disappearing. "She told me she wants you to be happy, Aden."

He nodded, smiling again. Because in that moment, despite the secrets, despite the pain of loss and the confusion of navigating a new life with Sadie, he was happy. Happier than he'd been in a very, very long time.

CHAPTER 15

The next morning, after nearly an hour's taxi ride to Middlefield, Sadie walked out of the elevator at Jones Rehabilitation Center and stopped in the middle of the hallway. The scent of antiseptic hit her straight on, reminding her of the hospital smell. Her stomach lurched at the memory, how worried she'd been during Joanna's surgery, how fresh the pain still was from her parents' deaths. She clutched the dark blue patchwork cloth bag she carried, one that Abigail had made for her fifteenth birthday, and said a silent prayer before seeing her sisters, not knowing what to expect.

She looked at the scrap of paper in her hand. Room 308. She searched for the sign on the wall that would direct her to Joanna's room. Once she found it, she followed the arrows until she reached the room.

She paused before walking in, still unsure of what to say to Abigail and Joanna about her marriage to Aden. On the ride to Middlefield she'd thought about how Patience had been right. She should have insisted on waiting until her sisters had returned home before she married Aden. Bishop Troyer would have fought her on it, but she should have stood her ground.

Maybe if she had waited, she wouldn't have had to marry him at all.

But marriage to Aden hadn't been as horrible as she had expected. Yesterday their lunch together had been nice, even though she was mortified that she'd blurted out what she'd been thinking about his smile. It was true, though. He had a gorgeous, genuine smile, and when he'd flashed it yesterday her pulse had raced. Then he looked at her as if she'd lost her mind, and she regretted saying anything.

They'd spent the rest of the day and evening apart—she'd spent the day in the store to make sure everything was ready for opening on Monday and then preparing for this trip, while he'd worked on the yard again. She'd been in bed by the time she heard him come upstairs. Instead of lying with the quilt pulled up to her chin, she had been relaxed. She no longer worried about him coming to her room. In the back of her mind she knew eventually they would have to address this part of their relationship. But Aden still hadn't pressured her. Perhaps he wasn't ready either.

She sighed. She'd stalled long enough. Taking a deep breath, she knocked on the door. It was open a crack, and she saw an empty hospital bed neatly made with white sheets. A beige curtain reached from ceiling to floor, dividing the room.

"Come in."

When she heard Abigail's voice, something broke inside her. She hurried into the room, eager to see her sisters. Assuming they were on the other side of the curtain, she pushed it slightly to the side. Sure enough, Abigail was sitting in a chair, but next to another empty bed. She lifted her head, her eyes growing wide, then jumped up from the chair.

"Sadie!" Abigail threw her arms around her. Sadie held her close, not wanting to let her sister go.

When Abigail released her and stepped back, Sadie saw the tears in her eyes, which made it more difficult for Sadie to keep her composure. "I'm so glad to see you," Abigail said thickly. "Why didn't you call and let me know you were coming?"

"I'm sorry. I should have. It was a last-minute decision."

"That's all right. I'm just glad you're here."

"Me too." And she was. Even though her stomach had been in knots the entire drive from Birch Creek, the sight of Abigail steadied her nerves. She glanced at the bed. "Where's Joanna?"

"At her morning therapy. She was up at 5:30 this morning, ready to get to work." She reached for Sadie's hand. "We need to talk. But not here. She'll be back in ten minutes, and I don't want her to hear our conversation."

Sadie set her bag on the small table near

Joanna's bed that also held a plastic pitcher, cup, and a newspaper. "Where should we *geh*?"

"To the courtyard. It's very pretty there, and I need to get out of this room."

Abigail led Sadie to a small garden retreat that was situated to the side of the rehabilitation building. Wooden benches were set in a square around a small brick water fountain. Leafy bushes and plants were everywhere, their vibrant green still untouched by the cooler evening temperatures that were signaling a shift to autumnal weather. Red, pink, purple, and gold annuals and perennials were interspersed throughout. Sadie had no idea what the names of the flowers were, but they were beautiful. She glanced up to see a clear glass ceiling enclosing the courtyard so it could be enjoyed all year.

"*Gut*, we're alone," Abigail said, motioning for Sadie to sit down on one of the benches. The backrest was engraved with someone's name and the words "In Memory Of." Abigail joined her.

"I'm missing home so much," Abigail said, angling her body toward Sadie. Sadie noticed Abigail's favorite dress seemed a little snug. Of course, she had been sitting at Joanna's bedside for almost three weeks instead of bustling around the store like she usually did. Sadie fought the lump in her throat at the thought of her sister's devotion.

"How is everyone? Anything new happen while I've been away?"

Sadie gulped. This was the opening she needed, but she wasn't prepared to talk about Aden just yet. "Everything is fine," she said quickly. "Tell me about Joanna."

Abigail nodded. "I had a chance to talk to her therapists yesterday. She's healing, but it's slow. Slower than they thought. But it's not due to lack of effort on her part."

"So she's upset about it?"

"That's just it, Sadie. She's *not* upset. She smiles all the time, she eats everything on her plate, she spends a lot of time in prayer . . ."

Sadie was confused. "Aren't all those *gut* things?"

Abigail shook her head. "She hasn't cried, Sadie. She hasn't mentioned *Mamm* and *Daed*. Not once."

Her fingers clasped together, Sadie cringed. Other than when she read *Mamm*'s letters, she hadn't shed a tear either. She also hadn't talked to anyone about her parents. It seemed like she wasn't behaving that different from Joanna.

But if Abigail and the therapists were worried about that behavior, did that mean there was something wrong with her too?

"There's more. She apologizes constantly. If she has to ask for help, she says she's sorry. If she falls asleep while I'm visiting, she promises never to do it again. I don't care if she sleeps while I'm here. She's so tired, she needs it." Abigail looked at Sadie. "But that's not the strangest part. Andrew sent her flowers. They arrived the second day she was here."

Sadie smiled at the sweet gesture. Since she hadn't talked to Andrew Beiler since the accident, he would have had to do a bit of sleuthing to find out where Joanna was. "That was nice of him."

"I found them in the trash the next morning. When I asked Joanna about it, she ignored me. I even started to pick them up, thinking someone had accidentally thrown them away." She pressed her teeth against her bottom lip. "That was the only time she's shown any real emotion. She yelled at me not to touch them. So . . . I left them in the trash can."

"Why would she do that?"

"I don't know. I mentioned it to the therapists yesterday, and they think she has survivor's guilt. She's upset that she's alive—"

"And *Mamm* and *Daed* aren't," Sadie finished for her. The words pierced her heart. It made sense. Joanna had been in the accident with them. Sadie had no idea what Joanna had witnessed or what she remembered. Her heart went out to her sweet little sister. "Did they say when she can come home?" Maybe being around familiar surroundings would help.

Then again, being home hadn't eased Sadie's pain.

"They're not sure." At Sadie's frown, Abigail added, "As much as I want to *geh* home, I don't want her to leave until she's ready. The good thing in all this is that Mary and her *familye* are wonderful. I don't know why we never visited them before. They've been very supportive of both Joanna and me." Abigail smiled, the first smile since Sadie's arrival. "I can't wait for you to meet them. I've also gone to church with them, and everyone is very friendly. They've welcomed me with open arms."

"That's *gut* to hear." The tightness in Sadie's shoulders eased a fraction. She was glad Abigail had family support, even if that family were almost strangers.

Abigail looked at her wrist, and Sadie noticed she was wearing a watch. "Where did you get that?"

"Mary gave it to me." She looked guilty. "Don't tell anyone, please? It's easier to keep track of time, especially if I'm somewhere like this courtyard, where there isn't a clock on the wall."

"I won't say a word." She knew Bishop Troyer wouldn't approve, though Sadie didn't care what the man thought anymore. But she wouldn't get her sister in trouble over something as insignificant as temporarily wearing a wristwatch.

"*Danki.*" She tapped the silver face of the watch. A thin black band was fastened around Abigail's wrist. "We should get back."

Sadie nodded, but she didn't move. Guilt threatened to devour her, not only because she hadn't been here for her sisters. She couldn't continue without telling Abigail the truth. She took her sister's hand.

"Sadie?" Abigail frowned and gripped Sadie's fingers. "Something is wrong, isn't it? I knew it."

"Not wrong, exactly." Oh, this was hard. "Abigail, I'm sorry I haven't called or visited sooner. I love you and Joanna. I need you to know that."

"We do." Abigail's eyes grew shiny. "Mary and her family are *gut* people, but you and Joanna . . ." She wiped underneath her eye with the forefinger of her free hand. "You two are all I have left."

The lump returned to Sadie's throat, and she could barely speak. "I hope you can forgive me," she whispered.

"Sadie, you're scaring me. What happened?"

"I got married."

Abigail's face remained completely still. "What?"

"I married Aden Troyer earlier this week."

Her eyes widened until Sadie thought she had to be in pain. "I must be more tired than I thought because it sounded like you said you *married Aden*."

Sadie nodded, wincing. "I did." She quickly explained—more accurately, lied—to Abigail about how she and Aden had courted in secret.

That they had fallen in love. She repeated the same story Aden had told his father—the same story she would be telling everyone before long.

Her sister continued to gape at her in disbelief. "Oh my—"

"Don't say it," Sadie warned.

"I can't believe it." Abigail removed her hand from Sadie's. "I don't know which is more shocking, that you got married or that you married Aden." Then her stunned expression turned hard. "I can't believe you kept this from me. From us. You know *Mamm* wanted you to get married. She worried that *nee mann* would put up with you."

"Thanks a lot," she mumbled.

"You lied to us."

Sadie clasped her hands tightly together. She was still lying to them. To everyone. But she couldn't go back now. It was too late to revise the story into the truth. "I'm sorry."

Abigail shot up from the bench. "How could you get married without me and Joanna being there?"

"I—we couldn't wait any longer."

"You couldn't wait a month?" Abigail started to pace, then froze. "*Nee*," she said. "You're not . . ."

Sadie realized what Abigail was getting at and held up her hand. "I'm not pregnant," she said, her face flaming.

"Then why the hurry? I don't understand."

Sadie had to tell her a bit of the truth. "I'm being practical," she said, ironically using the same word the bishop had used when he'd told her she had to marry. "Aden has been a big help to me." Which was also true. He'd cleaned the barn, taken care of the horses, tended to the yard . . . and saved her from Sol.

Abigail plopped back down on the bench. "You're the most independent of us all," she said, looking dazed. "You're the one who said you were going to take over the store when *Daed* retired. That you didn't need a *mann*."

"That was before the accident," Sadie said softly. "Everything changed after that."

Her sister turned to her. "*Ya*," she said softly. "It did." She finally smiled. "I want you to tell me everything." Abigail faced her, a curious—and slightly mischievous—spark in her eyes. "What's it like to be married? What do you love about Aden? How did you know he was the one for you?" She sighed. "I've wondered if Joel's the one for me. He called me earlier this week. We couldn't talk long, but it was *gut* to hear his voice."

Sadie felt an unexpected pinch of jealousy. Both her sisters had young men who cared about them. Yes, Aden was kind, polite, considerate, and as he showed yesterday, protective. But he didn't care for her, not in the way Joel and Andrew cared about Abigail and Joanna. There were no feelings between them. No romance. They were both victims of his father.

The thought used to fill her with resentment. Now it saddened her. They both deserved more than a forced marriage.

Abigail nudged Sadie, dragging her out of her thoughts. "Here's a little secret. I always thought Aden liked you."

Sadie's head jerked up. "You did?" Sol's words rattled around in her brain. *He loves you. That's why he married you.* At the time they hadn't registered, and she hadn't recalled what he'd said until now. *He was drunk. I can't take anything he says at face value.*

But now Abigail was saying he liked her. And not in the polite, considerate way either. "You never said anything," Sadie said, rubbing the end of one of the *kapp* ribbons between her fingers.

"Pot, meet kettle."

Sadie couldn't help but chuckle. "Noted."

"It wouldn't have mattered anyway." Abigail waved her hand. "You'd have argued with me and told me he didn't like you. Little did I know I was right." Her grin turned sly. "What I never would have guessed is that you liked him. I didn't realize you were so *gut* at keeping *yer* feelings to yourself."

But Sadie was barely listening to her. "Why did you think that?" she blurted. "About Aden. That he, uh, liked me."

"There were little things. I'd see him watching you during the service. He always managed to sit on the bench directly opposite of you."

She'd noticed him there, too, but thought it was coincidence.

"And at the singing at the Troyers'—the night before . . . the accident. He was trying to hide it, but he couldn't stop staring at you. At the time it didn't make sense, but now I see he can't keep his feelings a secret as well as you can." She squeezed Sadie's hand. "Don't get me wrong. I'm still upset you got married without us there. But if you're happy, then I'm happy."

Sadie hugged Abigail. While she couldn't admit to being happy, she didn't feel as desperate. After Aden sent Sol away, something had shifted between them. She wasn't sure what, just like she couldn't bring herself to believe Abigail was right about Aden's feelings. Her sister was a true romantic, down to her core. If Aden had cared anything about her, he wouldn't have left her alone at the cornfield.

But hadn't he made up for that? More than once?

Abigail released her. "We should get back. I'm sure Joanna's finished with therapy by now."

As they walked back inside the building and to Joanna's room, Sadie felt lighter than she had in long time. She had no idea how Joanna would react to the news, but it felt good that Abigail was on her side.

When they reached Joanna's room, it was still empty. "She had a roommate," Abigail said, gesturing to the empty bed nearest to the door. "She was discharged yesterday. Joanna gave her a huge hug and said she was so happy for her. I think the woman was shocked, but she hugged her back." She turned to Sadie. "I hope she's not overdoing it again. We can meet her in the therapy room. Sometimes they'll let me wheel her to her room when she's finished working with the physical therapist."

Sadie nodded and followed Abigail down the hall to a large room. When they walked inside, Sadie saw Joanna right away. She was standing between two parallel bars, struggling to drag one foot in front of the other. As they neared, she could see the trickles of perspiration sliding down the sides of her face. She and Abigail stopped a few feet away and watched their determined sister fight to walk to the end of the bars.

Joanna started to turn around when a short, whipcord-thin woman with a long gray braid down her back went to her. "That's it for today, Joanna."

"One more time." Joanna's chest was heaving and her arms were shaking underneath the long sleeves of her plum-colored dress.

"No," the woman said sternly. "You're risking injuring yourself further."

"That's Mrs. Triskett, the physical therapist," Abigail said to Sadie.

"I'm sorry," Joanna said and allowed Mrs. Triskett to help her to the wheelchair. Joanna collapsed in the chair, although a strained smile remained on her face. "Thank you for taking such good care of me."

"You don't have to thank me, Joanna." The wrinkles around her red-painted lips deepened as she smiled. "I wish all my patients were as determined as you." She glanced up, her gaze meeting Abigail's, her smile dimming slightly.

Sadie watched as her sister exchanged a knowing glance with Mrs. Triskett before the woman said, "Abigail's here, and it looks like you have another visitor."

Joanna turned, her hands going to her mouth as her eyebrows lifted. "Sadie!" She whirled around, nearly bumping into Mrs. Triskett. "Sorry!" she called out as she rolled over to Abigail and Sadie.

Although she knew her sister was struggling, Sadie couldn't keep from smiling. It was so good to see Joanna despite the wheelchair and the healing scar on her face. She bent down and hugged her, feeling the heat coming from Joanna's sweat-soaked skin.

"I'm so glad you're here."

Sadie pulled away and crouched in front of the wheelchair. "I'm sorry I didn't come sooner."

"It's okay." Joanna's smile stretched across her face.

The surgical thread had been removed from the cut that traveled from the top of her cheek to her chin, but Sadie could see the small red slashes and holes where the stitches had been. Tears instantly welled up in her eyes, but she refused to let them fall.

"I'm sure you had a *gut* reason," Joanna added.

"She did," Abigail said. "Sadie got married."

For a split second the smile slid from Joanna's face and something flared in her eyes. Sadie wasn't sure what it was, and it was gone before she could figure it out. "That's wonderful!" Joanna said, her voice echoing in the empty physical therapy room. "I'm *so* happy for you!"

"Guess who our new brother-in-law is?"

Sadie glanced over her shoulder and up at Abigail. Her sister was enjoying this a little too much.

"I'm sure whoever he is, he's perfect."

Gripping the sides of Joanna's wheelchair, Sadie fought to keep smiling. She now understood what Abigail was talking about. Joanna was too bright, too excited. Her sister's skin had to hurt from being stretched into such a huge grin, but she kept looking at Sadie with intense love and an overabundance of joy.

"Aden," Sadie said softly. "Aden and I were

married last week. We should have waited for you and Abigail, I know. But I'm being practical—"

"You married Aden?" Joanna's voice rose another decibel. "He's soooo *schee*, Sadie. And nice. Very nice."

"I wish you could have been at the wedding."

"Oh, it's okay." Her smile widened, although how Sadie had no idea. "It's just a ceremony, after all. A moment in time compared to the rest of *yer* lives."

Abigail put her hand on Sadie's shoulder and squeezed. "You must be hungry, Joanna. Looks like you worked really hard this morning."

"We can eat lunch if you want to."

"Joanna, what do you want?" Sadie asked.

Joanna tilted her head, her smile in place. "Whatever you and Abigail want."

Abigail said they would all eat lunch in Joanna's room. As Abigail wheeled her back to the room, Joanna kept up a steady buzz of conversation in between telling everyone she saw in the hallway "*Gut* morning" and wishing them a happy day. After lunch, they visited until Joanna dozed off.

Sadie stood. "I should get back home," she said, looking at Joanna.

"To *yer* husband?" Abigail grinned.

A knot formed in Sadie's stomach. She wished she could joke about her relationship with Aden. That would be the normal thing to do.

Abigail stood and hugged Sadie. "*Danki* for coming."

"You don't have to thank me." She pulled back and looked at Abigail, who had suddenly become serious.

"*Ya*, I do." Her voice lowered and she glanced at Joanna, who was still asleep. "I know things are hard for you too. You're keeping everything going back home so Joanna can focus on healing." Her lower lip quivered slightly. "I'm so glad you don't have to do it alone."

Sadie squeezed Abigail's hand. "I'll come back soon."

"You better. I'll tell Joanna you said good-bye."

Thirty minutes later Sadie was headed back to Middlefield, her emotions in turmoil. She was worried about both of her sisters, with an extra dose of fretting over Joanna. She leaned against the backseat of the car and stared out the window as they zipped down the freeway, her brows knitted together. If she were honest with herself, she'd have to admit it wasn't just her sisters who had her feelings whirring around. She was looking forward to seeing Aden . . . and she didn't know how to deal with that.

CHAPTER 16

After Aden saw Sadie off to Middlefield Saturday morning, he turned and looked at the property. Earlier that week he had posted a sign at the end of the driveway, letting any potential customers know the store would be open on Monday. The sign had done its job—since he'd set it up, no one had stopped at the store.

It felt strange to be here without Sadie. Although she'd said the house belonged to him now, it didn't feel that way. It was like he was in some kind of limbo. At times he felt at home, and other times he was just . . . here. He realized that he'd also felt the same way at his father's house. His home had never truly belonged to him. He didn't have a place of his own.

Yet he did feel a spark of hope. Sadie had trusted him enough to leave for the day. Since her parents had died, he felt sure she had stayed home and at the store, venturing out only to visit Joanna at the hospital and for the wedding. But now she was able to be away, and hopefully she knew she'd left the place in good hands.

Which made him more than reluctant to think about what his father wanted him to do.

The day was beautiful, sunny with a breeze that carried the earthy scent of the nearby dairy farm.

It was the kind of day he liked best, and he often spent time in the sunshine to work on his hives. Yet despite the cloudless sky, a gray cloud hung over him as he continued to think about the papers he was supposed to find. How could he betray Sadie like that? Yet he couldn't disobey his father. And then there was his brother to consider.

Sol's buggy and horse were still here. Aden had been taking care of Jasper since Sol left yesterday morning. Aden had told Sol to stay away, but he had expected him to come get his horse and buggy, even if he had to sneak into the barn to do it. It didn't make sense. If Sol didn't pick up the buggy by the end of today, he would go to his parents' house and find him. He didn't want Sol's possessions still here when Sadie returned.

He walked past the store and stopped, looking at the door. He could hear his father's voice in his head, urging him to go inside, to look through Matthew Schrock's papers. But Aden couldn't bring himself to do it. The idea of riffling through those personal items made him queasy. Instead he set about chopping firewood.

An hour later he was soaked with sweat but had a good pile of wood split. He was stacking it up when he saw Timothy approach. He'd been so focused on his task he hadn't heard a buggy pull into the driveway.

"Hello," Timothy greeted, stopping in front of Aden.

"Timothy." Aden set down the axe and wondered what had brought the man by this time.

After shaking Aden's hand he said, "Stopped by to tell Sadie that Patience wouldn't be at the store on Monday. She's come down with some kind of flu bug. She didn't think it would be a *gut* idea to be around customers."

Aden saw the wisdom in her decision. He shoved back his hat and wiped his damp forehead with his palm. "Sadie's not here. She went to visit her sisters. But I'll make sure to tell her when she gets back."

Timothy looked at the pile of wood. "You need some help with that?"

Aden wasn't surprised by the offer. He'd have done the same if he was at Timothy's place. "Sure."

As they stacked the firewood, Timothy said, "There's another reason I came here."

Aden picked up a slab of wood in each hand. "*Ya?*"

"The other day I asked you about the community fund . . . I wasn't asking just because I was curious." He set two chunks of wood on the growing pile. "I guess there's no *gut* way to do this but to come out and ask. Do you know anything about *yer* father's dealings with natural gas rights in Birch Creek?"

Aden stilled. "Not sure," he said, inwardly cringing at the partial truth. He measured his next words. "I know there's natural gas all through this area."

"Do you know how much?" When Aden shook his head Timothy said, "I hit the library and did some research about Birch Creek. There are numerous gas deposits around here. They were recently discovered, about five years ago. They're worth millions."

Aden struggled to keep his jaw from dropping. Millions? He couldn't wrap his head around that kind of money.

"Apparently the gas companies have been in a bidding war over the past year, trying to acquire the rights. I have some on *mei* property."

"I see." Aden didn't know what else to say. This had to be the reason his father was so insistent on getting Sadie's father's papers. But a bigger question loomed—why didn't Sadie know about this? If she had, she wouldn't have gone to his father for help. She wouldn't have been forced to marry him.

Timothy chewed his bottom lip. "I hope you don't think I'm stepping over the line with this question, but it's something I really need to know. What is *yer* father doing with those rights?"

"As far as I know he doesn't have any." Which was true. All he knew was that his father wanted

Sadie's rights, probably because he didn't trust Aden to handle them. *Not exactly a surprise.*

"Did you know he's been asking several people in the church to sign over their rights to him?"

Aden shifted on his feet. "I'm not privy to his business matters."

"It's not the money I'm worried about, although realistically it would be nice to have a secure future. I just want to make sure that whatever I turn over to *yer* father will be distributed among the community when the time comes."

So Timothy had suspicions about Aden's father too. That made sense, considering he was an outsider. Everyone else in the community took his father at face value. "I'm sure whatever money is in the community fund is handled honestly and correctly," Aden said, his tone even.

"That's what I needed to know," Timothy said. "I appreciate you being honest with me. I know this is a sensitive subject. I'm just glad you're not upset that I brought it up." He put on his straw hat. "I should get back and check on Patience."

Aden nodded, maintaining his outwardly non-committal stance. "Tell her I hope she feels better."

"I will." He started to walk away, then turned around again. "I have one more question, if you don't mind."

He did mind. No one had ever questioned him

about his father before, and he didn't want to be in this position. "Sure," he said.

"Is there a reason we don't have any ministers or deacons in this community? I asked Patience about it, but she said that's always how it's been in this church."

"We're a small district. *Mei* father says there is only need for a bishop."

"I see," Timothy said. "But it seems like it would be helpful to him and everyone else if we had a minister or two. To spread out the ministering, that is, so it's not on one person's shoulders. I imagine *yer* father is extremely busy with all his duties."

Aden shrugged. "That's not really *mei* business."

"*Ya.* I guess it's not mine either." He waved at him. "I'll see you later."

Aden watched him walk away, his thoughts warring inside him. On the one hand, Timothy didn't understand how things worked here. His father had been the sole authority in Birch Creek for over twenty-five years. Aden hadn't known anything else. Yet Timothy wasn't wrong. The community had grown in two decades. It would be wise to have someone else in charge. But to Aden's knowledge, no one had ever brought up the subject. Would his father even allow an election process? He couldn't imagine the bishop giving over any control.

But that didn't bother him nearly as much as the

natural gas rights. Had others signed their rights over to his father? *Daed* had often said he had to be frugal with the dispensing of community funds, since it was difficult to come by extra money in such a small community. If he had cashed in the natural gas rights, then the community fund should be bursting. Perhaps his father was talking about Amish frugality, which was important. Greed had a way of worming into a man's soul.

Yet hadn't he thought of his father as greedy when it came to taking Aden's money from the honey sales?

He went into the house, passing by the patio. He thought about the stray dog he'd met the day he and Sadie married. The mutt hadn't returned. Then again, Aden hadn't set out any more food or water. He went inside, filled up a bowl with water and opened up another jar of canned meat, dumping it into another bowl. He put them on the back patio and went back into the kitchen.

Taking a glass from the cabinet, he got some water from the tap. As he drank, he thought about the papers. About what they meant, and how they were so important to his father that he'd gone as far as threatening Sadie. He couldn't put off looking for them.

Moments later he was standing in front of the store, turmoil churning within him. Could he betray Sadie like this, even for her own good?

More importantly, could he disobey his father?

He put his hand on the doorknob. Started to turn it. Then let go. He didn't care about his father's threat. His loyalty was to Sadie. *For this cause shall a man leave father and mother, and shall cleave to his wife . . .* The Scripture repeated in his mind. This decision was biblical. What his father was asking him to do was not.

When he walked away from the store, an unexpected peace washed over him. He would protect Sadie against whatever consequences his father would dish out. Regardless of the circumstances of their marriage, he and his wife would stand together as one against the bishop.

It was nearly dusk by the time the taxi turned into Sadie's driveway. She paid the driver, thanked him, and got out of the car. Behind the house the sun hovered above the horizon, streaking the clear sky with a rosy-orange hue. She stopped, gazing in appreciation at the beauty of the sunset.

"Get back here!"

She frowned at the sound of Aden's voice coming from behind the house. He didn't sound angry—he actually sounded a little amused. Her eyebrows lifted when she saw a flash of white and brown streak across the top of the driveway, then streak back. Then she heard a bark.

Surely Aden hadn't gotten a dog while she was gone.

She hurried up the drive, and as she neared the house she wrinkled her nose and groaned. She recognized that smell. Skunk. From the strength of the stench she wondered if there had been more than one lurking around the yard.

Sadie rounded the corner in time to hear another bark, then Aden's hearty laugh. She halted, the deep, pleasant sound moving over her like a soft wave. She blinked. She'd known him all her life . . . and she'd never heard him laugh.

Her gaze took in the scene in front of her—Aden crouched in front of a large metal tub filled with soapy water, and one sopping wet dog squirming under his hands. Now she knew the source of the skunk smell. The dog wasn't too big—in between a Beagle and a Lab, with unusual brown spots all over its body.

The animal suddenly dashed out of the tub and ran to Sadie. He put his dripping paws on her knees.

"Homer!" Aden said, his tone only partially stern. He rose, his hands covered in bubbles. "I'm sorry," he said, then snatched up the panting dog and plopped him back into the tub. "He's not too happy with me now." Aden rubbed the dog's belly, which seemed to make him stay still for a few moments. "I don't think this bath is working," Aden added, a look of amused disgust on his face. "He smells more like skunk than before."

"What are you washing him with?"

"Dish soap." He tilted his head in the direction of the generic bottle.

She shook her head. "That kind won't work." She neared the tub. "You need a special brand—"

Homer picked that moment to shake every square inch of his body. Sadie squealed as she was sprayed with skunk-scented soap suds.

Aden, who had been crouched down again, popped up from beside the tub as Homer took off for the woods. "Sadie, I'm so sorry . . ."

She glanced down at her dress, which was covered in large splashes of water. Then she looked at Aden. While he'd been apologetic, the grin on his face and the twinkle in his eyes told another story. He smelled like skunk. Or was she smelling herself? Unable to stop herself, she started to laugh.

Homer came dashing by them again. Aden chuckled and ran off after him. Sadie laughed as she watched the game of chase, which Homer was clearly winning. The dog paused and Aden jumped to tackle him, only to miss him and land with a belly flop on the grass.

But Aden didn't seem to mind being bested by a dog that was quickly becoming more adorable by the second. He jumped to his feet and ran after the dog again.

Sadie's laugh faded into a smile as she watched the chase. Aden's reddish-brown hair lifted from the top of his shoulders as he sprinted. He was fast, but Homer had a two-leg advantage on him. Aden's speed wasn't what caught her attention, though. It was the sheer joy on his face. His exuberant laugh as he barely missed capturing Homer—again. He seemed like a totally different person. *Is this the real Aden Troyer?*

Homer's tongue hung out of his mouth as he slowed down long enough for Aden to scoop him up again. Sadie put her patchwork bag on the patio and went to help. Bathing this dog was a two-person job.

Aden didn't say anything, just flashed her another grin as Sadie knelt on the other side of the tub and thrust her hands into the water. Ugh, the dog's fur was really rank now that she was up close. "What happened to him?"

"Other than getting sprayed by a skunk, I don't know." Aden pulled out a sponge and scrubbed Homer's back while Sadie circled her arms around the dog's neck. She was already wet, she might as well get soaked. "This is only the second time I've seen him."

"How do you know his name?"

Aden dipped the sponge into the water. "I had to call him something. 'Dog' seemed too obvious."

Sadie giggled as Homer licked her cheek. She loved dogs, but her mother had been allergic, so they never had any pets. "He's so cute."

"I think he'd prefer to be called handsome,"

Aden said, continuing to scrub the dog's stinky fur.

She paused, thinking the dog wasn't the only handsome one she was near. She stiffened for a moment, only to relax when Homer licked her again. It was impossible to be tense around this goofy dog.

Aden tossed the sponge back in the tub. "I guess that's the best we can do for now. He still smells, but I think it's not so bad now."

"Or we're used to it. I've got some of the other soap in the store. I can run and get it."

As if Homer understood her words, he broke free of her grip and jumped out of the tub, this time disappearing into the woods.

"I guess that's a *nee*," Aden said. He looked at Sadie, the mirth in his eyes contagious.

She couldn't help but smile back, unable to look away from him, trying to reconcile this happy man with the Aden Troyer she'd known all her life.

He suddenly grew serious. "How are *yer* sisters?"

His kindness touched her. She touched a soap bubble on the surface of the water, breaking it instantly, unsure how much to reveal to him—not because she didn't trust him, but she didn't want to burden him. "Joanna is working hard on her physical therapy," she finally said. "Abigail likes Mary and her family."

"But you're still worried."

Her head lifted. "*Ya*," she said softly. "I am."

"We'll keep praying for her." He rose and held out his hand. The gesture was so natural, she didn't hesitate to let him help her up. As soon as she was on her feet he let go. "I'll take care of the tub if you want to shower first."

"Do you think Homer will come back?"

"I hope so." He picked up the tub and tipped it over. "He's a little ornery, but fun." Aden emptied the tub and headed for the barn.

Sadie went into the house, noticing the bowl of half-eaten hamburger meat next to another bowl of water. They stocked dog food in the store, along with the blue dishwashing liquid that would help get rid of the skunk smell. She'd have to get both after she had her shower, just in case Homer decided to return.

She showered and changed into a fresh dress. Her *kapp* was a little damp, but fortunately it didn't smell of skunk. She set it on her dresser to dry, quickly braided her freshly shampooed hair, pinned it into a bun on the crown of her head, then put on a light green kerchief. She held the dirty dress away from her body as she stepped out into the hall at the same time the bathroom door opened. Her gaze met Aden's and locked.

Sadie couldn't pull her gaze from him. He paused when he saw her, the ends of his wet hair grazing the top of his clean yellow shirt. She couldn't stop her eyes as they traveled from his square shoulders to his lean waist. His legs were clad in dark blue broadfall pants, but his feet were bare. Catching herself, she lifted her head, making sure to keep her eyes on his face and not on anything else.

He didn't seem unsettled by her frank perusal, though. "I can throw *yer* dress in the washer with *mei* clothes," he said, gesturing to the shirt, pants, and socks he held. "I used it the other day. While you were working in the store. Hope you don't mind."

Guilt surfaced as she realized he'd been left to his own devices for the most part since he'd been here. "I should have taken care of them for you."

"You've been busy."

"That's not an excuse."

Aden went to her, taking her dress from her hand. "I'm not saying it is."

He went to the head of the stairs, and she called out to him. "You need a haircut." Her lips folded in. She hadn't meant to sound so blunt.

His fingers slipped through his wet mass of hair. "I suppose I do."

"I . . . I could give you one." She swallowed. "I used to cut *mei daed*'s hair."

He looked down at the clothes in his hands, then at her. "All right." His voice was low, hesitant. "I'll put these in the washer then."

Sadie leaned against the wall as he hurried

down the stairs. Why had she offered to do this? Giving her father a haircut was one thing, but cutting Aden's hair . . . *my husband's hair* . . . The thought of it made her stomach flutter.

She pressed the back of her head against the wall. She was being ridiculous. It was only a haircut, another task similar to making supper or doing laundry or washing windows. Sadie closed her eyes. Giving Aden a haircut wasn't anything like her other chores. But that didn't mean she had to make a big deal about it.

After retrieving an old sheet from the linen closet next to the bathroom and a comb from her bedroom, she went downstairs to the kitchen. The hair shears were in the drawer, and she set them on the table along with the sheet. She hugged her arms as she waited for Aden to come up from the basement. A few moments later he did, and without a word he sat down in the same chair he used when he ate at the table.

The soft rustle of her shaking out the sheet was the only sound in the kitchen. She swooped it around his neck and tied it, leaving the rest of the sheet to cover his torso. "Too tight?"

"*Nee*," he said, his voice sounding weird. He cleared his throat. "It's fine."

She nodded, even though she was standing behind him and he couldn't see her. She took the comb from the table and combed his hair, which had partially dried. Despite the messy appearance, the comb easily ran through the strands. She relaxed as he remained still.

"I guess you need these," he said, handing her the scissors.

"*Danki*." She took them and started to snip. His hair smelled like his skin and clothes—clean, fresh, and appealing. Her hands flinched at the thought, and she forced herself to focus on his hair and not on him.

After a few minutes, when she was about a third of the way done trimming the ends of his hair until they were level with his earlobe, he spoke. "I have something to tell you."

She stopped mid-snip. He sounded serious. Tense. In other words, typical Aden. But she'd seen another side of him. *Maybe not so typical after all.*

"Sol's buggy and horse are still here."

Sadie straightened, scissors in one hand, comb in the other, and a fully formed knot in her stomach. "What?"

"He hasn't been back since yesterday morning. Which is a *gut* thing, but I thought he'd have gotten Jasper by now. I've been taking care of him in the meantime."

Sensing her hands starting to shake, she ran the comb through his hair again.

"I'll *geh* to *mei* parents' in the morning, if Sol hasn't—"

"Hasn't what?"

"Come back." He moved for the first time, craning his neck so he could glance up at her. "Don't worry," he said. "If he comes back tonight, I'll make sure he won't get to you." He gave her a lopsided smile. "He has to pass by *mei* bedroom first, anyway."

She knew he was making a joke, but it wasn't funny to her. Instead it churned up more guilt, which overrode the fear that Sol would return. She started cutting again, the knot in her stomach tightening with uncomfortable awareness. How long would he be patient with her? How much time had to pass before she would be able to share a bed with him?

The sharp swishing sound of the scissor blades filled the silence. She made quick work of the rest of the haircut, eager to get away from him. Putting space between them would hopefully temper the rising emotions she'd had since she'd returned from Middlefield. "Done," she said, swiping the loose hair off his neck before untying the knot.

He stood, giving her an inscrutable look before stepping away from the table. "I think I'll head over to *mei* parents' now. Could you, uh, get the clothes from the washer?"

She couldn't look at him, her face flaming with heat at the thoughts running through her mind. Folding up the sheet to shake outside, she kept her head down but nodded. How had so much changed between them so fast? Like the rest of her life, her emotions were out of control, and she was desperate to rein them in. How could she be thinking about attraction, about something pleasurable, while Joanna suffered and Abigail yearned to be home?

Worse, how did she dare to be even a little happy so soon after her parents' deaths?

"Don't worry about supper," he said. "I'll grab something at *Mamm*'s."

She nodded, latching on to the broom and sweeping the floor with furious strokes.

Aden paused again, then left.

Sadie leaned her forehead against the top of her hand and leaned on the broom handle. He probably thought she was an idiot. Or *ab im kopp*. Maybe a bit of both. And for the first time in her life, she realized she actually cared what Aden thought.

CHAPTER 17

Darkness had descended by the time Aden reached his parents' house. He turned into the driveway, still trying to understand what had happened between him and Sadie. On the surface things were simple—they'd tried to bathe Homer, and then she'd given Aden a haircut. But like everything else in his life, it was more complex than that. He and Sadie had fun together during Homer's bath. He'd seen a light in her eyes that hadn't been there before.

He'd also seen her looking at him in the hallway. Had felt the tug of attraction that had been so one-sided on his part finally reciprocated, if only for a brief instant. For once he dared to hope that maybe his marriage could be something other than a forced arrangement.

Then he'd mentioned Sol, and that changed everything.

He brought Rusty to a halt and jumped out of the buggy, then shook his head. Hard. They had been married less than a week. How could he expect anything from her in such a short time? He had to remind himself of her loss. That pain still had to be fresh, even though she never mentioned her grief, at least not to him. He also had to remember that her parents' deaths had brought them together.

How could he be so selfish as to want so much from Sadie when he could give her so little?

But it was becoming harder to keep that in the forefront of his mind now that he'd seen her smile. Heard her laugh. Had felt her delicate fingers against his skin as she cut his hair.

Had seen the darkening of her eyes when she looked at him.

Aden tethered Rusty near the barn. Leaving the Schrocks' when he did had been the right thing to do. She'd been unnerved when he mentioned Sol, and he didn't blame her. But he wondered if something else had thrown her off balance too. He'd never thought his relationship with Sadie would be easy. There was too much history and too many bad circumstances between them. What he hadn't expected was how confusing it was. Or how much those small, happy moments he'd experienced meant to him. He didn't only want more from their relationship, he wanted to *give* more. He wanted her to be happy. Problem was, he didn't know how to make her happy.

Aden stared at his parents' house, seeing hazy lamplight shining through the front window. Now wasn't the time to puzzle over his marriage. He had to focus on figuring out what was going on with Sol.

He went to the front door and knocked. His mother opened it, and Aden could immediately see that something was wrong. Her expression was difficult to read in the low light of the lamp and the darkness outside, but her body language wasn't. Her shoulders were hunched more than usual, and she was rubbing her hands together, something she did when she was upset. "*Mamm*?" he asked.

"*Kumme* inside, Aden." His father had appeared behind *Mamm*. She stepped aside and Aden walked in.

"What's going on?" Aden asked, his gaze darting from his mother to his father.

"Aden, sit down." His father gestured to the hickory rocker near the doorway.

After seeing his mother's red-rimmed eyes, he shook his head. "I'll stand." Dread pooled in his stomach. "What happened to Sol?"

"He's gone. Since yesterday," his father said, with little emotion in his voice.

Mamm drew in a sharp breath. "Excuse me," she said hoarsely and rushed out of the room.

Aden started to go after her, but stopped when his father grabbed Aden's forearm and squeezed. "She'll be fine."

Aden glared at him. "What do you mean Sol's gone?"

"He's in the *bann*."

"*What?*"

The bishop eyed him evenly. "Do not pretend that you don't know Solomon's drinking has gotten out of hand."

"It's been out of hand for a long time." Aden glanced at the entrance to the kitchen, where his mother had gone. No wonder she was so upset. He turned back to his father. "You're the one who's been pretending." The words flew out of his mouth.

"Watch *yer* tone." His father's jaw jerked beneath his long beard.

"I can't believe you put him in the *bann*." Ignoring his father, he started to pace.

"Solomon made a choice. He chose drink over his family, community, and faith."

"And you couldn't have tried to help him first?" Aden spun around, his anger rising. Part of him couldn't believe he was defending Sol after everything his brother had done. Yet it wasn't until now that he realized how alone Sol was. The one person who could help him the most not only refused to but sent him away. "How could you, *Daed*?" he muttered. "He needs—"

"To be excised from our lives, before his poisonous behavior affects others."

"What about *Mamm*? Can't you see she's heartbroken?"

"Solomon broke her heart, not me."

Aden stood there, staring at his father. He didn't think his *daed* could be any more coldblooded than he was at that moment. "Where did he *geh*?"

The bishop shrugged. "That isn't *mei* concern.

You know the rules of the *bann*, Aden. If Solomon comes to you, turn him away."

"His horse and buggy are still in *mei* barn."

"Return them to me."

"They belong to Sol."

"Enough!" His father's cheeks turned red as he took a step forward. His glare shot through Aden like a bullet. "You dare argue with me? Question *mei* authority as *yer* spiritual leader?"

Out of habit, Aden shrank back. He'd been on the receiving end of his father's anger and biting glares. But this time it was different. This time the rage seemed barely contained. The bishop's shoulders twitched, his mouth pressed so thin it was almost invisible. His words made him seem unaffected by sending Sol away, but he wasn't.

His father suddenly relaxed, the angry glare dissolving into his usual disengaged expression. "Did you find the papers?"

Are you kidding me? Sol was gone, his mother was hurting, and his father's main concern was those stupid papers. *And the money. Don't forget this is all about money.* "*Nee*," he grumbled.

The bishop's eyes narrowed. "Then I suggest you keep looking." He started to leave the room.

"Can I at least see *Mamm*?"

His father turned. "Find the papers first." Then he left the room.

Aden put both hands on the back of his neck. He wanted to yell. He wanted to punch something. He wanted to shake sense and compassion into his father. So many things didn't make sense. Wasn't Sol the favored son? A shiver ran through him at the reminder that his father was going to let Sol marry Sadie. He hadn't cared at the time about the drinking. Of course he wouldn't. His *daed* would do anything to get his hands on those papers, including uniting Sadie with an alcoholic for the rest of her life, all in the name of money. The realization chilled him.

He looked around the familiar living room. Saw the plain, old furniture. The lack of any kind of décor. His mother had been wearing the same dresses for years, although she continually mended them to make sure they looked present-able. Aden had worn Sol's hand-me-downs because, according to his father, "they were perfectly fine, and it's unnecessary for both *buwe* to have new clothes." They had always eaten simple, inexpensive food, mostly vegetables grown and canned from his mother's garden. His parents owned one horse and buggy. There were no signs of wealth anywhere. The only signs of greed had been his father's insistence that Aden turn over any money he made from his honey business. But after what Timothy had told him, after his father's threat to Sadie, and now him *banning* Sol . . . something deeper—and darker— was going on.

"Aden?"

He turned at the soft sound of his mother's voice and hurried to her. "Are you all right?"

She nodded, but didn't speak, her eyes welling up.

He put his arm around her shoulder. "Where's *Daed*?" he said quietly.

"Outside." Her voice sounded like it was moving through a rusty screen. "Smoking his pipe." She looked up at him. "Whatever *yer vatter* tells you to do, Aden, you need to do it."

"But Sol—"

"Has chosen his own path." Her lower lip trembled and she pressed her teeth against it. "I have always put *mei sohns* in the Lord's hands. Solomon is loved, Aden. You might find that hard to believe right now, but he is. As are you." She put her hand against his cheek. Please . . . don't argue with *yer vatter*. Don't fight against him. It will *geh* easier for you . . . for all of us . . . if you don't."

Aden shook his head. He'd taken the easy path all his life. He'd cowered in fear from his father and brother, had believed them when they said he was weak. A coward. Worthless. But would he be all those things if he had stood up for himself? If he'd refused to keep the family secrets?

He looked at his mother, his heart constricting at the pain and pleading in her eyes, and he knew he couldn't refuse her. If he were the only person at risk, he'd challenge his father. But he wasn't. Others could be collateral damage. His mother. Sadie. Even Sadie's sisters could be brought into the fray. He wouldn't put that past his father. He wouldn't put anything past his *daed* again.

He bent down and kissed his mother's cheek, something he hadn't done since he was a little boy. "I love you," he said softly, not wanting the bishop to hear. She needed to know she was loved too.

The tears flooding her eyes spilled. She wiped them quickly away, nodded, and pulled out of his one-armed embrace to hurry out of the room.

Sadie's eyes opened when she heard the kitchen door shut. She sat up from the couch, not realizing she'd fallen asleep. It was late, late enough for her to have been in bed already. But she couldn't bring herself to go upstairs, not when she knew Aden was at his parents', trying to find out about Sol. After she composed herself when he left, she had a moment of panic. What if Sol came back while Aden was gone? Maybe that was what he was waiting for, to get her alone. And for an instant she was angry with Aden for leaving her by herself. He had promised to protect her. How could he do that if he wasn't here?

Then she'd had a moment of clarity. She couldn't keep living in fear. She couldn't put her dependence and faith in Aden. Not because she didn't trust him, but because it wasn't fair to him. *God is my rock . . . in him I will trust . . .*

So she had prayed. She'd prayed for courage, for her sisters . . . and for Aden.

She rose from the couch at the same time Aden walked into the living room. He looked haggard, his shorter hair matted from wearing his hat. He stopped when he saw her, and she remained by the couch, unable to move, but unable to deny that she wanted to go to him.

He shoved his hands into his pockets. "What are you doing up?"

The sorrow and heaviness in his voice propelled her to him. She stopped a few feet in front of him, clasping her hands together. "Waiting for you."

She thought she heard him sigh. He raked a hand through his hair, pulling a thick hank back from his forehead. Conflicting emotions flitted through his eyes, barely discernible in the low light of the gas lamp. He didn't say anything, just looked at her with quiet desperation.

"Do you want something to eat?" she asked. The question seemed so inconsequential, yet she didn't know what else to say.

"*Nee.*" He rubbed a patchy spot on his reddish beard and continued to look at her.

Something strong tugged inside her. She couldn't go upstairs and leave him alone. Not now. "What happened?"

"Sol's gone," he said flatly. "He's in the *bann*."

That news shocked her. Only two other people had ever been put in the *bann*—both men, both in their thirties. They left the community and never returned. Sadie hadn't seen or heard about them again. The bishop hadn't divulged the reason they were in the *bann*, just that they had been disobedient. That definitely summed up Sol.

"I'm not sure what to do," Aden said, shaking his head.

Sadie clenched her hands tightly together. "Do you have to do anything?"

"He's *mei bruder*, Sadie."

"I'm aware of that." She calmed the bite in her tone. "Maybe it's for the best."

He walked past her, and she thought she'd upset him. But instead of going upstairs like she expected, he sat down on the couch. "Part of me believes that. Another part of me . . ." He put his head in his hands.

She sat next to him as he struggled with his emotions. "Aden," she said softly, not wanting to upset him further, but unable to keep her thoughts to herself, "why do you care?"

He lifted his head and looked at her. "How can I not care?"

She licked her suddenly dry lips. "I know he hit you."

He looked away, his jaw tensing.

She clutched her knees, squeezing them

through the skirt of her dress. "He is a terrible person," she said, years of resentment rising to the surface. "Cruel, selfish . . ." Anger tightened inside of her as she spoke. "Whatever he did to get put in the *bann*, I'm sure he deserved it."

Aden gazed at her, his complexion paling, making his freckles stand out. "Oh, Sadie," he whispered. "How he must have hurt you."

The compassion in his voice touched the knot of anger in her chest, threatening to unravel it. She steeled herself against it.

Aden shifted on the couch, facing her. He was so close, near enough for her to touch his hand, to wrap her fingers around his and never let go as she started to drown in the past. Her throat tightened. She should be furious with him right now. For years she had clung to her grudge against him, blaming him for what had happened in the cornfield almost as much as she blamed Sol. Yet as he looked at her, and she saw her pain reflected in his eyes, she felt that blame slipping away. "He never told you what happened?" she asked, barely able to say the question out loud.

"*Nee*." He glanced at his lap. "I never asked." He looked at her again. "Now I know I should have."

"Would it have changed anything?"

He pressed his lips together and shook his head. She turned from him, fighting a losing battle within herself. She'd vowed not to tell her secret, and she had kept that promise. *If Aden wanted to know, he should have asked Sol.*

But Aden didn't pry. Didn't push. She knew it wasn't from lack of interest that he kept quiet. It was out of respect. The secret suddenly felt like a boulder sitting on her chest, stifling her until she could barely draw breath.

"He kissed me," she whispered. "And I let him." Shame consumed her, making her face hot and every nerve ending rigid. She couldn't look at Aden, but she felt him tense, as if he were a wire strung tight enough to snap. "He said if I let him kiss me he would let me *geh*."

"Did he?"

She shook her head. "He wanted more. So . . . I kicked him. Where it hurt the most." When Aden didn't respond, she finally looked at him.

His eyebrows were lifted, his eyes wide. "You kicked him?"

"*Ya.*"

"That's why he was walking funny when he came home."

Knowing that didn't give her any satisfaction. Neither did the ghost of a smile teasing Aden's lips.

"He got what he deserved," Aden said. "I'm glad you defended yourself."

"I shouldn't have had to. You shouldn't have—"

"Run." His voice cracked on the word, all traces of humor gone. "I know. And I've lived with being a coward every day since."

She stood and looked down at him, the mixed emotions he'd displayed earlier changing into something else. Shame, possibly even deeper than her own. But she refused to pity him, not when her admission opened a raw wound. She was the one who was wronged, not him. "Is that why you married me? To put *yer* guilt to rest?"

Aden looked up at her. Never had she seen such sorrow in a person's eyes. "Sadie . . . I married you because I wanted to."

Her breath caught, his answer stunning her.

He disconnected their gazes and stood. "*Daed* wants Sol's horse and buggy, but I'm not turning them over. Sol still might come back for them."

"But—"

"Please, Sadie, trust me on this. I know the rules of the *bann* as well as you do. But if Sol returns, I want to make sure he's all right." He sighed. "I'll take care of Jasper. You won't even know he's here."

Didn't she have a say in this? It was her barn, after all. *Nee . . . it's our barn.* And Sol was his brother. She had to trust that Aden was making the right decision. Despite anger from the past still clouding her thoughts, she nodded. "All right."

Then he put his hands on his slim waist, his

gaze intent. "There's something else I have to do," he said. "Something *mei vatter* wants."

Her teeth clamped down until she felt pain. How much more was the bishop going to demand from her—from them both?

CHAPTER 18

Aden searched through a cardboard box filled with expired brochures, slips of scrap paper, old newspapers, and some broken pencils. Matthew Schrock had put pack rats to shame. No wonder Sadie had been spending so much time in the store—and in the office in particular. When he had told her about the natural gas rights papers, she had been shocked. Her father hadn't said a word about them, and now that she knew they existed, she'd been eager to help him search.

"I don't think they're here," Sadie said, tossing another stack of old invoices on top of the already over-piled desk.

"Have we looked through everything?" He slid the box to the side.

"Almost. Like I said, I'd already gone through the desk last week, and I've been sorting through all the other stuff. I haven't had a chance to organize any of it yet."

He heard her sigh and looked up. She was leaning against the desk, exhaustion creating shadows under her beautiful brown eyes. "It's getting late. We should stop."

She shook her head. "I'm too curious now. And confused." Sadie glanced around the mess in the office. She gestured to the paperwork nightmare around her. "If there were any documents, I have *nee* idea where he would have put them."

"He didn't have a filing system?"

"You're looking at it." She went to a high shelf that was near the ceiling of the office. "There's a small box up here. Can you reach it? Maybe we'll find something in there."

Aden stood close to her and stretched to reach the box. He ended up having to stand on his tiptoes, and his body wavered a bit as he caught his balance. He brushed up against her. She smelled good, sweet, like a fresh field of flowers, despite the smudges of dust on her face. "Sorry," he said, grasping the box and pulling it down.

She barely nodded as she took the box from him and set it on the floor. She sat down next to it, folding the skirt of her dress underneath her legs, her focus completely set on the box in front of her.

While their searching hadn't revealed the paperwork his father demanded, it did tell him something else: Sadie's father had owed a lot of money, and now he had a clearer picture of why Sadie had gone to his father that night. She'd been desperate, and he couldn't blame her. The debt fell on both of them now. However, if the natural gas rights were worth as much as Timothy said, then they needed to find those papers, not for his father's sake but for their own.

She lifted the lid off the box. Her hand went to her mouth. "Oh!"

"What is it? Did you find something?"

She shook her head. "Sorry." She lifted up a piece of paper covered with basic addition problems. At the top was an A+ written in bright red. Schoolwork, it looked like. "I had *nee* idea he kept these."

Aden crouched next to her as she continued to remove several drawings and school papers. All three of the Schrock girls had been good students in school, but Sadie had been exceptional. She also had a special talent for art. He picked up a pencil drawing of a horse standing under a large oak tree. "I remember this one," he said, looking at it with admiration. "Fifth grade. *Frau* Yutzy pinned it on the board in front of the room so everyone could see how terrific it was."

"She pinned a lot of pictures on the board," Sadie said, not looking at him. But in the meager light of the office lamp, he could see she was blushing.

"She never pinned mine." He carefully set the paper aside. "Of course, my drawings were always terrible."

"I'm sure they weren't."

He looked at her and smirked. "Trust me, they were."

She didn't say anything for a moment. "I'm surprised you remembered the drawing," she said softly.

"I remember a lot of things about you." The

words slipped out, but he didn't care. He was tired of hiding how he felt about her. He wanted to be free—free to be himself, free of fear, and free to express what was in his heart. Now wasn't the time for any of that, but he wasn't about to apologize for the truth.

If his words bothered her, she didn't let on. They continued to rummage through the box, finding more papers her father had saved from school but nothing relating to natural gas rights.

He glanced at Sadie occasionally as she spent a few minutes lingering over several of the papers. Were the memories affecting her? Concerned, he asked, "Are you okay?"

She looked up, her eyes dry, her tone brittle. "*Ya.*" She started to put the papers back in the box. "This is all just a bunch of junk."

He put his hand on hers, stilling her movements. "They're memories, Sadie. Not junk."

She pulled out of his grasp, shoved the rest of the papers in the box, and placed the lid on it. "*Daed* never could get rid of anything." She stood and picked up the box, then tilted her head in the direction of the drawing of the horse. "Can you hand me that?"

"What are you going to do with it?"

"Put it in the burn pile with the rest of this stuff."

Her voice sounded hard, like chipped ice. The memories had quickly triggered not only her temper but also affected her demeanor. A few moments ago she'd been singularly focused on finding the papers. Now she looked on the verge of fleeing. He'd rescue the box later, not wanting her to do something she would regret.

"Can I keep this?" he said, picking up the picture.

She shrugged. "Suit yourself." She walked away from him and dropped the box on the large pile of trash they would burn later.

Aden noticed the stoniness of her profile, the stiff way she moved. His stomach suddenly growled and he cringed.

She turned to him. "I take it you didn't eat supper at your parents'?"

He shook his head. "Lost *mei* appetite while I was there."

She grimaced. "*Kumme.* I'll make you a snack."

Figuring she was also using his hunger as an excuse to get out of the office, he nodded. After locking up the store, they walked back to the house together. Aden put the picture on the counter and washed his hands while Sadie went to the pantry.

After he dried his hands he saw what she had set out—a loaf of bread, a jar of peanut butter . . . and something else that surprised him. He moved to the table and picked up the small jar of honey, seeing the homemade label. He remembered the hours he'd spent carefully handwriting his last name and the type of honey that would be in each jar. The effort was crude, and after seeing the neatly labeled products the Schrocks sold, he was a little embarrassed.

Sadie finished washing her hands and stood next to him. "Honey with peanut butter is my favorite snack," she said. "Do you want something else?"

He shook his head and set the jar down. "I've never had honey and peanut butter together."

"Really? It's delicious. Especially with *yer* honey. It's so much better than what we sell in the store."

She'd relaxed since they'd come into the kitchen, and he couldn't help but smile as he pointed to the jar. "The label is the worst, though."

Sadie picked up the jar. "It's not that bad. Maybe if you had a drawing of a bee, or a beehive, or some honeycomb on it, it would look better."

"I can't draw, remember?" Looking at his horrible penmanship, he saw he couldn't write either.

She shook her head. "You're too hard on yourself." She picked up the sandwich fixings and went to the counter. While she prepared the snack, he retrieved two glasses from the cabinet and filled both of them with tea. They sat down and Aden looked at the sandwich, which was sliced in fourths. He picked one up and took a bite. Not bad, but it wouldn't fill him up.

Sadie picked at the crust of her sandwich. "What made you decide to grow bees?" she asked.

Aden swallowed. "You don't grow bees, you raise them."

"Oh." She lifted her shoulders in a non-committal shrug.

"I raise them because I like them. Did you know there are twenty thousand known species of bees in the world? And some bees don't sting at all."

She tore a small portion of crust off her bread. "I wouldn't mind those bees."

He grinned. "Too bad they don't produce honey."

"You never did tell me why you didn't bring *yer* hives over," Sadie said.

His smile faded. "Something happened to them." He didn't want to tell her that Sol had destroyed them. But if she asked, he wouldn't lie.

She remained silent for a moment. "I'm sorry about *yer* hives," she said, sounding sincere. "I know they meant a lot to you."

"I'll build new ones in the spring. Bigger ones, probably. I always wanted to expand *mei* honey-making business. This will set me back, but eventually the new hives will produce."

"You sound optimistic."

"I am. I have to be."

She tapped her fingers against the table, her sandwich left uneaten. "You could sell *yer* honey products in the store. Once you get everything going again."

Her idea made sense. He'd never sold his wares in a store, always at a roadside stand or by word of mouth in the community. "I'd probably have to double *mei* hives then."

"As long as they're far from the house, that's fine."

"Don't worry, they will be." He crammed another quarter sandwich in his mouth. Actually, honey with peanut butter wasn't half bad. Maybe he'd make himself another sandwich.

"We'll have to do something about those labels though," she said.

He took a drink of tea before he answered her. "I thought you said they weren't bad."

"They're not. But *yer* honey deserves better."

She continually caught him off guard with her compliments. He smiled again, glad that for a short while they could put everything behind them and have a normal conversation. "I bet you could draw a lifelike bee."

She nodded, but looked unsure. "Maybe. I haven't done any drawing in a long time." Her expression turned somber. "I've been too busy with the store."

That reminded him of the bills, which in turn

made him think about the paperwork they still had to find. Stone-cold reality was never far away. He finished his sandwich as she sat in the chair, not speaking, not even looking at him. She stared at her lap, her mind clearly occupied with something else.

"Are you going to finish that?" he asked gently, gesturing to her sandwich.

"*Nee.*" She pushed the plate toward him. "You can have it."

He took the plate. "You're right about this snack," he said, sliding his finger over the honey that had dripped off the sandwich. "It's delicious."

She stared at him as he licked his finger. His movements stilled as he felt the spark of attraction ping-pong between them.

Sadie shot up from her chair and took his plate. *So much for attraction.* But it had been there. He'd *felt* it. Maybe she wasn't aware of it, but he definitely *was.* Not that he could do anything about it.

He shoved the rest of the sandwich away, downed his tea, and brought her his glass. He was about to offer her some help, but she took the glass and washed it quickly.

He stood awkwardly in the kitchen, unsure what to do. He could go upstairs, but he didn't want to leave her. Not yet. He'd be alone in Abigail's room soon enough.

Once the dishes were done, Sadie turned off the

light and he followed her to the stairs. The night had grown chilly, and the temperature in the house had cooled. As they climbed the stairs Sadie asked, "Do you need another blanket? *Mamm* has some in her hope chest."

"*Nee*. It's not cold enough for me yet."

"Let me know when you need one." They stopped in front of Abigail's room. She crossed her arms over her chest and looked at him. "*Gut nacht*."

He paused, willing her to meet his gaze, wishing they didn't have to part. Instead she almost turned her back to him, and he knew it was more out of self-preservation than rudeness. "*Gut nacht*, Sadie."

He leaned against the door frame of Abigail's room until she had disappeared down the hall. With a heavy sigh he turned, knowing it would be a long night.

Patience sneezed as Timothy brought her a cup of lemon tea and set it on her bedside table. He rounded the bed and got under the covers next to her.

"Maybe you should sleep on the couch," she said. "I don't want you to get sick."

"I don't mind. And I don't want to sleep on the couch."

She sneezed again and blew her nose. "Maybe I should sleep on the couch."

He brushed a strand of her hair from her forehead. "Definitely not. I rarely get sick, Patience. I'm not afraid of a few germs."

"If you're sure—"

"I'm sure."

She picked up the tea, glad he hadn't taken her up on her idea. She didn't want to be alone. She felt better than she had yesterday, which was a shade higher than miserable. At least tonight she could breathe a little bit. She took a sip of tea but didn't taste the lemon. Or the tea. It was like sipping hot water. But it did soothe her throat. "You're a *gut* nurse," she joked.

"Only when I'm taking care of someone I love." He lay on his back and stared at the ceiling, something he'd done for the past few nights. Since his talk with the bishop at the wedding, he'd been troubled, but had kept it to himself. Or at least tried.

"Timothy?"

He popped up to a sitting position. "Do you need something else?"

"*Ya.* I need you to tell me what's wrong."

He looked at her, his blue eyes uncertain. Then he reclined on his side, his head propped on his elbow, brushing his fingers along the sleeve of her nightgown. "I'm still trying to figure out what to do with the natural gas rights."

She nodded. "I thought that might be it." She set down her cup. "Maybe you should talk to someone else about it. It might help to get another opinion."

"I did, sort of." She listened as he told her about his conversation with Aden. "He didn't seem to know what I was talking about, although I thought he was hiding something."

"Aden? I can't imagine that."

"I didn't get the impression it was anything bad. More like he was protecting something. Or someone."

Patience frowned. "I don't like the sound of this."

"I know." He looked up at her. "That's why I didn't want to talk to you about it. I shouldn't have brought it up anyway, with you feeling this sick."

"Timothy, you know you can tell me anything. And when it's something this important, it's only fair that I know." She started to touch his cheek, then pulled back. He might not be afraid of germs, but she was more cautious. "I don't want you to have to bear anything alone."

His smile was rueful as he sat up in bed. "I've already made *mei* decision. I'm not going to sign the papers over. I truly believe that's the right decision. If I thought it was God's will to turn over the rights to the bishop, I would. But I don't think it is. There are too many unanswered questions, and Bishop Troyer seems too eager to get his hands on the paperwork." He looked at her. "Patience, that means I'm going to have to disobey him. I'm not sure what that will mean for us."

She let his words sink in. This was new territory for her. No one had ever defied the bishop before, as far as she knew. His guidance had helped keep Birch Creek together, without the splits that sometimes plagued other church districts. Her own parents had come here after their district had split. But that had been over major disagreements about the *Ordnung*—not because one member had refused to do what the bishop had asked him to do.

The bishop was the highest authority in the church. No one was above him—except God. And if God was telling her husband to disobey, then she had to accept that. Timothy had proved to her throughout their relationship that he was a godly man. His decision wasn't about following Emmanuel Troyer or any other man. It was about following God's lead.

Despite her concern over him catching her illness, she took his hand. "Whatever you decide, Timothy, I'll support you."

"I would hope so, you being *mei frau* and all." His lips tilted in a half grin.

"*Nee*, it's not that. I'm supporting you not because I have to, but because I want to."

His expression grew serious, yet the strain from the past few days slipped from his face. "That means more to me than you know," he said, his eyes holding so much love she thought her heart would burst. Then he released her hand. "I'll let you rest. Hopefully you'll have kicked this flu bug by the morning." He gave her one last peaceful look before turning off the lamp on the nightstand, plunging the room into darkness.

Patience felt him shift beside her as she lay with her pillows propped behind her head to help her breathe through the congestion. She became drowsy, not knowing if it was because of the tea or finally getting better. Perhaps it was because her husband had found some peace about his decision.

Just as she closed her eyes, she heard Timothy's voice.

"I love you."

He sounded groggy, and she realized he probably had spoken the words in his sleep. "I love you too," she whispered, closing her eyes again and putting the situation with the bishop completely in God's hands.

CHAPTER 19

On Sunday, Sadie thought she would have to find excuses to avoid Aden. Since there wasn't service that day, they would be home. Alone. But Aden left on foot early in the morning, saying he was going to explore the woods and would be back by the end of the day. She couldn't help but feel relieved that he had spared her several awkward hours. Yet when he returned that night, she had to admit to herself that she had missed him. The house had been lonely and empty without him. As usual they went to their separate bedrooms, and Sadie's thoughts shifted from him to the store's reopening the next morning.

Sadie had expected business to be brisk when they reopened on Monday, but she'd been floored by the steady stream of customers who had come into Schrock's Grocery and Tool. Many customers were Amish, mostly from their church but a few from surrounding districts who had heard about what happened to her parents and Joanna. Each one of them, whether or not they bought anything, had asked after Sadie and her sisters.

"We're fine," she said to everyone, giving them each the cheeriest smile she could while quickly refusing their offers of help. She'd discovered that Bishop Troyer had spread the word that she and Aden were to be left alone not only due to her grief but so they could have some time to themselves. Still, that didn't stem the flow of questions her surprised friends had peppered her with.

I had nee *idea you and Aden Troyer were a couple.*

If we had known about the wedding, we would have been happy to help.

You two sure do know how to keep a secret.

Yer mudder *and* vatter *would have been very happy.*

It was that last sentiment, expressed by several people, that had her chest compressing. Their intentions were good, and Sadie had no choice but to smile and agree with them, all while knowing that she and Aden were only married because her parents had died.

Shortly before lunch she was ringing up an *Englisch* customer who was buying a fifty-cent candy bar. "Nice store you have here," the woman said, pulling out a coin purse from her small brown leather handbag.

"Thank you." Sadie wished the woman were buying more than a candy bar. While they'd had more customers in the store than she'd ever seen, not many were purchasing items.

"I've never been in this area before. I'll have to come back when I have a bit more money." She handed over her fifty cents. "I'm a diabetic, but my granddaughter loves chocolate."

Sadie took the money and punched the amount in the cash register. She glanced up to see Aden talking with another *Englisch* man. He pointed to the back of the store where the tools were, and the man took off in that direction.

"Is that your husband?" the woman asked as Sadie tore the receipt from the register.

"Yes."

"He's a nice young man. He's been helping customers from the moment I walked into the store."

With a nod Sadie put the candy bar in a small paper bag. Aden had been very attentive since they opened, not only to the customers but to straightening the store shelves. During the short time they weren't busy, he had gone outside to sweep off the small slab of concrete in front of the door.

"It must be nice to be able to work with your husband," the woman continued, taking the bag from Sadie.

"I'm still getting used to it," she mumbled, unnerved by the woman's remark—and the confusing accuracy of it.

Around noon Aden came to the front counter. "Why don't you get some lunch?"

She shook her head. "We still have customers."

"Not that many." He looked around. "There's a

lull right now. You *geh* eat and I'll mind the register."

She hesitated. "I'm not really hungry."

He put his hand on her forearm. "You need to eat, Sadie."

A tingle traveled through her skin at his light touch. Throughout the morning she'd been catching glimpses of him, watching as he talked to customers with an ease she'd never seen before. His lean body was relaxed, his expression calm but not standoffish. She could almost say he was in his element—which shocked her nearly as much as her reaction to his touch.

He stepped back. "*Geh* on. You need the break."

"I won't be long," she said, hurrying from behind the counter.

"Sadie," he said, stopping her in her tracks. "Everything will be fine. I promise."

She nodded slowly.

After a quick lunch, she returned, telling him it was his turn to eat. A few of the customers had brought meals for her and Aden, so she had heated up a hamburger casserole and had left a plate for him, along with several slices of bread and butter.

Traffic continued to be good all afternoon, and by the end of the day she was exhausted, mentally and physically.

That evening, after they closed the store, Sadie totaled the receipts. Despite the crowd, sales had been disappointing. Then again, her expectations had been high. She knew she couldn't make enough money to cover the bills in a day. Still, it was disheartening to see that the profit they made would barely make a dent in one of Joanna's medical bills. She heaved a sigh.

Aden came up to her. "What's wrong?"

"This," she said, gesturing to the receipts. She rubbed her forehead with her fingers. "I know, I have to be patient. God will provide—"

"He already has, Sadie."

Her head shot up at his words. "What?"

"The natural gas rights. They're worth something."

Why didn't he tell her this before? "How much?"

"I don't know. But if *mei vatter* wants them, I'm sure they're worth a lot." He leaned forward. "Whatever money the rights will bring in, it will at least be something. Don't worry." He reached for her hand. "We'll handle this together."

The warmth and security of his touch flowed through her, giving her more hope than she'd felt in weeks.

He pulled away. "I've got to see to the horses. I'll put some more food out for Homer. I think he snuck here in the middle of the night because what I put out last night is gone. He's probably avoiding another bath." He gave her a crooked grin, then walked out of the store.

Sadie looked at her hand, remembering the feel

of his skin against hers. *We'll handle this together.* Ever since her parents' deaths, she had felt alone despite Aden's presence. She tried so hard to keep him at a distance, but he kept gently moving closer, slowly drawing her to him with his kindness and loyalty.

She grabbed the receipts and the money drawer and headed for the office. Everything with Aden was happening too fast. Her parents had died only three weeks ago. She'd been married for less than a week. How could she be this affected by Aden in such a short time? It wasn't possible. She couldn't have any feelings for him.

She was afraid to.

When she finished in the office, she would find those papers. Then she would contact whoever she had to and find out what needed to happen to get whatever money the rights were worth. Once she was able to settle her father's accounts and pay off Joanna's bills, she would be able to stand on her own feet. She wouldn't need Aden's help or support. She wouldn't need him, and that would stop the terrifying stream of emotions he instilled from overtaking her.

Later that evening, she walked down the hallway and stopped at her parents' room. Aden had already turned in for the night. She'd said very little to him at supper and had barely looked at him. She couldn't let him in any more than she already had. She had to protect herself.

Taking a deep breath, she opened the door and walked into the darkness. She hadn't been in this room since her parents died. She went to the dresser and turned on the small lamp her mother had always kept there, then flicked on another battery-operated lamp on the nightstand. The room flooded with light. She turned from the lamp and stared at the bed. Sadie was suddenly unable to move.

The bed was still the way her mother had made it the morning of the accident. The geometric quilt pattern blurred in front of Sadie as memories came spilling over her in painful, unrelenting waves. When she and her sisters were little, they would run to their parents' bed during a thunderstorm and crawl under the warm covers. Their father would grumble a bit, tweak one of their noses and tell them they were fraidy cats, then roll over and fall back asleep.

But their mother would snuggle them close and tell them stories. Bible stories. Made-up stories. Stories that had been handed down through her family. Each one featured a brave young woman or man who was able to overcome fears with God's help. Abigail and Joanna would always drift off before *Mamm* finished, but Sadie would stay awake for every word, enthralled.

She had to force her gaze from the bed. Her head throbbing, she turned and walked to the closet. Swallowing, she opened the door. Her parents' clothes were still there, her father's on the left, her mother's on the right. She touched the skirt of her mother's favorite dress, a light pink one that barely got past the bishop's rule of no bright colors for women's clothing. Her fingertips ran over her father's church shirt, which her mother ironed every Saturday night. She pressed a sleeve to her cheek, her father's faint scent still on the fabric.

Her eyes burned as if they were on fire.

"Sadie?"

She dropped her father's sleeve. Heard Aden move closer to her. She refused to turn around. Her throat squeezed shut and she was unable to speak. She flinched as his hand touched her shoulder.

"You're not doing this alone," he said.

He knew exactly why she was here, as if he were inside her skin. She should send him away. He didn't have the right to be here. She didn't need him here.

"There are two boxes in the closet," she said, barely able to force the words out. "We can look through those."

Aden nodded, and she stepped aside as he retrieved the boxes. She still couldn't look at him. "Where do you want me to put them?" he asked.

"I don't care."

She waited until he had set them on the bed before she turned around. Her feet felt like lead as she propelled them toward the first box. *I have to find those papers . . .* She repeated the words over and over in her mind, as if they would give her the strength to continue.

The box was her mother's. The papers wouldn't be in there. Yet she found herself reaching inside. Her fingers touched a book, and she lifted it out, seeing the old cookbook with its cracked binding and dog-eared pages. Sadie took more items out of the box—a carefully folded paper dress pattern, a sock *Mamm* had given up knitting on, a stack of greeting cards from *Mamm*'s friends, a folded pile of fabric . . .

The pressure in her chest grew, flaring out all over her body until her head spun. She jerked in a breath, but it wasn't enough. Her lungs were closing and she could feel them shutting down as hot tears flooded her eyes.

"Sadie . . ."

Aden's voice reached her. Calm, just like he was. But he seemed far away as spots appeared in front of her, huge black dots threatening to steal her vision. She felt his arm, sturdy and strong, around her shoulders. She couldn't push him away even if she tried. He led her out of the room, into the hallway, and then to her own bedroom.

"Sit down," he said in a gentle, but firm, tone.

She didn't argue, since her legs were on the verge of collapsing under her. She perched at the edge of her bed.

He crouched in front of her. "Do you need some water?"

Shaking her head, she said, "I'm fine."

He moved a little closer to her, peering at her face. "You're pale."

The spots dimmed and her breathing eased. She had no idea what had come over her. As she drew in air, she finally looked at him. Saw the concern—no, worry—in his eyes. She didn't want him to worry or be concerned with her at all.

"I'm tired." She lifted her heavy arms and crossed them over her chest. After another long drag of breath she said, "It's been a long day and I need some sleep."

He tilted his head, and she knew he didn't believe her. But his closeness was threatening to take away what little breath she had. "I want to be alone, Aden."

His eyes didn't leave hers for a long, drawn-out moment that seemed to last for hours. "All right," he eventually said, rising from the floor. "If you need anything, let me know."

She looked away, keeping her gaze from his until she heard her door shut.

Aden stood outside Sadie's doorway, unsure what to do. Since their wedding day, he'd made it a point never to push her, to always give her the space she needed. But today was different. Something had changed in him. Maybe it was the fact that for the first time he'd felt needed and respected. He'd enjoyed working in the store, helping out the customers, even making small talk with a few of them. Some were men from church, and he could tell they hadn't heard about Sol's shunning. He wasn't surprised. His family was expert at keeping secrets.

But while he'd felt more comfortable as the day passed, Sadie had grown more uncomfortable, and he didn't know why. He thought it might have something to do with him taking her hand when he'd seen how worried she was over the receipts. She'd flinched when he touched her, though she didn't let go. He didn't regret reaching out to her even though it might have set their relationship back several steps.

He'd told Sadie they would handle things together, and he meant everything, not just their financial situation. She needed comforting. Reassurance. And after what happened in her parents' bedroom, she needed to grieve. For some reason, she wouldn't allow herself any of that.

They had more in common than he'd realized. He knew what it was like to keep emotions so tightly wound and hidden that they threatened to suffocate. He understood the risk of letting someone get close to you. His father's and brother's abusiveness was only part of the reason Aden had kept his distance from everyone. Now he knew something else had driven him to stay separate from the community—the fear of getting hurt. He'd experienced so much pain in his life that he didn't have room for any more.

Yet some of that pain was easing. Being free of his father and being married to Sadie had opened the door to healing, and he drank it up like a man dying of thirst.

He wanted to show Sadie that she didn't have to bear her grief alone, that letting someone in wouldn't be opening the door to hurt, but to healing.

Aden stared at the door, struggling to decide whether he should go to her or honor her request to be left alone. After a few moments he went downstairs, turned out the lights, and returned to his room.

Yet he didn't stay there. He took the quilt off Abigail's bed and walked into the hallway to Sadie's room. He wrapped the quilt around his shoulders and sank to the floor, leaning against the wall next to the door. If she had a nightmare or another attack of emotional distress in the middle of the night, he would at least be close. She may have pushed him away . . . but he would never be far from her.

Sadie woke the next morning and grimaced. Another night spent in her clothes. She had managed a small amount of sleep, but she still felt tired—and embarrassed over what had happened last night. Aden had seen her weak, and that unsettled her. Yet she couldn't forget how he'd been there for her. The flash of worry in his eyes as she told him she wanted to be alone. She didn't understand him. She was letting him know he didn't need to be obligated to her. That she could handle herself.

I really handled myself last night . . .

She shook her head. This morning she would pretend nothing had happened. They would continue through the day as normal . . . at least as normal as possible. If Aden didn't bring it up, she doubted he would.

She rose and quickly dressed, shoving the last bobby pin in her *kapp* as she opened her bedroom door. Her bare foot touched something warm and solid. Sadie looked down, her mouth dropping open when she saw Aden lying on the hardwood floor next to the threshold. Abigail's quilt was halfway around his shoulders. His back was to her, and he was sleeping on his side. A flash of guilt ran through her as she realized how uncomfortable he had to be. He didn't even have a pillow.

"Aden?" She knelt down and touched his shoulder. When he didn't move she gave it a nudge.

He rolled over on his back, his eyes barely opening. "Sadie?" Then his eyes opened fully. He sat up. "What? Is something wrong?"

"It's morning."

He scrambled to his feet, then yawned, pulling the quilt around him. He looked a little endearing with his hair sticking up and wearing a girly-looking quilt.

She quickly averted her gaze.

"How did you sleep?" he asked.

"Okay." Another slash of guilt forced her to look at him. "Why were you on the floor?"

He yawned again. "I tried sleeping against the wall. Floor's more comfortable." He still sounded drowsy.

"That's not what I meant—"

"Better get to the horses," he said, walking away and effectively not answering her question. "Jasper eats twice as much as the others, which figures."

"Aden—"

But he walked into Abigail's room before she could say anything else. Before she had a chance to thank him. *So much for me ignoring what happened.*

Patience arrived shortly after eight in the morning to help Sadie in the store. When Sadie saw her friend, she almost fainted with relief. Aden had remembered to tell her Patience was ill, and Sadie hadn't thought her friend would be back so soon. When she went to hug her, Patience held off. "Just in case. I don't want you to get sick."

"I don't care," Sadie said, tears threatening to well up in her eyes again. She was disgusted with herself. Why wouldn't the tears stay at bay? It was becoming harder and harder to keep them locked inside.

"That's what Timothy said." Patience sniffed. "But now he's got a cough."

Sadie frowned. "Are you sure you want to be here?" She stopped just short of saying Aden could help out.

"I'm going crazy stuck in the *haus*," she said, smiling. "Plus, I feel so much better. I haven't coughed since yesterday morning, and last night I slept for over nine hours."

"As long as you're sure. I don't want you to wear yourself out."

Patience nodded. The store sign was turned to Open, but they didn't have a customer yet. Sadie was behind the counter, and she reached to straighten the pencils in the pencil can, only to pull back at the reminder of her mother. The strain in her throat returned.

"I need to apologize," Patience said, putting her purse on the counter.

Sadie frowned. "For what?"

"I was short with you when I was here the other day. I'm sorry for that. I promise I won't ask about you and Aden anymore."

Her hands gripping the side of the counter, Sadie regarded her friend. Again the unwelcome sting in her eyes came without warning, and she looked away. But not fast enough.

"Sadie." Patience's gentle, sweet voice brought welcome warmth. "What is it?"

Sadie clenched her hands together. "I don't know how to do this," she managed.

"Do what?"

"Be a wife."

With a compassionate smile Patience walked to the other side of the counter and hugged Sadie.

"What about getting sick?" Sadie said, surprised but glad for the hug.

"You need this more." She pulled back, still smiling. "I can't teach you how to be a wife. No one can. Only God can guide you and help you realize what *yer* husband needs."

Deep down she knew what Aden needed even though he hadn't asked for it. But she felt it with every tender expression, every light touch, every gesture of . . . what? *Love?* No, that couldn't be it. Desire, maybe. Yet she knew what desire looked like. She had seen it in Sol's eyes before. Aden had never looked—never leered—at her that way.

"I'm sure Aden is trying to figure out what you need too," Patience said, breaking into her thoughts. "You've always been strong and independent. Perhaps he's searching for his place in the marriage, just like you are."

Sadie nodded, but she thought Aden seemed more confident in their relationship than she was. He seemed to have blossomed since their wedding day, while she shrank more into herself.

"God brought the two of you together for a purpose." Patience's smile widened.

"Why would he do that?" Sadie asked.

"Because he knows what's best for us. That doesn't mean everything will be easy and *gut*." She grew serious. "Now you don't have to face life alone. You have someone who loves you standing by *yer* side."

Sadie gulped as a customer walked into the store. Patience said hello and moved from behind the counter, leaving Sadie alone with her thoughts. Of course Patience thought Aden loved her. Everyone else did too. Only a few people knew the truth.

And God. He knows.

Patience's words were meant to be comforting, but they stirred up more confusion. Aden had also told her she didn't have to be alone. When her parents died and then her sisters left for Middlefield, that's exactly what she'd been—alone. Until Aden married her.

Is that why you married me? To put yer *guilt to rest?*

Sadie . . . I married you because I wanted to.

Her heart tripped as she remembered what Abigail had told her when she visited her and

Joanna. *There were little things. I'd see him watching you during the service.* And then what Sol had said. *He loves you. That's why he married you.*

She closed her eyes. *He spent the night lying on the floor outside your bedroom. Without a pillow.*

Her eyes flew open, and something broke loose inside her heart.

Aden pushed open the back door of the barn, which faced away from the store. Good thing, too, since he had to add to the growing pile of manure a few feet away. It wouldn't take much of a wind to catch the strong scent and send it wafting toward the store, which wouldn't bother Amish customers but might offend the *Englisch*.

As much as he liked working in the store, he was glad to see Patience arrive this morning. Not only did he have work to do, but Sadie needed her friend.

He walked inside the barn. Since caring for Sol's pig of a horse, the manure had multiplied in the stalls. Actually he didn't mind—Jasper was gentle and eager to please, the exact opposite of his owner. As he mucked out the stall, Aden pondered what to do, if anything, about Sol. Admittedly it was a relief to know that he didn't have to be always on guard, expecting Sol to show up any minute. But where had he gone? His

306

brother had left four days ago . . . the same day he was shunned.

The back of his teeth crashed together at the memory of the way his father had told him about Sol. Then he remembered his mother's pain, her plea not to go against his father. He could only imagine what she was going through, and she had to do it practically alone. Aden was sure the bishop was of no comfort.

Aden continued cleaning out the stalls, losing himself in the work as he often did when he performed a task. He was taking out the last wheelbarrow of manure to the huge dung pile when he saw a figure approach. He dropped the handles of the wheelbarrow, realizing who it was.

Sol.

CHAPTER 20

Aden's mouth fell open. His brother looked terrible—his body gaunt, his clothes soiled, and from a few feet away Aden caught a whiff of horrible body odor. Sol continued to walk toward Aden, his shoulders slumped, carrying none of the haughty confidence he'd always had.

"Sol," he said, almost too stunned to speak. His brother looked like he'd been through a fight—and lost.

Sol halted. "I won't come any closer."

Aden shook his head and went to meet him. "Don't worry about that." He looked Sol up and down. "Where have you been?"

"That doesn't matter." He looked at Aden, his eyes eerie . . . yet serene. "I came to apologize."

Aden's eyes widened. "What?"

He held out his hands. "I'm sorry, Aden. For everything. For what I did to you. What I did to Sadie." He hung his head. "I'm asking for *yer* forgiveness."

His brother had never said he was sorry. Ever. Aden peered at him, trying to sense Sol's angle. "Is this a trick?"

"*Nee.*" Despite his appearance, Sol's voice sounded strong. Genuine. "I'd understand if you sent me away. You must already know I'm in the *bann*. Those are the rules, and I will abide by them."

Removing his hat, Aden pushed back his hair, trying to comprehend the outward and apparently inward change in Sol. It was strange to see his normally clean-shaven brother with a scraggily mustache and beard. But it was even odder to see the sincerity in his apology.

"I have only one favor to ask of you," Sol said.

Here it comes. Of course there would be conditions to his "apology." Aden crossed his arms, pushing away any sympathy he had felt for his brother.

"I need a place to stay tonight. Somewhere warm." He shivered. "Safe. Can I sleep in *yer* barn? Sadie won't know I'm here. I'll leave in the morning and you can keep *mei* horse and buggy as payment and restitution."

Aden's mind spun. He'd never seen Sol like this. He was vulnerable. He was humble.

Tend to your brother.

The voice in the center of his soul, the one that had spoken to him so many times over the years, was louder than he'd ever heard it. Could his brother have changed? Could he have become a different person in a few short days?

Did it even matter?

Sol was hungry, ragged, and had nothing to his name. In spite of the past and impelled by an unseen force, Aden went to his brother. He wouldn't turn him away. "You'll not sleep in the barn," he said, putting his arm around Sol's thin shoulders, a lump coming to his throat as the man who had always been taller, stronger, and better than Aden leaned against him. "You're welcome in *mei haus*."

Sol turned into Aden's shoulder . . . and wept.

While Sol was upstairs taking a much-needed shower—Aden could hardly stand to be near him —Aden was pulling food out of the pantry and putting it in a big, empty fruit basket. Crackers, bread, a jar of peanuts, an apple, peanut butter— anything he could find that would give Sol a bit of nourishment. He opened the large cooler where Sadie kept the milk, cheese, and lunch meat. He set those in the basket too, grabbed a glass out of the cabinet, and went upstairs.

Sol met him in Abigail's room, wearing the clothes Aden had given him—a long-sleeved blue shirt and dark blue denim pants. They were snug, as Sol had always been thicker and more muscular than Aden. But they would do for now. Sol sat on Abigail's bed as Aden shut the door, then gave him the basket of food.

"*Danki*," Sol said, then began wolfing down the food—a chunk of cheese, a slice of bread, a handful of peanuts, whatever he could grab fast. Aden had never seen anyone so hungry.

"When did you last eat?"

Sol shrugged. "Four, five days ago, I think," he said with his mouth full. "If I don't count the alcohol."

Aden poured him a glass of milk and Sol gulped it down. Then Aden stood back and waited, still unsure if Sol was being genuine about what he'd said or if hunger had brought him low enough to come back. Maybe once his brother got his fill he would be back to his old—and unpredictable—self.

"Why did *Daed* put you in the *bann*?"

"He had his reasons. Mostly because of my drinking." Sol looked down at his lap. "He was right, at least about that. I was out of control and not thinking clearly. I haven't been for a long time." He looked up at Aden. "I'm ashamed of the things I've done . . . mostly what I did to you."

Aden swallowed. "You didn't have a choice."

"There's always a choice. I know that now. If I had stood up to *Daed*, if I had told him *nee*—"

"He would have beat you," Aden said matter-of-factly. "Then he would have beaten me. He'll never change, Sol."

"But *we* can change." He pounded his fist against his chest. "We can be better. We can live as God truly wants us to, instead of how *Daed* expects."

Shocked, Aden regarded his brother. He couldn't remember the last time Sol had mentioned God. Yes, Sol had joined the church. Not joining was unthinkable for either one of them. But while Aden had always felt that being Amish was right for him, he'd never been sure about Sol. Then again, they'd never had any meaningful conversations until now. "Why did you come back?" he asked.

"Because I have to make things right, starting with the person I hurt the most." He cleared his throat. "I don't know how I can make it up to you when I am in the *bann*, but I'll try. I'll do everything I can to convince you how sorry I am." Sol slid from the bed to his knees. "Aden, I hope one day you can forgive me."

Aden's heart contracted. As a kid he'd hoped to hear those words from his brother. As an adult, he'd never expected to. Now, seeing Sol on his knees and hearing his apology given with complete humility, Aden couldn't bear it. "Get up," he said, going to Sol and helping him to his feet. "Don't ever do that again."

"Aden—"

"You have my forgiveness, Sol. All you had to do was ask." The words poured out with no reservation, stunning him. As an Amishman he'd been taught to forgive. It was at the core of his faith. Yet he'd expected it to be more difficult than this. Years of abuse from Sol, verbal and physical, suddenly melted away. *How is this possible?*

Then he realized why. Sol had changed. Something had happened to him while he was gone, something miraculous. Aden not only could see it, he could *feel* it. "We are both victims of our father," he said, tears pooling in his eyes. "We have both suffered pain at his hands." He clasped Sol on the shoulder. "I need *yer* forgiveness too."

Sol wiped the back of his hand across his nose. "There's *nix* to forgive."

"I should have stood up to him too. We should have banded together."

"We were *kinner*, Aden. We didn't know any different. Or any better."

Aden yanked Sol's weakened body into a fierce hug. "We do now, *mei bruder*."

Sadie locked the store door and headed for the house. She hadn't seen Aden all day, not even when she thought he'd take a break and perhaps share the lunch she'd made for herself and Patience. He knew how to keep himself busy, but she'd expected him to come into the store at least once. She'd kept watching the door all day, but he never walked through it. She needed to see him. To talk to him. To thank him for everything he had done for her. After that . . . she wasn't sure what to do.

Her pulse sped up as she entered the house. She started supper, putting another casserole from one of her *mamm*'s friends in the oven, this time chicken noodle. While the casserole cooked, she went to the living room and called Aden's name. There was no response. Thinking he was in the barn, she went outside and noticed his buggy was gone. He'd left? Why hadn't he told her where he was going?

She went back inside, a nugget of worry forming in her belly. Then she chastised herself. He was a grown man. There was no need to worry about him. But she did care that he wasn't here. That much she had to admit to herself.

An hour later she pulled the casserole out of the oven and glanced at the clock on the wall for the tenth time. It was past seven and almost dark. What if he'd had an accident? She flinched, the back of her hand touching the hot casserole dish.

"Ow!" She yanked back and hurried to the sink, turning on the tap and running cold water over the burn. The pain didn't stem her rising panic as she imagined Aden's buggy, overturned and in pieces, his body mangled from the impact of the accident—

"Stop!" she yelled, forcing herself to stay calm and finding it hard to do. What would she do if he were gone?

I can't lose anyone else . . .

She paced the kitchen, looking out the window, praying he would walk through the door any minute. Halting her steps, she put her palm against her abdomen, willing her stomach to settle, trying to slow her heartbeat. Nothing worked.

She was about to hitch up Apple to her own buggy and search for Aden when the back door opened. As soon as he walked in she practically tackled him, throwing her arms around his neck. "Where have you been?" she wailed. His arms tightened at her waist for a brief moment, and she closed her eyes, feeling the urge to bury her face in his neck.

"I went to get some wood for a new door." His voice was low, almost a grumble in her ear. "It took longer than I expected."

"You should have told me where you were going."

"I didn't want to bother you at the store."

She should have pulled away. But she couldn't. She couldn't move out of his embrace, which felt better than anything she had ever experienced.

"I'm sorry." He stepped back, but his hands remained at her waist. "I didn't mean to worry you."

"I wasn't worried," she said. At his arched brow she added, "More like a little concerned." She looked at him, not pulling away from his gaze. Although he held her, his expression seemed unusually distant. "We need to talk, Aden."

"*Ya*, we do . . ."

She didn't hear the rest of what he said . . . because Sol walked through the door.

CHAPTER 21

"What is he doing here?" Sadie scrambled backward, away from the Troyer brothers. She could feel her throat starting to close, the terror rising within her. "Get out!"

"Sadie, it's okay. Sol's not going to do anything." Aden went to her.

But she moved away, not wanting him to touch her. Moments ago she'd felt so safe in his arms. Now the distrust she'd managed to set aside came slamming back into her. "You promised he wouldn't come back. You promised he'd leave me alone."

"Sadie," Sol started to say. "I'm—"

"Stay away from me!" she yelled, tightly hugging her body with her arms. She turned to Aden, his betrayal popping something inside her, a painful breaking of confusion and emotion, pain and sorrow. She rushed past both men and ran out of the house and into the yard, not knowing where she was going—and not caring where she ended up.

She tripped over her own clumsy feet and fell to the ground. As she tried to scramble up, she felt steady arms around her waist.

"Sadie . . ."

Aden's voice pierced through the haze. When

he pulled her to her feet, she turned in his arms and started shoving against his chest. "How could you do this to me?" she screamed, every nerve in her body excruciatingly alert.

"Shhh," he said, drawing her against his chest. "It's not what you think."

She wanted him to let her go, but instead she leaned into him. The soothing sound of his voice, the strength of his arms around her, the way he was rubbing her back and whispering that everything would be all right . . .

Every bit of strength she possessed drained from her. She was tired of fighting against him, against her feelings, against a pain that was now so acute and oppressive she could barely stand. All she could do was bury her head in his chest and sob.

Sol stood in the kitchen, peering into the night at Aden and Sadie, seeing only their shadows outlined in the darkness. When he saw Aden pull Sadie into his arms, Sol shut the kitchen door.

He looked around the room, not really paying attention to anything, his mind on what he had witnessed. The terror in Sadie's eyes had torn at him. He shook his head at the irony—a few days ago he would have been too drunk to care that she was melting down. Now all he could feel was guilt for causing it. After their talk upstairs, Aden had told him to stay in the barn until he had a chance to talk to Sadie that evening, after the store closed. Then Aden left to pick up wood for a new kitchen door—the one he'd broken the day Sol cornered Sadie. When Aden returned from the lumberyard, he told Sol to give him five minutes.

Sol should have waited longer.

He sat down at the table and let his face fall against his hand. He hadn't meant to cause more trouble between Aden and his wife. Even when his intentions were good, he seemed to mess up. No wonder he was a disappointment to his father.

His head lifted as three words derailed his train of thought: *you are loved.*

Four days alone, cut off from everyone, had sent him through his own crisis and a blinding rage that had sent him deeper into the woods, vowing he would never return to Birch Creek. Eventually he sobered up and calmed down enough to realize he was lost, something that had never happened to him before. He was a good tracker, having spent years hunting deer and turkey in the woods surrounding Birch Creek. But no matter what he did or where he walked, it was as if he walked in circles.

Then the sickness came. Vomiting, sweating, panic. When night descended he couldn't sleep. He saw shadows in the dark and heard echoing voices, which terrified him. He thought he was going crazy. He thought he was going to die.

Until only one voice remained. Clear and strong, it calmed his fear and soothed his tortured soul. *You are loved.* He heard the words over and over, for hours on end, until he finally believed them. Finally understood what they truly meant, and who was saying them. His mind cleared as his past rolled through his brain, shaming him into submission. When he was able to stand on shaky legs, he suddenly knew where he was and found his way out of the woods. He ended up in a field near the Schrocks' house, and he knew what he needed to do.

He had so many sins to make up for, and he was scared. Just approaching Aden had been difficult, not because he didn't want to be restored to his brother. For the first time in his life, he craved forgiveness. No, he'd been terrified of Aden's rejection—one that would be well deserved. But he shouldn't have worried. Aden was a good man. He always had been the strong one no matter what his father had said. Sol had been the coward.

Now his brother was out there, cleaning up another one of Sol's messes. But Sol couldn't do anything about Sadie right now. Hopefully she would come to see that he had changed, and she could forgive him. Now she needed to be with Aden, who truly loved her. Sol had always known how Aden felt about Sadie. He'd known since he'd returned home from the cornfield that day, limping and sore from where Sadie had kicked him. Since that day Aden had changed, had borne the burden of guilt that was Sol's to carry. Only out of love had Aden lied to their *daed* to marry Sadie. Sol had been willing to marry her for his freedom. Aden had married her for love.

No, he couldn't reconcile with Sadie, not for a while. But he could do something else. He thought of the money stashed in Aden's barn. In his fury he'd broken his father's strongbox and taken all the cash, intending to use it for his new life outside Birch Creek. Now he knew that was wrong—the money didn't belong to him or his father. It belonged to the community. Somehow Sol had to return it to the rightful owners.

The door opened and he turned in his chair. Sadie didn't look at him, her body tucked close to Aden's while he held her protectively. Aden glanced at Sol, shook his head, and left the kitchen.

Sol stood. He looked at the casserole on the stove. The kitchen was filled with the savory scents of chicken and herbs, causing his stomach to growl. The plates were on the table and all he had to do was serve himself.

The way he'd done all his life.

He turned and walked out into the night.

Aden led Sadie up to her room, torn between leaving her side and telling Sol to leave, and trying to make Sadie understand why his brother was here. The decision wasn't that hard. Even if Sadie didn't believe Sol was a different man—and he doubted she would—he couldn't leave her side. Not when she was so fragile.

He guided Sadie to the bed and turned on the lamp. Her whole body trembled against him. While they were outside she had scared him, until he realized what was causing her breakdown. Sadie was always strong, always stoic. She never cried. And he was almost positive she had never grieved.

She didn't move as he kept his arm around her. Tears streamed down her cheeks, and he wiped them away with his thumb. Her tears tugged at him, but he knew she had to let them flow. He pulled one of the bobby pins from her *kapp*, readying himself for her protest. When she didn't respond, he removed the other three and took off her *kapp*, setting it on the bedside table. Wayward strands of light brown hair framed her face. The rest of her hair was pulled up and bound tight. She suddenly tensed and he said, "It's all right. I'm not going to do anything else."

He pulled down the covers on the bed. "You're exhausted," he said, guiding her into the bed. She had stopped crying, but she still looked at him with round eyes, liquid eyes. "I'll bring you something to eat."

She shook her head. *"Nee,"* she whispered.

"All right." He started to get up from the bed. "I'll sleep by *yer* door again tonight."

"*Nee!*" She clutched his shirt.

"I'll tell Sol he has to *geh*." And he would. His wife's peace came first.

"What if he doesn't listen to you?"

Aden paused. "He'll listen. Lie down, Sadie. You need to rest." He moved to leave.

"Please." Her tears started again. "Don't leave me."

He hesitated, not knowing what she wanted him to do. She scooted over in the bed, then her gaze dropped to the empty spot. He looked at her to make sure, then slipped off his boots and lay next to her. The twin bed didn't allow for any space between them.

"I'm sorry," she whispered.

"There's *nix* for you to be sorry about."

"Can you . . . will you turn off the light?"

He reached over and shut off the battery-operated lamp. Darkness filled the room. He felt her put her head against the side of his shoulder. He didn't move.

"I don't know what happened," she said after a long stretch of silence.

"How do you feel now?"

"A little better. Strange, isn't it?"

"*Nee.* Not so strange." He took a risk and lifted his arm slightly. She moved her head, and he wrapped his arm around her shoulder, holding his breath to see what she would do. With a short pause she laid her head against his chest. He let out a long breath.

Then she started talking. She told him about Joanna, about how much she missed her and Abigail, how she ached because she couldn't be in Middlefield to help them. About how she had promised her parents she wouldn't let them down. About how guilty she felt that she couldn't relieve Abigail and spend time with Joanna because she was worried about finances. She gave him details about the store debt and the huge medical bills. As she spoke he rubbed her shoulder. He hadn't realized the extent of what she'd been holding in.

When she stopped talking, the room was silent except for their breathing. Sadie's became steadier, and he thought she'd fallen asleep. He closed his eyes. Even in the tight quarters and knowing he was literally being a shoulder for her to cry on, he wouldn't have moved from this bed for anything.

"I miss them."

His eyes opened at the sound of her teary voice. "*Yer* parents."

"*Ya.* I miss them so much it hurts. I don't know if it will ever stop hurting."

He thought about his own pain, how it had lessened since he married her, and had decreased even more with Sol's apology. "I pray that it will."

She didn't reply, and by the stillness of her body he knew she was asleep. His hand moved up from her shoulder to her hair. He brushed his palm against the soft strands, thinking she probably wouldn't appreciate him touching her like this. It was a little beyond simple comfort. But he couldn't help himself. When she shifted in his arms, he put his hand back on her shoulder. He was aching for more—he couldn't deny that. But he wouldn't take advantage of her.

As his eyes drifted closed and sleep overtook him, he thought he heard her whisper in a drowsy voice, "Thank you."

Light streamed through the curtains when Sadie woke up the next morning. Her eyes felt heavy, her mind groggy, her body tired. She was spent. But she had also slept a dreamless sleep for the first time since the accident. As she moved, her cheek brushed against Aden's shirt, and everything that happened last night returned in acute detail.

She looked at Aden's profile. He was still asleep, sunbeams sliding across his face. His reddish beard was still growing in, some places in thin patches. She'd never been this close to him before, and she could see every light brown freckle that covered his forehead, cheeks, and nose. She was aware of the weight of his arm around her waist, which had somehow slipped from her shoulder last night. The last thing she remembered was falling asleep next to him, feeling safer and more secure than ever before.

He hadn't asked anything of her. He hadn't tried anything. He hadn't given her answers or platitudes. He had listened. He had been there when she needed him.

She drew in a breath when he moved, opening his eyes. He turned and their gazes met, their noses nearly touching. She felt an unfamiliar pull deep inside herself, more acute than any attraction she'd felt for him before. Scared by the intensity, she shuddered. His arm immediately fell from her body.

He stared at her for a moment, his eyes moving from her face to her hair. The light green irises darkened before he pulled away and sat up. "I need to check on Sol."

She cringed at hearing the name, but she wasn't as furious or frightened as she'd been last night. He hadn't explained why Sol was here. Instead he'd spent his time comforting her. She trusted him, despite the angry words she'd hurled at him last night. That meant she had to let him deal with his brother in his own way.

His back was to her, and she fought the urge to touch him. Physically they were so close, but a chasm seemed to emotionally separate them. He finally stood up, turned, and looked at her. "Are you okay?"

Her bed felt empty and cold without his presence. She didn't want him to leave. "*Ya*," she said. "I am."

Aden gave her one last look, then left.

Sadie hugged her body. A full day stretched in front of her—cleaning the kitchen, working in the store, washing clothes when business was slow. Mundane tasks that seemed so insignificant in light of spending last night in Aden's arms.

She wasn't at peace. Far from it. But she wasn't angry anymore . . . and she had Aden to thank for that.

CHAPTER 22

Before he went downstairs, Aden checked Abigail's room, expecting to find Sol. When he didn't, he hurried down the stairs but didn't see his brother in the living room either. The food and supper dishes from last night were untouched. Frowning, he went outside, expecting Sol's buggy to be gone. His frown deepened when he saw it was still parked near the barn.

As he walked into the barn, he heard rustling sounds. He went to the first stall and saw Sol pouring feed into Apple's trough. "You don't have to do that."

"They're hungry. I'll get to Rusty and Jasper in a minute."

Aden wasn't going to argue with him. "Where did you sleep last night?"

"There." Sol pointed at a short stack of hay bales in the corner of the barn. "I rearranged them a bit. I'll put them back."

Aden clasped the back of his neck, still coming to terms with the changes in his brother. He was reminded how God could make the impossible possible. Now he was witnessing it firsthand.

"How's Sadie?" Sol asked, his voice tentative. "I didn't mean to upset her last night."

"She's okay."

"I thought it would be better if I stayed out here." He pushed open the stall door and stepped out. "She's really scared of me, isn't she?"

"Do you blame her?"

"*Nee.*" He went to Rusty's stall and gave the horse his feed.

Neither of them said anything for a long moment. "Have you eaten?" Aden asked.

Sol shook his head.

"I'll be back in a minute."

He went into the kitchen and found Sadie cleaning up. He stopped near the back door. Maybe he should wait until she was working at the store to get food for Sol. But he was done with secrets. The truth always seemed to come out anyway. "Sadie."

She turned and looked at him. The circles under her eyes were still there, but her posture was less tense. She didn't seem happy or content, but she didn't seem angry either. *That's something, at least.* "Sol spent the night in the barn," he told her, trying to break the news to her gently.

She paled, but only slightly. "So he's still here."

Aden nodded. "I wondered if he could come in and have breakfast."

Sadie's lips pinched together.

"He's changed, Sadie."

"Maybe he just wants you to think he's changed."

"That could be true. But I want to give him the benefit of the doubt."

Turning from him, she said, "After all he's done to you? To me?" She paused. "To *us?*"

Aden scrubbed his hand over his face. She would be within her rights to say no. He was asking a lot, and she had already given up so much. He was about to tell her never mind when her words stopped him.

"All right." She faced him. "I trust you know what you're doing."

He couldn't help but smile. She had given him a gift, whether or not she knew it. "If there's a problem, I'll make sure he leaves. I promise."

"You always keep *yer* promises, don't you?"

Aden saw something in her eyes that made his heart do back flips. *Respect. She respects me.* Grasping to keep his composure, he said, "I always try."

Sadie pushed around the scrambled eggs on her plate. To her right sat Aden, to the left sat Sol, who had eaten his meal in silence. Although she didn't want to, she couldn't help but watch him, her nerves on edge as she waited for him to do something, anything that would give her and Aden an excuse to ask him to leave. Aden seemed to believe Sol had changed, but Sadie didn't. No one turned his life around in a few days . . . especially not Sol. He didn't have it in him.

But all he did was eat his meal, keeping his gaze on his plate and almost inhaling the food. He didn't try making small talk with Aden or throw a sarcastic backhanded compliment at Sadie. When he was finished he barely glanced at her. "*Danki*," he said, his voice nearly inaudible.

She blinked but didn't respond. He was probably lulling them into a false sense of trust. She couldn't blame Aden for falling for it. Sol was his brother. Family ties ran deep, even when they were torn and frayed. It also wasn't lost on her that they were disobeying the bishop and the *Ordnung* by eating with Sol. Even allowing him in the house was forbidden. Aden hadn't mentioned his father at all, and Sadie wasn't about to. How much trouble would they be in if they were caught? Was Sol worth it?

Aden seemed to think so.

"I have to get to the store," she said, rising from her chair, eager to get out of the room and away from Sol. She started to pick up the dishes when Aden stopped her.

"I'll take care of these. You don't want to be late."

"I can help," Sol added, gathering up his plate and utensils.

Sadie froze. Had the world turned upside down? Doing the dishes was a woman's job, and their father had stressed the delineation between male and female work more than once in his sermons. Of course, Aden had broken that ideal already, mostly because she'd been too focused on the store—and on herself. But she hadn't expected Sol's offer of help at all. "Okay," she mumbled, not knowing what else to say, and left the kitchen and headed to the store.

The steel gray sky threatened rain, and a swift wind swirled a few dead leaves around her ankles. She pulled her navy blue sweater around her mauve dress, warding off the sudden chill. Next week she would turn the calendar page to October, and fall seemed to have finally arrived. The faint scent of smoking wood hovered in the air, carried by the fall wind from a nearby chimney. Last night had probably been cold, but she'd been warm and snug in the cocoon of Aden's arms.

She paused, putting her hand over her heart to steady its thrumming beat. Even Sol's presence couldn't completely douse the embers of yearning for Aden that had been stoked last night. Suddenly she resented Sol's presence for another reason. How long would Aden allow his brother to stay? Would she and Aden ever have time alone? Because, despite herself, that's what she wanted.

A bark sounded behind her, and she turned to see Homer barreling toward her. She knelt down as he pounced on her, his tongue licking her face in one long stroke. He smelled much better.

Earthy, as if he'd been rolling in mounds of dirt for a week. "Where have you been, *bu*?" she said, scratching him behind the ears.

Another lick was her answer, then he took off and disappeared in the woods. "What a strange dog," she muttered as she opened the door to the store. But he'd been a welcome diversion and had given her the short time she needed to gain her composure and face the day.

Facing tonight would be a different story.

"I wonder what *Daed* would say if he saw us." Aden handed a wet dish to Sol, who grabbed it and haphazardly ran a towel over it.

"We both know what he would say," Sol said in a bitter voice.

They were nearly done with the dishes, and Aden was glad. This wasn't his favorite chore. Not even in the top ten. But since he married Sadie he had cooked, washed dishes, and done his own laundry, tasks his mother had always taken care of. While he didn't mind doing them, he would rather be working outside.

"Do you think Sadie will ever forgive me?"

Aden glanced at Sol. "I don't know. I'm still not sure she's forgiven me yet."

"What do you mean?"

Aden yanked his hands out of the soapy water. He turned to Sol. "For leaving her with you."

Sol leaned against the counter. "She shouldn't have held that against you."

"Well, she did." He pulled the plug out of the drain. "I should have stayed and stuck up for her."

"I would have pounded you into the ground."

Aden looked at him. "It would have been worth it."

Sol still looked concerned. "What if she tells *Daed* I'm here? I don't want to get you in trouble."

Oh, how the tables had turned. Sol had never worried about Aden getting into trouble. In fact, sometimes Sol had told on Aden for the purpose of getting him in trouble. He pressed down the sudden resentment, reminding himself that he had forgiven his brother. Someday he might be able to forget. *I hope.*

"She won't say anything to *Daed*," he said. "She's busy with the store, so she doesn't have time to see him." He didn't want to add that he knew Sadie no longer thought much of their father.

"*Gut.*" Sol yawned. "Sorry. I didn't sleep well last night."

"You can take a nap in Abigail's room." He wasn't about to admit to his brother that he and Sadie slept in separate rooms. He'd figure out what to do about that tonight. But right now Sol looked like he was going to drop from weariness.

Sol went upstairs, and Aden sat down at the table. He drummed his fingers against it, deep in thought, his mother coming to mind. She would want to know Sol was okay, but he also remembered her warning about not crossing his father. *Too late.* He'd already broken more than a few rules. He wasn't only tired of secrets . . . he was also tired of regrets. Too many times in his life he had thought about what he should have done instead of doing the right thing. His father had also threatened consequences for Sadie if he didn't have that natural gas rights paperwork by now, and he needed to tell him how hard he had tried to find it. He had to protect Sadie from whatever his father had in mind.

Aden rose, put on his boots, grabbed his hat, and went to the store. He wasn't going to skip telling Sadie he was leaving this time. She had worried about him last night. His lips lifted into a smile.

"Sadie's in the office," Patience said from behind the counter as Aden walked in.

Aden nodded his thanks and strode to the back of the store, feeling more confident about his decision to see his mother. He knocked on the door and opened it, unsure about Sadie's mood. He wished they'd had more time to talk about Sol, but she didn't need to get upset while she was at work. "Sadie?" he said, peeking into the office.

She looked up. To his surprise, she smiled and motioned him in as she jumped up from the chair.

Instinctively his arms lifted, half expecting—and half hoping—she would run into them like she had last night, before Sol had showed up. When she stopped a few feet in front of him, he winced and dropped his arms. Clearly he expected too much.

"I found something," she said, holding a thick envelope. She opened it so he could look inside at the stack of bills.

Now he understood her excitement.

"They're all ones," she said, still smiling. "I found it way in the back of the middle drawer of the desk. It was stuck and I had to yank on it a few times. It's not marked, of course, so I have *nee* idea what it's for. But it's fifty dollars I didn't have before."

His pulse settled. "That's great, Sadie," he said, meaning it, but unable to hide a slight note of disappointment in his tone.

She nodded and sat back down. "I think I'm going to tear this desk apart. Who knows what's hidden in here." She looked up at him, her eyes widening. "Maybe I'll find the natural gas rights paperwork. Do you mind helping me?"

Her request surprised and pleased him. Maybe their relationship was changing after all. "When I get back," he said.

Her expression turned serious. "Where are you going?"

"To see *Mamm*. I have to tell her Sol is okay."

"What about the bishop?"

He shrugged. "I'm concerned about *mei mamm*. I'll deal with *mei vatter* if I see him."

Apprehension tugged at her mouth. "And Sol?"

"Sleeping in Abigail's room. I reckon he'll be asleep for the rest of the day. He won't bother you." He waited for her to protest. To insist that Sol leave. To tell him at the very least that Sol had to stay in the barn.

"I saw Homer this morning."

He took her changing the subject as tacit approval. "He came back?"

"For a minute. Then he went back into the woods."

"Strange dog."

She gave him a half smile. "That's what I said."

Chuckling, he put his hand on the office doorknob. "I'll be back soon."

"Aden?"

He glanced at her over his shoulder, noting she'd become serious.

"Be careful," she said.

And he could tell she meant it.

Sadie watched as the door shut behind Aden. She didn't like the idea of him going to his parents' house. She liked it even less that Sol was in Abigail's room. Yet she had promised herself she would trust Aden, and so far he hadn't done anything to break that trust.

She considered Sol for a moment. He wasn't Aden, and she didn't trust him at all. Her only comfort was in knowing that he wouldn't risk anyone finding out he'd returned to Birch Creek. Not yet, anyway. She hoped he wouldn't be around long enough to cause any more trouble or put Aden at risk with his father.

Shoving all that out of her mind, she looked for a screwdriver, finding one in the pencil tray in the center drawer of her father's desk. The tray held everything but pencils—two more screwdrivers, several thumbtacks, two sticks of gum, a box of matches, and, inexplicably, an orange crayon. She picked up the flathead screwdriver and started to remove the screws holding the desk together. Then she realized they weren't screws, but bolts. With a sigh she put the screwdriver on the desk and yanked on the top drawer, then shook it a little bit, trying to pry it loose from the sliding track.

Half an hour later she had finally removed all the drawers, but found nothing except a few stray pieces of paper. She leaned back against the chair and blew out a breath. All that work for nothing.

"Sadie?" She heard Patience's muffled voice through the door.

"*Ya?*" She wondered why her friend didn't walk into the office, like she had all week. "Bishop Troyer is here," Patience said.

Sadie felt the blood drain from her face.

"He wants to talk to you. Now."

She stood, clutching her hands together. "All right. Let him in."

The door opened and the bishop walked into the office, wearing his usual unruffled, serene expression. "Hello, Sadie." He took in the desk drawers on the floor. "Looking for something?"

"Not really." Now she was back to lying again, and it was almost as unsettling as the intense look the bishop was aiming at her. "Just cleaning up *mei daed*'s desk. He was a bit of a pack rat."

"I see. Mind if I sit?"

Why can't you leave us alone? Sadie shook her head. "Not at all."

He sat down, then folded his hands over his abdomen, which was quite lean for a man his age. "Do you know why I'm here?"

"To see how Aden and I are faring?" That would be the last thing he'd be interested in, but she knew she should act ignorant of his real purpose.

He studied her for a moment. "Did Aden bring up the subject of your father's paperwork with you recently?"

"*Mei daed* had a lot of paperwork. Which papers are you referring to?"

He smiled, but Sadie saw it more as a smug smirk. "Ah, so he didn't tell you, per my request. At least he did one thing right," the bishop said, almost under his breath, but loud enough for Sadie to hear.

She bristled. "I would appreciate it if you didn't insult *mei* husband."

The bishop arched his brows. "A little protective now, I see. Interesting." He touched his chin.

Sadie fought to stem the anger growing within her.

"I'll get to the point." He unfolded his hands and sat up. "Right before *yer vatter*'s untimely death, he was in the process of signing over some paperwork to me. Perhaps you've seen it as you've gone through his things."

"I'm sorry, Bishop Troyer. I still don't have any idea what you're talking about." But as he continued to look at her, she felt her cheeks heat. She averted her gaze as she saw the smirk slide off his face.

"A lying tongue doesn't become you, Sadie." He leaned forward in the chair. "Now, let's try this again. Where are the natural gas rights papers?"

"I don't—"

"*Ya*, you do know what I'm talking about. Because Aden told you."

She snapped her gaze to his. "*Nee*, he didn't."

The bishop scowled. "I can tell you're lying, so stop playing games. It doesn't matter anymore if Aden told you. I never expected him to actually follow through on his promise to me. That's why I'm here." He lifted his upper lip in a sneer. "Ah, now you're looking confused. I see I have *yer* attention."

"I promise, *Daed* never said anything about natural gas rights, or paperwork . . ." She held out her hands. "And we haven't found it either."

"So you and Aden have looked." The bishop stood. "It's imperative that you find those papers, sign them, and give them to me." When Sadie started to shake her head, he lifted one finger. "That's not a request."

"I can't give you what I don't have."

The bishop moved closer to her. "You won't have anything if you don't find those papers. I can guarantee it."

When Aden arrived at his parents' house, a strange feeling came over him. For some reason the simple house, with its plain white paint and slate gray roof, wasn't welcoming. He relaxed a little when he saw his father's buggy wasn't in the driveway. But that also meant there was a good chance his mother wasn't home either.

He knocked on the door. No answer. He waited, then knocked again. He turned the doorknob, and it was locked. He went to the back and knocked twice, but there was no answer. That door was also locked.

Aden walked to the area where his hives used

to be. Near the base of a dead pear tree—one he'd planted when he was a kid that had never produced any fruit—he started to dig, first with the toe of his boot, then with his hands as he removed a layer of grass and dirt. Years ago he'd been locked out of the house overnight, another one of his father's lessons. Shortly after, his mother secretly gave him a spare key, telling Aden to hide it carefully and not to use it unless it was an emergency.

He found the key, unlocked the door, and went inside. He quickly made his way through the house, calling out for his parents until he was sure neither was there. Then he stopped at his father's office. As usual, the door was closed. He never left it open, even when he wasn't home. Aden paused, then went inside.

Guilt bubbled up the moment he walked into the room. This was his father's personal sanctuary. He spent his time here in prayer, preparing for sermons, reading books in German about their Amish ancestors. Yet this was Aden's chance to find out whatever he could about the natural gas rights other members of the church had signed over to his father.

In a short time, he found what he was looking for. *Daed* didn't need to hide anything in here—he never expected it to be searched. In the top drawer Aden found three documents signing over natural gas rights to his father. So Timothy had been right. He found check stubs from dividend payments, some of them showing staggering amounts. He also found a stack of bank statements for an account called Birch Creek Fund. There was less than two thousand dollars in the account.

But the math didn't make sense, not according to the dividend payments. Where was the rest of the money?

"Aden, what are you doing in here?"

He looked up to see his mother standing at the door, shock on her face. Aden shut the top drawer and turned to her. "*Nix*," he said, putting his hands behind his back, as if she'd caught him sneaking a cookie from the jar, not snooping through his father's private papers.

"You shouldn't be in here," she said, going to him. She put her hand on his arm. "You need to leave before *yer vatter* gets back."

"Where did he *geh*?" Not that he expected her to know—or admit that she knew.

"He had church business to take care of." She was practically dragging him out of the room.

Aden pulled out of his mother's grasp. "I'm going," he said, following her hurried steps out of the office. He shut the door behind him. "Why didn't you answer the door?"

"I was out for a walk."

She didn't normally take walks. As she looked up at him, he could see the worry lines deepening on her face. "Sol's okay," he said, taking her hands.

Her eyes widened. "What?"

"He's at *mei haus*." That was becoming easier and more natural to say. "He's thin and tired, but he's *gut*." Aden squeezed her hands. "He's better than *gut*. Something happened to him while he was gone. He's changed, *Mamm*. He's stopped drinking. He's sorry for everything he's done."

Relief crossed her features for a brief moment, then disappeared into uneasiness. "*Yer vatter* can't know," she said. "You can't tell him Solomon's with you."

"I know. But that doesn't keep you from going to see him. I'll take you to Sol right now."

She pressed her lips together, shaking her head.

"Okay, I'll *kumme* back later—"

"Aden, he's in the *bann*. I can't see him at all." She turned her back on him. "*Geh*, Aden. I'll forget what I saw you doing. I'll forget what you just told me."

"*Mamm*, listen. Things have changed—"

"It doesn't matter." She crossed her arms over her chest. "I will not *geh* against *yer vatter*."

Fury rose within him. "Not even for *yer sohns*?"

She turned and looked at him, glassy-eyed. "Not even for *mei sohns*."

CHAPTER 23

Later that evening, Sadie stirred her beef barley soup with her spoon, but she couldn't bring herself to eat any of it. The only person who seemed to have an appetite was Sol. When Aden had returned home from his parents' house, he'd been sullen. She'd seen Aden angry. Frustrated. Resigned. But never brooding. She didn't dare bring up the bishop's visit, especially in front of Sol, who hadn't said a word since they sat down at the table.

Outside a thunderclap sounded, making Sadie jerk. She glanced up and met Aden's morose gaze. Something had happened with his mother, and it seemed to set Aden back on his heels.

Sol wiped his mouth on his napkin and stood. "I'll take care of the horses," he said as driving rain sounded against the roof.

"I'll do it." Aden started to move back from the table, his soup bowl still close to full.

But Sol walked out the door before Aden could stand.

The rain pounded outside, interspersed with thunder. This was the first storm they'd had since their wedding day. She looked at Aden, willing him to talk to her. Instead he stood, picked up his bowl, and put it on the counter.

"Aden?"

"Not now, Sadie." He stormed out of the kitchen.

Dread filled her. He'd never been rude to her before. She pushed back from the table and left the kitchen, then went upstairs, determined to find out what was going on. She knocked on Abigail's closed door. "Aden?"

He didn't say anything. She turned the doorknob, but it was locked.

"Aden, please. Talk to me." When he didn't answer she said, "*Yer vatter* came by today."

He threw open the door, anger flaring in his eyes. "Why didn't you tell me?"

She took a step back, not because she was afraid, but by the sheer power of his reaction. "Because you haven't exactly been in a talkative mood."

He took her arm and led her into the bedroom, shutting the door behind him. "What did he want?"

"The papers."

Aden groaned and walked the length of the room. He spun around. "Did he threaten you?"

Should I tell him? He looked angry enough to burst, but she couldn't keep this from him. "*Ya*," she said softly. "He did. But I'm not afraid of him."

"You should be."

She went to him, touching his firm arm. "What can he do to us?"

"He can put us in the *bann* for hiding Sol."

Her lips pursed. She couldn't believe she'd forgotten about that. "Then we'll ask Sol to leave, and we'll ask the church for forgiveness. There's nothing else he can do."

"He has power, Sadie."

"Not over us." She touched his cheek, feeling the soft hair of his beard under her fingertips. "He doesn't hold that kind of power anymore." She watched as Aden closed his eyes, and she ran her fingers down the length of his jaw. A bold move on her part, but she couldn't pull away. She didn't want to.

He needed more than her words and her reassurances. He needed *her*.

His eyes opened, and he gazed at her, the color of his irises deepening to almost emerald. Then he stopped her hand with his.

"Sadie," he said, his voice raspy. "Don't."

Hurt coursed through her. He was rejecting her? Had she made a mistake? She withdrew, resisting the urge to pout, to make this about her. Regard-less of her misinterpretation of his feelings, he was hurting. He'd done so much for her—now she wanted to be here for him. "What happened with *yer mudder*?"

He turned from her, but not before she saw him swallow. "Nothing I shouldn't have expected."

She started to reach for him again, but put her hands at her sides. "Do you remember what you told me the other day?"

"I've said a lot of things, Sadie. You can't expect me to remember them all."

She bristled, but continued. "You said that we would handle things together."

"I meant the bills."

"Really? Because I got the impression you meant everything."

Aden turned slightly.

"Or were you only talking about *mei* problems?" Her palms fisted as tears slipped down her cheeks. "*Mei* brokenness?"

He faced her completely, shock and remorse shading his expression. "Sadie, *nee*," he said, going to her. "I didn't mean that at all."

"Then why won't you tell me what happened?" She took his hand, for once not embarrassed that he saw her crying. "Why won't you open up to me?"

Tears welled up in his eyes, and he looked away. But she wasn't going to let him off the hook that easily. She touched his chin and guided his face toward hers. "You're *mei* husband," she said softly. "How we got here doesn't matter anymore. What we do from this day forward does."

Aden cupped her cheek with his hand, wiping away her tears with his thumb. "I've never had anyone on *mei* side before," he choked.

"You have me. And you have God."

His eyes held hers for a moment before he dropped his hand. "I told *mei mamm* about Sol. I thought she'd be happy. But all she was worried about was how *mei daed* would react. I even offered to bring her here so she could see him, but she refused." He shook his head. "She chose *Daed*. She always has."

"Is it because she's afraid of him?"

"I think so. I'm not sure. All I know"—he swallowed again—"it hurts, Sadie. And I feel guilty about that because *mei mamm* and *daed* are here, and *yer* parents aren't."

Pain slashed at her. How many times had she questioned God about her parents' deaths? Why would he allow it? But God had also allowed Aden to suffer at the hands of his brother, and although he never said it out loud, she suspected his father's too. She and Aden were both suffering. Both broken.

Yet they could help each other fit the pieces back together. Maybe that had been God's plan all along.

Sadie took his hand, her insides shaking even though she knew what she was doing was right. She led him to Abigail's door and opened it. Without letting him go, she walked into the hallway and headed for her bedroom. He didn't say anything until they went inside. She released his hand, shut the door, and leaned against it, not turning on the light.

A flash of lightning lit up the sky, brightening the room for a second, long enough for her to see the questioning in his eyes. She stepped toward him, her legs trembling, and searched for his face in the dark. When she found it, she put her hands on either side.

"Sadie . . ."

The warmth of his skin seeped into her palms. Another flash of lightning illumined his face, highlighting his confusion. A booming crash of thunder followed, surprising her, causing her to jolt against him.

His arms wrapped around her waist. "Sadie, what are we doing?"

She answered him with a kiss, her lips featherlight on his mouth. He didn't respond right away, and she thought he might push her away. She still wasn't completely sure he wanted this.

She just knew she did.

Then his hands tightened around her as he responded. She felt so much emotion pouring from him as he continued to kiss her, his hand rising up her back to cup her neck as she put her arms around him. They ended the kiss at the same time. She heard only their rhythmic breathing as the raindrops splashed against the windowpane.

He moved away from her and turned on the light. He remained by her nightstand, keeping his eyes on hers. "I need to know something," he said, wariness entering his voice.

She touched her lips, still feeling the heat from

his kiss. "What?" she asked, confused by his withdrawal.

"I need to know . . ." He took a few steps toward her. "That you kissed me because you wanted to. Not because you felt sorry for me."

How could he even think that after what they'd both just experienced? But she held her tongue as she searched his face. He meant the question. He really doubted her intentions. "Did you kiss me out of pity?"

He shook his head. "Definitely not."

She took his hand again, liking how it felt in hers, marveling how much had changed in such a short period of time. How she'd gone from nearly hating him to . . . loving him. Admitting it to herself wasn't that hard. But she wouldn't say it to him, not yet. A simple—okay, not so simple—kiss had thrown him off balance. No telling what a proclamation of love would do.

But . . . she could show him. "Stay with me, Aden."

His hand jerked in hers, but he didn't let go. "I can't. Not after that kiss. Not when I feel . . . the way I'm feeling."

"I feel it too." And when she kissed him this time, she made sure he understood exactly what she meant.

The rest of the week had been uneventful, which had both surprised and relieved Sadie. Sol had managed to keep himself hidden for the most part, appearing only for breakfast and supper. She didn't know where he spent the days, and she didn't ask. Aden never brought it up, and she was content to be in the dark when it came to her brother-in-law's activities, since he'd done nothing that she knew of to put her and Aden at risk.

Patience had remarked a couple of times that Sadie seemed different. She had replied to her friend with a smile but nothing more. She was different, and it wasn't because she and Aden had consummated their marriage. She was in love, and while nothing in her life had changed since then, she had. She still marveled that she could fall for him after less than two weeks of marriage. Then again, now that she knew the real Aden, how could she not love him?

That Saturday after the store closed, she and Aden had searched for her father's papers again. They had looked everywhere, including her parents' bedroom. It hadn't been as difficult to be in the room as it was the first time, but she had cried when she opened her mother's hope chest and saw everything *Mamm* had saved over the years. Having Aden there with her helped. He never told her to stop crying or made her feel weak because of her tears. He merely held her, rubbing her back, letting her use his shirt as a handkerchief until she was done.

But they hadn't found the paperwork. Sadie had surrendered. Obviously it wasn't in the house or the office. She had no idea where to look next.

As she prepared for church on Sunday, Sadie pinned the front of her best dress closed. The dark green color had been her mother's favorite, and this was the last dress she had made for Sadie. With unsteady hands she slid the last pin into place, her nerves a little wracked at attending church for the first time since she and Aden had married. There would be questions, but she could face them now with Aden by her side. They were a united front. She was securing her *kapp* to her head when she heard a knock on her bedroom door.

"Is it okay to come in?"

She smiled at Aden's question. Her room was small, and he had left to let her dress in private. Despite the intimacy they shared, there was still some awkwardness between them. It wasn't unpleasant, and technically they were still getting to know each other.

We have the rest of our lives to do that.

"*Ya. Kumme* in."

He walked into the room, and she could barely breathe. Over the years she'd seen Aden in his church clothes, which weren't any more special than the typical clothes all Amish men wore to church. Yet Aden looked more than handsome in slim black pants, a fitted black vest, and a crisp white shirt.

He frowned when she didn't move. "Is something wrong?"

She shook her head, finally able to tear her gaze away from him. "*Nee*. Just finishing getting dressed. I'll be ready to *geh* in a minute."

"Sol's gone." Aden sat on the edge of the bed.

"For *gut*?" She could feel him watching her and she hid a smile. She finished pinning her *kapp* to her head.

Aden shrugged. "I have *nee* idea. He hasn't said much the past couple of days. He's put on some weight at least from *yer* cooking."

She turned to him. "Do you think he's drinking again?"

He shook his head. "He's not acting like he did when he drank. He's just . . . quiet."

She nodded and slipped the last bobby pin between her hair and *kapp*. She couldn't worry about Sol, although Aden was concerned. She took one last look in the mirror before going to him. "He'll be okay, Aden. You have to believe that."

But he didn't move. He kept looking at her, long enough to make her blush. She glanced down at her black-stockinged feet.

"I'm sorry," he said, rising from the bed. "It's just that . . ."

She looked up. "Just what?"

He swallowed. "You look beautiful." Before

353

she could say anything, he kissed her . . . and it wasn't awkward at all.

When they got to the Yutzys', the service was about to start. They went to the barn where the service was being held. Sadie sat on the women's side, finding a seat next to Patience on the hard wooden bench. Aden sat across from her, giving her a quick wink while everyone was milling around. Once they were all seated, Joel Zook, who had a fine singing voice, led the hymns.

After the singing, Bishop Troyer began his sermon with his usual confidence. For almost an hour he preached on so many topics it made her head spin. Honesty. Respect of elders. Doing the Lord's will. Striving for peace and not division in the church family. More than once he had pointed his gaze in Aden's direction, but Sadie didn't dare look at her husband. She wouldn't draw more attention to him. His father was doing enough of that.

"I believe we have such dissension in our midst," the bishop said. "In fact, the Lord has spoken to me about it. There are young men and women here who have sinned against the church. They've sinned against me personally." He looked at Aden. "They have allowed a former church member who is in the *bann* into their home."

Sadie gasped. She looked at Aden, who also seemed stricken.

The bishop narrowed his gaze at Sadie. "They

354

have let him eat at their table. They have given him shelter. They have listened to his lies."

Patience whispered to Sadie, "What is he talking about?"

"God is calling for *yer* confessions," the bishop said, his voice rising. "Clear *yer* conscience and *yer* spirit. *Kumme*, Aden and Sadie Troyer. *Kumme* forward and tell us all *yer* sins."

Sadie's mouth grew dry. The entire church congregation was staring at her and Aden, their shocked voices surrounding her in murmured dissonance. Some of them knew Sol was in the *bann*. How they found out she didn't know. But apparently no one had known he'd been hiding out with Sadie and Aden.

Her eyes met Aden's as her stomach churned. *What do we do now?*

"They are not at fault. I am."

Sadie turned to see Sol enter the barn, carrying a cloth bag. She watched as he headed up the aisle, his steps steady, his profile strong and sure.

The bishop looked shocked, and for once, he was speechless.

Sol went to the front of the church and set the bag on the ground. "I have sinned," he said. "Because of that sin, I was put in the *bann*. Which I deserved."

Sadie's gaze kept bouncing from Sol to the bishop. Aden's father's face had turned completely white.

"I've been a drunkard for years. Whiskey is *mei* drink of choice, but I've been known to consume anything that will get me drunk." He looked at Aden. "But that's not the only sin I've committed."

Aden balled his hands into fists. *Sol wouldn't dare confess to everything . . . not in front of the church.* But he had shocked Aden by showing up this morning. Aden wouldn't put anything past him. And if he admitted to the abuse, both he and his mother—and Sadie—would be brought into it. He would shame them all.

Had it come to that point? Did he hold his family's shame and their secrets higher than the truth? *Lord, forgive me.*

He looked at Sadie again. She was transfixed by Sol, leaning forward and practically perched on the edge of the bench. Then, as if she sensed him looking at her, she turned in his direction . . . and gave him an encouraging smile that settled his nerves. He knew whatever the fallout of the day entailed, she would be by his side. He'd never loved her more than at that moment.

"I've committed so many, many sins." Sol's shoulders slumped a bit, as if the burden were physically weighing on him. "I've been cruel. I've been selfish. I've been physically abusive." He glanced at the bishop before continuing. "I'm also a thief."

Murmurs started throughout the congregation. Aden couldn't believe the courage Sol was showing. He'd seen confessions in church before, but never anything like this. His brother was stripping himself bare in front of everyone.

He picked up the bag from the ground, opened it, and took out a handful of bills. "This money belongs to you." He looked around at the congregation. "To everyone in the community. *Mei vatter* had a special place where he kept it. But I knew where it was. And when I was put in the *bann*, I took it. I stole from all of you, my church family, and I was going to use the money to start a new life." He looked at the bishop again. "Far away from Birch Creek.

"But God dealt with me." Sol approached his father. "He dealt with me severely. He brought me low. He showed me what a weak man I truly am. He corrected me . . . and then he set me free." He dropped the bag at the bishop's feet, then shoved the cash into his hand. "Take these ill-gotten gains from me, *Vatter*. Put them in the church *bank account,* where they belong, and make sure whoever needs the funds will get them."

Aden studied the standoff between his brother and father. There was something underlying Sol's words. He could tell by his father's silence. The bishop stood there, holding the money, as if he couldn't believe what Sol was saying.

Before his *daed* could say anything, Sol faced

the congregation again. "Please forgive me," he said, his head hanging low, his hands clasped loosely together.

The congregation waited for the bishop to move. Aden looked at his father, who was still staring at the money in his hand, guilt awash on his face. Aden was still confused by Sol's confession, and from the mumbling of the churchgoers, he wasn't the only one. However, that didn't matter right now. Sol had confessed. He'd asked for forgiveness. He would be granted it, and welcomed back in the church.

Why wouldn't his father move?

Sol turned to the bishop. "Am I forgiven, *Daed*?" The pleading in his voice spread through the barn.

After an almost endless pause, his father finally spoke. "*Ya*," the bishop said, strain evident in his voice. "You . . . are forgiven."

Sadie couldn't move when the service ended. She was still in shock over what Sol had confessed, still bewildered by the bishop's strange reaction.

"Sadie, did you know about any of this?"

Patience's question brought Sadie out of her stupor. She shook her head. "I had no idea." Several of the men were at the front of the church with Sol, including Timothy and Joel. Freemont was talking with the bishop, and from the frown of frustration on Aden's father's face, it was clear the bishop didn't like what he was hearing. "I need to find Aden," she said.

Patience nodded. "*Geh.*"

She got up, ignoring the questioning looks from the other women, and searched for her husband. She jumped when she felt a hand cupping her elbow.

"We need to leave," Aden said, low in her ear.

"But Sol—"

"He'll be fine."

She followed him out the door and to the buggy. Neither one of them said anything as they pulled out of the Yutzys' driveway. The horse spirited back toward the house as if he was as eager to get home as they were.

The pin oaks and maples were almost in full autumnal bloom, but Sadie couldn't enjoy it, not when Aden was sitting next to her as tense as she'd ever seen him. After they'd ridden a little more than a mile Sadie said, "Aden, are you all right?"

"I don't know." He let out a long breath. "I didn't know Sol was going to do *that*." He shook his head. "That wasn't *mei bruder* up there, Sadie."

"What do you mean?"

"I mean what we just saw was a miracle." Aden's voice broke. "Sol has never apologized for anything, ever, except to us the day he came back to Birch Creek. He's never had to." He

paused. "He took the blame for everything."
Aden rubbed a hand over his face. "What will *mei vatter* do to him?"

"Aden, he forgave Sol. *Yer bruder* is reconciled with the church now."

"*Ya*, but I can't see him letting Sol get away with it."

"I don't understand." She waited for him to reply, but he didn't. He was silent the rest of the way home.

Sadie went inside, prepared a cold lunch, and waited for Aden to return from caring for the horse. When he seemed to be taking too long, she went out to the barn and found him sitting on a hay bale. To her surprise, Homer was lying at his feet.

"He came back," Sadie said, sitting next to Aden on the hay bale. Homer remained at Aden's feet, barely lifting his head in her direction, as if his focus was solely on Aden.

"*Ya*." Aden reached down and absently patted the dog's head.

Sadie put her hand on Aden's shoulder. "I fixed lunch."

"I'm not hungry." He glanced at her. "But *danki*."

She nodded. "Do you think the bishop will do anything to us? He was asking us to confess before Sol showed up."

Aden shrugged. "Maybe. Everyone knows we

disobeyed." He leaned forward and rubbed his hands together. "I'm so confused."

"You're not the only one."

He chuckled, and that caused Homer to look up at him, then rest his furry chin on the toe of one of Aden's black boots. "I know I shouldn't say this, but I'm proud of what Sol did today. He showed a lot of courage."

"*Ya.*" Sadie nodded. "I didn't think he had it in him."

Aden looked at her. "He's hoping you'll be able to forgive him."

"I do." She fidgeted with her fingers. "It's hard, holding on to so much anger. I'm a different person now. I can let it go." She took his hand. "I've made room for something else in *mei* life."

"What's that?" he said, running his thumb across the base of her thumb.

"Love."

His movements stilled as he gaped at her. "Love?"

"*Ya.*" She angled toward him. "I love you, Aden."

He pressed a kiss against her mouth. "I never thought I'd hear those words from you," he whispered, touching his forehead to hers.

"But you're so easy to love." She grinned.

Aden laughed, then kissed her again. "I love you too."

Homer barked, causing Aden and Sadie to look

at the barn entrance. Sol stood there, but didn't walk in.

Sadie rose, giving Aden's shoulder a squeeze. "I'll leave you two alone." She walked past Sol, who as usual barely looked at her. She stopped in front of him. Touched his hand. Then walked out of the barn.

"I didn't mean to interrupt you two."

Aden looked at Sol, who still seemed dazed by Sadie's gesture. Aden was a little dazed himself, mostly because his heart was soaring. Sadie loved him. Hearing the words thawed the last barrier of ice around his soul, allowing the warmth he'd been missing all his life to flow in. "It's all right."

"You two looked pretty cozy there," Sol said, entering the barn. Homer approached him and sniffed his boots. "I'm happy for you. You've changed, Aden."

"Not as much as you have."

Sol walked to the hay bale and sat down beside Aden. "Getting away from me and *Vatter* has been a *gut* thing for you. That and the love of a *gut* woman."

He didn't want to talk about his relationship with Sadie. "Sol, what happened back at church? What was that all about?"

"Confession, Aden."

"But there's more to it. I can tell."

Sol sighed. "When I get real drunk . . ." He

paused. "When I *used* to get real drunk, I would wander the back roads and the woods. I'd black out, wake up a few hours later, and find my way home. One day a couple of years ago I was on a bender, and I woke up inside this shack. I had no memory of finding it, but since I have a *gut* sense of direction I wasn't too worried about being lost. I left, still hung over—more likely still drunk. I'd only taken a few steps when I heard someone in the woods. It was *Daed*.

"I ran behind the shack to wait him out. He'd been on me about my drinking." He looked at Aden. "He never stopped abusing me, Aden. Up until he put me in the *bann*. It was more subtle, though. And not that often. I think because I was bigger than him by the time I was twenty-one."

"I'm sorry, Sol." He really had no idea what his brother had truly been through with their father.

"This shack, it's so old you can see through the gaps in the wood, so I watched him," Sol continued. "*Daed* went to the corner, lifted up a couple of loose boards, and pulled out a safe box. He keeps the key on a cord around his neck. When I saw what was inside . . . I couldn't believe it."

"Money?"

"Lots of money. Stacks of it. The day I saw him, he was putting another stack in the box. That's when I went inside and confronted him about it." He let out a bitter chuckle. "If I hadn't been so drunk, I probably wouldn't have."

"What did he do to you?"

"*Nix*. He didn't do anything to me. In fact, he told me everything, about the natural gas rights, about how he was going to make sure the community fund was safe and prosperous, and how we would both financially benefit. He wanted to include me in his plan, but I had to sober up first."

Aden rubbed his beard. "That was two years ago?"

"More or less. And yeah, I hadn't sobered up. My drinking got worse . . . as you well know. I think *Daed*'s intentions might have been *gut* at one time. It wasn't like he was spending the money on himself."

"He was hoarding it, though."

Sol nodded. "And I did steal it. Everything I said about taking the money and leaving Birch Creek was true. When I came back—when God led me back—I knew I had to return the money. But I couldn't give it to *Daed*. Not because I was scared about what he was going to do, but because I didn't trust him to do the right thing."

Aden nodded. "When has he ever done the right thing?"

"He has to now. Everyone knows."

"What are you going to do now?" Aden asked.

"I can't *geh* home, that's for sure. Don't have *mei* job, either."

"You know, I could use *yer* help. I've still got to replace that door I busted down in the kitchen."

"Because of me," Sol said.

"And I've got to rebuild the frames for *mei* bees."

Sol took off his black hat and threaded his fingers through his hair. "Again, because of me. I'm sorry I busted those up. I was drunk—"

"So if you're willing," Aden said, holding up his hand, "you can stay on here for a while until you figure things out."

"You sure that's okay with Sadie? And aren't her *schwesters* going to be home soon?"

"We'll make room," Aden nodded, clapping his brother on the back. "That's what families do."

CHAPTER 24

Everything had fallen apart.

Emmanuel paced the length of the decrepit shack, his glare shooting to the corner where the strongbox had been pried open. How could Sol have betrayed him this way? How could he have shamed him in front of the congregation? In front of *his* church?

He stopped pacing and glowered up at the splintered ceiling. This wasn't part of God's plan. It couldn't be. He had done everything he could to make Birch Creek a prosperous community. He'd built this district from the ground up! Now he had people like Freemont Yoder and Joel Zook questioning his authority. Freemont told him they should start ministerial elections as soon as possible. Joel had agreed with him. So did a few of the other men. Emmanuel didn't want a minister and deacon looking over his shoulder. He didn't need them. He could handle everything himself.

The only thing he'd miscalculated was his unpredictable son. Solomon ruined everything with his selfish confession.

A high wind suddenly kicked up, rattling the shack. Wood cracked and splintered as the wind grew intense. Emmanuel shielded his eyes as the force sent him to his knees. A plank of rotting lumber tore loose and smacked against his head. Emmanuel toppled over, his face hitting the ground. Blood trickled from his mouth, and the wind roared in his ears as his eyes drifted shut.

Then . . . he began to dream.

Sadie felt a feather-like touch brushing against her cheek. She opened her eyes to see Aden sitting on the edge of the bed, running the back of his hand over her skin. She smiled. "How long was I asleep?"

"Most of the day. And part of the night."

She started to sit up. "What time is it?"

"Nine. At night." He put his hands gently on her shoulders and pressed her down on the bed. "Next you'll be asking if I ate, which I did. Sol and I had supper a little while ago. I can bring you up something if you're hungry."

"*Nee*. I'm not hungry." She yawned. "I don't know why I'm still tired. I took a *gut* nap."

"Making up for lost time," Aden said. He smiled. "Mind if I join you?"

She could see he was already in his nightshirt. She scooted over until her back was against the wall. He climbed under the quilt. They would have to get a bigger bed . . . or move to a different room. She put her head on his chest as he wrapped an arm around her shoulder.

"Sol's going to stay on for a little while," he said.

Sadie looked up at him. He hadn't turned out the light yet, and it shined behind him, making the tufts of his reddish hair resemble the color of flame. "All right."

"Just until he figures things out. I'm sure it won't be long."

"He can stay as long as he needs to."

He moved his arm and rolled over on his side until he was facing her. She listened as he told her what Sol had revealed about the shack, the money, and the natural gas rights. "When we find that paperwork, we're not signing anything over to *mei vatter*."

"If we find the paperwork." She brushed aside his bangs. He had a small scar at the end of his eyebrow. She hadn't noticed it before, and she made a mental note to ask him about it. "I'm beginning to think we never will." She frowned. "We could use the money."

"We could." He took her hand and threaded his fingers through hers. "But if we can't find it, we'll be okay. I believe that."

She nodded, because she did too. God had taken them both through some dark times, and she was starting to believe they might be coming out the other side. That didn't mean she would stop missing her parents. Or that Aden would never struggle with the pain of his past. When Joanna returned home, she would need help. But Sadie and her sisters were no longer alone. They had Aden and Sol, a fact she was still trying to wrap her head around. Plus they had a community that would be there for them. Out of grief and confusion she had pushed so many of them away after her parents died. She would never do that again.

Aden leaned over and kissed the tip of her nose. "What are you thinking about?"

She was about to tell him, but his tiny kiss, coupled with the way he was looking at her, had her thoughts going in an entirely different direction. She tilted her head up to kiss him when a pounding sounded on the door.

"*Ya*?" Aden said, sounding as annoyed as she felt.

"It's *Daed*," Sol said, sounding breathless through the door. "He's here."

Aden scrambled out of bed, picking his pants up off the floor and yanking them on. His nightshirt was tucked halfway inside his waistband. "Stay here," he said to her, then flew out the door.

Sadie sat up in bed. She was still wearing her church dress, but she had taken off her *kapp*. Worry propelled her from the bed, and she quickly wrapped a kerchief around her head. She paced the room, but after five minutes she couldn't stand it anymore. Aden might be mad at her for not listening to him, but she had to find out what was going on.

She hurried down the stairs and saw the living room was empty. So was the kitchen. Where were they? She went to the front window and looked outside. In the dim light that came from a streetlamp a few yards down the road, she could see three people standing next to a buggy—Aden, Sol . . . *and their mother?*

"Sit down, *Mamm*," Aden said, pulling out a kitchen chair for his mother. He had finally convinced her to come inside. Sol had been mistaken, thinking it was their father who had come to see them. Their mother rarely took the buggy out by herself, and never at night. "We need to talk about this."

"There's not much more I can say." She did sit, though, and Aden saw that as a good sign. Her eyes were more bloodshot than he'd ever seen them. She'd been crying, and when she told them what their father had done, he couldn't blame her.

"He came home this afternoon and told me he had to *geh*. That God had told him to leave Birch Creek. And me."

Sol shook his head, his hands curling into fists, his tone reminiscent of "old" Sol. "I can't believe he would do this to you." He looked at Aden. "To us."

"*Yer vatter* is . . . complicated."

"Stop making excuses for him!" Sol unfolded his hands and put them under the table. "He's selfish and greedy, *Mamm*. That's why he left."

She shook her head. "You don't understand."

Aden reached for her hand. "Then help us, *Mamm*. Tell us why he ran away."

Mamm pulled out of Aden's grasp. "You never met *yer* grandfather. He was a cold, cruel man."

"Sounds familiar," Sol muttered.

Aden shot him a look.

"He treated his family horribly. Especially *yer* father and his brother, John."

Aden and Sol exchanged a look.

"They were poor, very poor. *Yer* grandfather wouldn't let anyone near his family. I'm not even sure of everything that happened between them. Emmanuel never talked much about that with me.

"I loved *yer vatter* since the day I met him. I knew he was special. I knew we would marry. We did, despite his *vatter*'s objections. He didn't want Emmanuel or John to succeed at anything." She looked at Aden, then at Sol. "You have to understand, the pain he carried from his childhood made him hard. He didn't get the love he needed from his father."

"And we did?" This time it was Aden's turn to be angry. "Is that supposed to be an excuse for the way he raised us?"

She shrank back. "There is *nee* excuse. I'm as much to blame as he is."

"You couldn't have stood up to him, *Mamm*," Sol said.

"But I should have." She looked at Sol. "When you were asking for forgiveness today, *mei* heart just broke." She touched his face. "You shouldn't have been in so much pain. Neither of you should."

"You can stay here," Aden said, feeling the thickness in his voice. Sol nodded his agreement.

"*Nee*, I can't. Emmanuel will be back."

"You don't know that."

She lifted her chin. "*Ya*. I do. He left to confront his past. The way you boys both have. He has to face it to move past it . . . to accept what he's done to you and to the community."

Aden didn't know what to say. He didn't like the idea of his mother living alone. But he couldn't force her to leave her home.

Mamm opened her purse, which had been sitting in her lap. "I didn't come here just to tell you about *yer daed*." She pulled out a thick envelope. "These are the papers Emmanuel has been looking for. The ones that belong to the Schrocks."

Aden's jaw dropped. "You've had them all this time?"

Mamm nodded. "Hannah Schrock gave them to me two weeks before the accident, for safe-keeping. She didn't explain why, she only asked that I keep them for her for a little while. When *yer vatter* was so set on Sadie marrying Sol, then you, I knew this was what he wanted."

"But you didn't give them to him."

"They weren't mine to give." She looked away. "I made a promise to Hannah, and I kept it." She handed the papers to Aden. "These are yours now."

Aden took them, too stunned to say anything. His mother was hiding something. He could tell. She'd never gone against his father . . . except for this. How had Hannah convinced her not to give the papers to *Daed*? Eventually he'd try to find out, but not now. His mother was too hurt, too raw from *Daed*'s abandonment. He had to keep himself from crumpling the papers in his hand. His father continued to wound the family even when he wasn't here.

Mamm stood. "I need to *geh* home."

"You're not going alone." Sol also stood. "Aden, I'll still keep my promise to help you with the door and the frames. But I'm going home with *Mamm*."

Aden waited for their mother to object. Instead she nodded. "*Danki, sohn.*"

Sadie brushed out her long hair as she listened for voices and movement downstairs. After she saw Aden, Sol, and their mother start for the house, she'd run upstairs to her room. She needed to give them their privacy, although she was curious about what was happening.

She set down the brush on her nightstand at the same time she heard Aden's footsteps outside the door. They were familiar to her now, and also welcomed. She stood as he opened the door and walked into the room, his eyes wide with shock and carrying an envelope. Without hesitation she went to him. He put his arms around her and hugged her close.

"*Daed* left," he said, stepping away from her. She listened as he explained what happened, ending the explanation by handing her the envelope. "*Mamm* had it all along."

Sadie took the envelope. "Why would *mei mamm* give it to *yer mamm*?"

"*Mamm* didn't know."

She looked at him and saw the stress and fatigue around his eyes. While she was thankful the papers were found, they could talk about it in the morning.

He met her gaze, and soon she was in his arms again. "I love you," he said fiercely against her ear. "I hope you don't get tired of hearing that, because I'll never stop saying it."

Melting against him, she said, "I love you too."

Epilogue

"Careful!"

"I'm sorry, Sadie," Joanna said as she got out of the taxi and leaned on her wooden crutches.

"Joanna," Sadie said, gentling her tone, "you don't have to be sorry. It's okay. I'm worried about you."

"Please don't worry," Joanna said. "I promise. I'll be fine."

As Aden helped Abigail with their bags and took care of the taxi driver's fare, Joanna looked up at the house. "Home," she whispered. "I can't believe I'm finally here."

Sadie hugged her lightly. "I'm so glad you are."

As the car pulled out of the driveway, Aden carried the bags inside while the sisters slowly made their way to the house. Joanna balanced herself well on the crutches. She had made great strides since Sadie's last visit a couple of weeks ago. She had been dismissed from the rehabilitation center yesterday. After spending the night at Mary's, Abigail and Joanna had come home.

In the month since Emmanuel Troyer left Birch Creek, the church had pieced itself back together. After a secret ballot, the new bishop of Birch Creek was none other than Freemont Yoder, who had said all along he'd never want the job. The new minister was Joel Zook's older brother Jacob, who wasn't thrilled with his new responsibility either. But both men had taken on their appointed duties with solemn enthusiasm once the shock had worn off, and the community had decided to hold a new ballot if they needed a second minister or a deacon in the future.

"You'll like *yer* new room," Sadie said as they neared the house. "Aden and Sol just finished it the other day. There's a bathroom nearby too."

"You thought of everything." Joanna's smiled dimmed a bit. "I wish I had *mei* old room," she whispered. Then she looked at Sadie. "Not that I'm ungrateful."

Sadie nodded. "I know. And it's temporary. Once you're able to get up the stairs easily, you can have *yer* old room back. We can use that room as a spare, or a sewing room, or a pantry, or—"

"Or a nursery." Abigail winked at Joanna and they both laughed.

Sadie smiled, her face flushing. Little did they know she had thought the same thing.

Once Joanna and Abigail had spent some time in their rooms and the family had lunch, Aden excused himself to work on his hive frames, which he wanted to complete by spring. Homer, who had by now decided to stick around, followed him outside. Sol had helped with some of the frames, along with making a brand-new

376

kitchen door and installing it himself. He had decided to open up his own carpentry and handyman business and devote the rest of his time to taking care of his mother, who was still convinced Emmanuel would come back.

Aden and Sadie didn't think he would.

"I want to *geh* see *Mamm* and *Daed*'s room," Joanna said after they finished cleaning the kitchen.

Sadie shook her head, remembering how difficult it had been for her the first time she'd gone in. "We can do that some other time."

"My last memories of them are when we picked apples. I need to see their room. I need to be closer to them."

Sadie looked at Abigail. Her sister nodded, and they assisted Joanna up the stairs. Other than putting some things away after searching the room, Sadie hadn't been in there. Everything remained the same, except for the two boxes she'd left in the middle of the floor.

Abigail and Joanna went into the room, and Abigail helped her sister sit on the floor. Together they started going through one of the boxes, Abigail lifting the half-finished knitted sock and commenting how their mother had tried to learn how to knit but could never master it. Joanna found the cookbook, and she carefully studied each page as if it were a lifeline to her mother.

Sadie held back, not wanting to intrude. Joanna

and Abigail had a special bond now, and while Sadie didn't feel exactly like an outsider, she wanted to give her sisters a chance to heal on their own terms.

She felt Aden's arm slip around her waist. "How are they doing?" he whispered.

"They're okay." She moved out of her husband's embrace and into the hallway. He followed.

She leaned against Aden, feeling his heartbeat against her chest, thankful once again that God had created a beautiful, loving relationship from the damaged pieces of broken hearts and souls.

"We're all going to be okay," she said. And she truly believed it.

ACKNOWLEDGMENTS

A special thank-you to Kelly Long and Eddie Columbia for their fabulous critiques and brainstorming sessions. Thanks to Eric Francis for generously providing his beekeeping expertise. As always, I appreciate my editors, Becky Monds and Jean Bloom, for their excellent editing skills, and my agent, Susan Brower, for her support.

Most of all, I thank you, dear readers, for joining me on another reading journey.

DISCUSSION QUESTIONS

1. Sadie chose not to tell anyone that Sol molested her in the cornfield. Do you think that was the right decision? Who should she have told? How would revealing her secret help her heal?

2. Aden also kept his abuse a secret. Could he have reached out to anyone? What do you think the consequences would have been?

3. Despite being the victim of abuse, Aden stayed true to himself and maintained strong faith. In what ways do you think his faith affected him?

4. Sadie had a difficult time letting go and grieving for her parents. Have you ever felt a time in your life when you had to be strong for others? How did that affect you emotionally and spiritually?

5. Do you believe Sol has truly repented? Do you think his change of heart will continue to have a positive effect on his behavior?

6. At the end of the story, Sadie believes that God brought her and Aden together to help

heal their brokenness. Do you believe God can use painful circumstances for healing? Have you experienced that kind of healing in your life?

7. Rhoda believes Emmanuel left Birch Creek to confront his past. She also believes he will return. Do you think Emmanuel will come back to Birch Creek? Can he be redeemed?

8. Sadie kept pushing people away instead of sharing her grief and pain. Eventually she realized she didn't have to bear her burdens alone. How important is family and community support in the grieving process?

ABOUT THE AUTHOR

Kathleen Fuller is the author of several best-selling novels, including *A Man of His Word* and *Treasuring Emma*, as well as a middle-grade Amish series, the Mysteries of Middlefield.

Visit her website at www.kathleenfuller.com.
Twitter: @TheKatJam
Facebook: Kathleen Fuller

Center Point Large Print
600 Brooks Road / PO Box 1
Thorndike, ME 04986-0001 USA

(207) 568-3717

US & Canada:
1 800 929-9108
www.centerpointlargeprint.com